A COLD DOSE OF MURDER

Books in the Cannabis Café mystery series

A Half-Baked Murder

A High Tide Murder

A Cold Dose of Murder

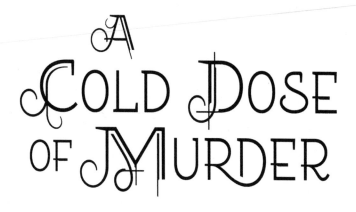

A COLD DOSE OF MURDER

EMILY GEORGE

Kensington Publishing Corp.
kensingtonbooks.com

KENSINGTON BOOKS are published by

Kensington Publishing Corp.
900 Third Avenue
New York, NY 10022

ISBN: 978-1-4967-4053-3 (ebook)

ISBN: 978-1-4967-4052-6

First Kensington Trade Paperback Printing: March 2025

10 9 8 7 6 5 4 3 2 1

Printed in the United States of America

To all the readers who took a chance on this series, thank you

CHAPTER 1

There was little more terrifying to me than being in the spotlight. It was a strange fear. Not as understandable as a fear of dying or sharks or heights. And certainly a strange fear for a business owner to have, where being in the spotlight was the entire point of marketing. After all, a successful business was one that people knew about!

But I *hated* it.

Or maybe it was simply a case of one fear disguising the more real fear beneath: failure.

Because what could be worse than tripping and falling flat on your face with the whole street watching? Or, in this case, any number of the approximately five billion people who used the internet.

I'd argue, nothing could be worse.

"It's live!" Aunt Dawn shouted as I flipped the OPEN sign to CLOSED on the front door of our business, Baked by Chloe.

"Don't hit play until Grandma Rose gets here," I called back. "I told her we'd wait for her."

Today was a big deal. Like, a *really* big deal. The kind of big deal that can make or break a small business like Baked by Chloe. When it came to the kitchen, I knew exactly what to do.

Temperamental pastry doughs? Not a problem. Perfect macaron shells? I could make them in my sleep. Preparing three different dishes at the same time? Child's play.

Learning to bake with cannabis after my grandma was diagnosed with breast cancer, so I could open my town's very first weed café catering to customers who enjoyed both medicinal and recreational use? Check it off the bucket list.

But when it came to marketing and promotion and trying to sell myself . . . well, honestly that made me want to crawl under a rock and hide.

Luckily for me—and Baked by Chloe's bottom line—Aunt Dawn had more balls than a juggling troupe, and she wouldn't hesitate to ask *anyone* to support our business. As business co-owners we're the perfect pairing: I made great food and she made sure we got people through the door. In this case, she'd reached out to the biggest food podcast on the internet, *Starch Nemesis*, to see if they would feature our little café.

And they'd said yes!

So I'd put on my big girl panties and allowed the podcast's host to come to the café for a personal taste testing session and now the episode featuring us was live, so Aunt Dawn, Grandma Rose and I were going to have a "listen party" over a batch of cannabis blondies and chai lattes.

Nervous butterflies swirled like a mini tornado in my stomach. To say I'd been anxious for the latest *Starch Nemesis* episode to air was putting it mildly. Like, milder than the lemon and herb marinade at Nando's. The host, Calista, was known for her viciously snarky humor—something that had won her millions of fans online—as well as her acute sense of what was hip and what was out in the food scene. Or rather, *who* was out. She'd been the final nail in the coffin of several restaurant businesses, and many lived in fear of being next on her hit list.

In our world, her word was gospel.

I had no idea if I'd managed to impress her. Only time would tell . . . and that time was less than five minutes away.

As I was sweeping the floor and wiping the tables down to prepare for the next day's trade, I heard voices coming from the kitchen and the distinctive tinkling of my grandmother's laughter. But it sounded like there were more people back there than just her and my aunt. A *lot* more people. Abandoning my broom, I pushed through the swing door that led to the area behind the serving counter, and rounded the corner into the kitchen.

"I hope you don't mind that I invited some extra guests to the listening party." She grinned.

My stomach somersaulted when I saw a cluster of people standing in the kitchen and not only because my hunky neighbor slash sort-of date was there. Jake stood a head above everyone else—*two* above Grandma Rose—and when he smiled the butterflies in my tummy flapped their wings a little harder. His smile exposed a dimple in his cheek and a delighted twinkle in his hazel eyes.

But before he could say anything, my best friend, Sabrina, elbowed her way through the group and grabbed me by the shoulders, giving me a little shake.

"I can't believe you didn't tell me you were going to be on *Starch Nemesis*," she said. "They're huge! They're, like, the most listened-to podcast on Spotify right now."

"They even got a mention on *Saturday Night Live*," Jake said with an impressed nod.

"I heard they're getting a cameo on the next season of *Only Murders in the Building*," Lawrence St. James added. He was my grandma's sort-of boyfriend. "Quite a good program, that one. I like Steve Martin."

"And Calista has written a book!" Aunt Dawn chimed in. "Anecdotes from her time in the food industry."

"Sounds juicy." Her girlfriend, Maisey, nodded. She was

tall, almost as tall as Jake, and had blond hair cut into a shaggy pixie cut. Whereas my aunt dressed like a hippie, Maisey was all American prep in a Ralph Lauren blazer, slim-cut blue jeans and ballet flats. "I bet she has all kinds of wild stories to share."

With each eager and excited comment I felt a boulder expand in my stomach. It was like a snowball, rolling itself in my fears and doubts, growing bigger and bigger until I could barely breathe from the pressure of it. I'd only intended the listening party to be my aunt, my grandma and me. I was already nervous about millions of people online hearing Calista's thoughts about our café, but somehow having people I know hearing what she had to say made me feel even more anxious.

"You're going to be *famous*." Sabrina linked her arm through mine.

For a brief moment I thought my lunch was going to rush back up and splatter all over the floor, but I pressed a hand to my stomach and managed to quell the nausea. *Famous* was not on my list of goals. Baked by Chloe had opened to an eager customer base and we had no trouble filling the seats and selling out of our products. *That* was what was important to me—not having people online know my name.

"Come on," Jake said, coming to my other side and reaching for my hand, giving it a reassuring squeeze. "There's nothing to be nervous about."

"I'm not nervous," I lied.

"You're just green in the face because it's some new beauty trend then?" He nudged me with his elbow. "You've got nothing to worry about, Chloe. Your baking is second to none."

I felt some of my tension ease a little. I *knew* my baking was top notch—one didn't graduate from Le Cordon Bleu with a fistful of job offers for no reason, after all. I was well trained, had been mentored by gifted chefs and knew the value of working my tush off. *That* I wasn't worried about. It was more the fact that I was a bit of an awkward turtle and tended to ramble when I was nervous. What if Calista said as much in her podcast?

The damage is done now. No point sticking your head in the sand.

"Let's get this party started," I said, with as much cheer as I could muster. Aunt Dawn had cut the blondies into smaller pieces so everyone could have a bite, and she'd also raided the refrigerator for some fresh fruit to go with it.

Blondies, for the uninitiated, are cocoa-free brownies which have a more buttery-vanilla flavor. I'd wanted to make a fun, summery twist on the traditional weed brownie and had mixed in some white chocolate, lemon and macadamia nuts along with a special strain of cannabis called Christmas Morning, which I had recently bought from a local grower. This strain of cannabis contained a set of sweeter terpenes which gave the cannabis a natural blueberry-like flavor profile, pairing excellently with the blondies' sweet ingredients. A sprinkle of salt and zesty lemon rind provided balance and stopped it veering into toothache territory.

Maisey helped with the drinks and soon we were settled at the tables usually reserved for our customers. Jake was pairing his phone to the portable speaker that usually lived in the kitchen, blasting my favorite late-2000s pop tunes while I worked early in the morning. Next to him, Lawrence St. James was readjusting the pocket square in his tweed sports coat and marveling over the power of Bluetooth while my grandmother looked on indulgently. Sabrina and Aunt Dawn were distributing plates and food, and Maisey and I made sure everyone had a beverage.

I glanced around the café, taking in the soft-pink wallpapered walls and white furniture, the vintage chandelier, the Parisian-themed art, including a beautiful watercolor painting of the Arc de Triomphe, and the wonderful group of people gathered at the tables we'd pushed together. No matter what *Starch Nemesis* had to say about my business, I could sleep soundly at night knowing my life was an embarrassment of riches. I had a wonderful grandma and aunt to call my family, amazing friends who supported me, a gorgeous café I was proud to invite townsfolk into and the knowledge that I was helping to destigmatize cannabis for the folks who used it.

That was what mattered to me.

"Are we all ready?" Jake asked. I could see the *Starch Nemesis* logo showing up on his podcast app, above some text.

Episode 143: small towns, strangers and smoking the reefer.

"Ready," I said, and my voice only cracked a little.

Jake pushed play and the familiar opening credits music drifted up from the portable speakers, filling the café with the cheerful melodic chimes. Then Calista's voice cut in.

"Hey folks, welcome back to another episode of Starch Nemesis, *the food podcast where we mince meat, not words. Warning: if you have delicate feelings, a predisposition for outrage or the tendency to write nasty comments when someone doesn't agree with you, then I guarantee this is not the podcast for you. So long and thanks for all the fish!*

"On today's episode I'm taking a trip to a very unlikely food mecca. Small-town America. I know, I know . . . I was thinking it, too. But, Calista, I hear you ask, what do small towns have to offer that aren't greasy spoon diners and leftovers of Ramsay's Kitchen Nightmares? *Well, I found a little gem, folks. A tasty little gem.*

"Let me tell you all about a place called Azalea Bay

and the best flipping weed brownies I've ever had in my life."

Twenty-five minutes later, I was glowing. Calista Bryant had given Baked by Chloe a fantastic review, saying that the pastries were better than most she'd had in Paris. The best compliment might have been that my talent for flavor went above and beyond what she'd expected; rather than hiding the cannabis away behind rich chocolates and caramels, I'd used other flavors to help the cannabis shine.

"This isn't your ordinary gummies and brownies, folks. This is taking weed and turning it into edible art. It's fine dining of the highest order—see what I did there? Even if you're not an unabashed stoner like me, I urge you to take a trip to the coast and try it for yourself. Get high or do it for the 'medical benefits,' if that makes you feel better. But try it out. Baked by Chloe is an experience. You heard it here first.

"And while you're off on your beach weekend jaunt don't forget to check out some of the other businesses that I mentioned in this episode, which are local to Azalea Bay. My top picks would be Oishi for sushi, Loafing Around for their caramelized onion bread specifically, Foam for a seafood lunch—make sure you ask for a table with a view—and the Dripping Cones ice cream parlor. You can skip Sprout . . . it's all hype and no substance. Crystal-charged smoothie bowls? Ugh! That's some Gwyneth Paltrow Goop-level BS. Definitely pass on this one, it's not worth your time.

"Now, speaking of ice cream, I'll be at the Azalea Bay Ice Cream Festival next week signing copies of my book, The Baddest B in Foodtown. *"*

Calista signed off the episode with her signature flourish and I slumped back in my chair, relief flooding my body. Sabrina let out an excited squeal and Jake reached out to squeeze my shoulder.

"Well, my dear, that was a total success," declared Grandma Rose. She had a bright pink silk scarf wrapped around her head as it was too hot to wear her wig today. Since starting chemo for breast cancer a few months back, she'd lost all her hair and preferred to keep her scalp covered up. "I am not at all surprised, mind you."

"I am," I muttered. "Did you hear how she ripped into Sprout?"

Sabrina made an eek face. "That was . . . rough."

Sprout was a local LA-inspired health and wellness café, as well as an Instagram haven with a menu that consisted of such items as antioxidant crystal-charged smoothie bowls, antitoxin charcoal bars, and anti–bad vibes power balls . . . I had no idea what ingredients could legitimately claim to get rid of bad vibes, so the Goop reference didn't feel far off. Still, even though I wasn't a huge fan of Sprout's capitalization on pseudo-science wellness trends, their food *was* good. Excellent, even. It was a super popular lunch spot in town and the owner did a roaring trade, with good reason.

"Starr is *not* going to be happy with that review," I said, shaking my head. "I wouldn't be either, frankly."

Calista had ripped the place apart, criticizing everything from the menu to the decor to the owner herself.

"I agree it was harsh," Aunt Dawn said. "But Starr can handle herself. And the most important thing is that Calista *loved* Baked by Chloe! Do you know how many people are going to listen to this episode telling people how great your food is? This could bring *huge* business to our door."

The nervous butterflies had thankfully vacated the premises, and left behind were some more excited, happy butter-flies. "You're right."

"And with Calista coming for the ice cream festival, I'm sure she'll give us a shout-out on social media." Aunt Dawn fluffed out her frizzy dark purple hair, making the thick stack of bangles on her wrist clatter and clank. "We're going to be busier than ever!"

"Congratulations, Chloe." Jake leaned over and gave me a kiss on the cheek. I felt my face heat up to approximately a billion degrees, but I was too thrilled to be embarrassed or to overthink what it meant for Jake to kiss me in front of my family. "You've got exciting things in front of you."

Under the table I reached for his hand. "I think so, too."

I'd turned my life around in the last few months and it was hard not to almost float off the ground with satisfaction. But little did I know that episode 143 of *Starch Nemesis* was about to become the center of attention . . . for all the wrong reasons.

CHAPTER 2

The next day Baked by Chloe was abuzz with chatter about the podcast. I'd had no less than ten customers mention that they'd popped in because they'd heard the episode and had decided to come check it out. One pair of friends had even driven three hours off course from their road trip plans just to visit! I was overwhelmed *and* overjoyed.

"See," Aunt Dawn said with a smug smile as the line of customers finally trickled down to nothing.

It was late afternoon and we were closing within the hour, so the rush had passed and now the people who remained were happily munching away on their cannabis baked goods and enjoying some of the beverages we made including our top favorites: the calming CBD chai latte (aka our "hug in a mug" drink) and the fruity canna-gria made with nonalcoholic sparkling pink wine. I'd also started putting out little bowls of "munchies mix" on the tables—which consisted of nuts, dried fruit, chocolate chips and broken cookie pieces—to encourage people not to overconsume the cannabis items, especially if it was their first time.

"See what?" I asked, knowing I was in for a full I-told-you-so moment.

"You were worried about me reaching out to *Starch Nemesis* and look at how well it went." She gestured to our dining area, where every table was full. There were even a few solo folks who'd paired up to share a table with someone they didn't know, just so they could dine in. That made me smile. "This is usually our quietest day and we're packed to the brim."

"You were right and I was wrong," I admitted.

"What was that?" Aunt Dawn cupped her ear, making a rather large pair of gold and purple enamel chandelier earrings shudder with the motion. "I couldn't quite hear you."

I laughed and gave her a playful shove. "You know I can admit when I'm being a scaredy-cat. I was terrified Calista was going to rip us apart with the whole world listening."

"You have to believe in yourself, girlie." Aunt Dawn grabbed some paper towels and started cleaning the serving area in preparation for closing time. We were just about sold out of everything—only two of my cannabis-infused "everything but the kitchen sink" cookies remained, along with a lone square of blondie—so there was no harm in getting a jump start on the closing procedure. "I knew people would come far and wide for your baking."

"The weed doesn't hurt, either," I said with a laugh.

The whole cannabis baking thing was so *not* the direction I thought my life would take. Not too long ago I was living in Paris, working as a pastry chef in an exclusive fine dining restaurant with my sights set on Michelin stardom. Oh, and I was engaged.

But in a matter of days my entire life had deflated like a poorly executed soufflé. I'd found out my fiancé had cheated on me with someone at work and had gotten her pregnant. Of course, it was *that* night a famous food critic showed up at the restaurant where we both worked and, I'm sad to say, I was not at the top of my game. When his review came out a week later, he'd called my dessert *a bitter disappointment better suited to a supermarket bakery than a 5-star restaurant.* Maybe that was why I was so scared for Calista to review us on her podcast. I'd been shredded before! Anyway, after that scathing critique, the universe had really wanted to kick me while I was down because Grandma Rose had been to the doctor and it wasn't good news.

The big C.

So I had abandoned my Parisian dreams and headed home to Azalea Bay, the cute Californian tourist town I'd called home most of my life, to look after my grandmother and figure out where I was headed next. Turned out I *wasn't* headed back to Paris or even back to a restaurant working for some talented but temperamental chef. After my usually straight-as-an-arrow grandma requested some weed brownies to help with the unpleasant side effects of her chemo treatments—*well, it's not like I'm going to* smoke *it*, she'd said when her doc had suggested that cannabis might help—I learned how to bake with weed.

Then suddenly I was running a weed café. Life was strange like that—just when you thought everything was going wrong, the right path opened up.

"Girlie, people would come to eat your food even without the chance to get high. That's just the icing on the cake!" She winked.

"Or should that be, the funk on the skunk?"

Aunt Dawn snorted. "Now you're talking like me."

While I was personally more into the medicinal benefits that cannabis provided for people like my grandma, Aunt Dawn indulged for the fun of it. She was the kind of person who lived life to the fullest and indulged every desire that came to her. Frankly, my type-A backside could probably learn a thing or three there.

But before Aunt Dawn and I could further devolve into trading puns, the front door to Baked by Chloe swung open and in walked our employee, Erica. I blinked in surprise. "What are you doing back here so soon?"

Erica had finished her shift at 2 p.m., and while she was a hard worker and the kind of person who always went above and beyond, there was literally no reason for her to be here when we were getting ready to close.

She raked a hand through her close-cropped blond hair, the ends of which were currently tipped with bright pink dye. "Uh, any chance we could talk?"

I glanced at Aunt Dawn with a worried expression and she waved a hand. "Go on out back, I'll hold the fort until we close."

I motioned for Erica to follow me out back to the kitchen. "You talk and I'll clean."

After years of formal training, I kept my kitchen neat and tidy as I worked, so there wasn't a huge mess to clean at the end of the day. But I still liked to give my food prep area a thorough wipe down and disinfect, as well as making sure all my tools were in the right spot so I could come in the following morning and get right to it.

"What's on your mind?" I asked.

Erica stood nervously at the edge of the kitchen, her hands jammed into her pockets. It wasn't like her to look so hesitant. Erica and I had first met when Sabrina invited me to join her Dungeons and Dragons group after I'd moved back home. I'd loved the group instantly and found Erica to be forthright and upbeat, if a little blunt at times. But I liked that—you always knew where you stood with her. Later, she had been looking for work and I had desperately needed an extra pair of hands. It was a match made in heaven!

But usually if she had something on her mind, it wouldn't take much for her to blurt it out.

"You're freaking me out, girl." I let out a nervous laugh as I wiped down the stainless-steel preparation table.

"Sorry." She shook her head. "I, uh . . . are you on Facebook?"

"I mean, I *have* an account. But it's gathering digital dust." Social media wasn't my favorite pastime, since I found it caused a lot of comparison-itis and I preferred to stay in my own lane. "I use Instagram sometimes, but even that hasn't been updated in a while."

Did Baked by Chloe need its own social accounts? Perhaps not, if our full seats were anything to go on. But did neglecting that make me a bad business owner? Possibly. Perhaps I could get Erica to take on some additional responsibilities for a raise.

"So you haven't seen Starr's post?" she said, dragging my attention back to our conversation.

I stilled at the workbench. "What post?"

It didn't take a genius to guess what the post was about. I'd already heard some folks gossiping about the absolute verbal smackdown Sprout had gotten from *Starch Nemesis*. I felt bad for Starr, honestly. Putting our differences in philosophy and taste to one side, I knew without a doubt that she took her business very seriously. It was her baby. Her pride and joy. And someone had just told the world they thought it was trash.

She had every right to be upset.

"She went *off* about the podcast," Erica said, her large eyes widening further. I noticed that she was already dressed for our Dungeons and Dragons catchup later that night, wearing a T-shirt that said "arcane trust fund kid" as a funny nod to her character's sorcerer class. "Like, totally freaking bananas."

"I'm not surprised. Starr likes to tell everyone she's all peace and light, but that *had* to hurt. It felt almost . . . personal." Calista hadn't pulled any punches with her opinion on Sprout. "But I guess that's kind of the *Starch Nemesis* MO, right? Calista knows how to whip the audience into a frenzy and she isn't afraid to polarize people. It's why the show is so popular."

Sadly, these days positivity didn't seem to garner as many

clicks online. If you wanted eyeballs (or in this case, auditory nerves), then it was better to be outrageous than to be kind. Thankfully, however, Calista had seen fit to bless Baked by Chloe with one of her rare totally glowing reviews. But those reviews were rare for a reason.

"Maybe it's better if I show you the post," Erica said, pulling her phone out of the back pocket of her light-wash jeans. One hole split across her thigh with shaggy frayed edges, allowing a peek of skin to show through. "Here."

She handed over her phone and the long diatribe was on display. The rant was riddled with spelling errors, likely because Starr had typed it out in such a rage that autocorrect hadn't a snow cone's chance in hell of keeping up.

"Calista Bryant is nothing but an ill-informed bully. She's the Wicked Witch of the West Coast and she won't be happy until she destroys anyone who dares challenge her." I raised both eyebrows and looked at Erica. "Yikes. Starr really went for it."

"Keep reading." Erica motioned with her hand.

I scanned on while Starr called the podcast "unethical" and "no better than cheap tabloid media" and a litany of other insults while defending both herself and her idol, Gwyneth Paltrow—which, in my mind, wasn't really helping her case.

"Calista should be ashamed of herself . . . blah, blah, blah. . . ." I scanned to the next paragraph where my stomach suddenly jolted. "I would bet that the businesses who receive positive reviews from Calista have done something *outside* the kitchen to deserve them."

I blinked. Did she . . .

"She's insinuating that you paid for your review," Erica said.

My mouth popped open. "That's ridiculous!"

"I know it is." Erica nodded. "But other people might believe her. You know Starr is very much a part of the community here and some people think she knows everything."

"You're totally right." A sinking feeling manifested in my stomach. Starr had a reputation around town for being "in the know," and if there was some kind of scandal regarding paid reviews then people would expect her to have the dirt. I continued reading the post.

I have never and will never do anything underhanded to get publicity for my business, and I stand on my own two feet as a businesswoman. Karma will come for Calista Bryant, you mark my words.

I stood for a moment, silently staring at Erica's phone, my earlier excitement about the podcast evaporating like smoke.

"I wanted you to know as soon as possible rather than overhear someone talking about it," Erica said as I handed the phone back to her. "I'll defend you and Dawn and Baked by Chloe until the cows come home. You *earned* that review fair and square. Starr is just jealous and angry."

"Thanks, Erica, I appreciate it. I'm sure it'll all blow over, right?" I said with a nervous laugh. "I mean, it's not like the internet is short on things to suck up people's attention. It's just a Facebook post."

But even as I said the words, I had a strange twinge of intuition that this particular Facebook post was going to cause a lot of trouble.

After work, I headed home to freshen up for our Dungeons and Dragons session. The group consisted of Sabrina as dungeon master; her boyfriend, Cal (short for Calix); Ben Wong and Matt Wilson, aka the most adorable couple ever; Archie Schwartz, who was hosting tonight; and, of course, Erica. Our adventuring crew—in which I role-played as a human cleric named Yasmine Fridenot whose goal was to atone for accidentally killing her twin sister with magic by becoming a master healer—was currently on the tail of an artifact-smuggling wizard. We were hoping to catch the thief and recover a long-lost Gnomish heirloom to win the favor of a rich merchant who might help us with passage to a walled city.

I was *never* that kid who was into fantasy stuff. While Sabrina had spent hours watching *The Last Unicorn* over and over and reading anything by Rick Riordan, I lost myself in Meg Cabot and *The Princess Diaries*. Sabrina played video games while I braided her hair and clipped in glittery plastic butterflies. I painted her nails and she came up with creative ideas for our Halloween costumes.

But despite that, I'd found myself really enjoying Dungeons and Dragons, not least of all because it was really cathartic to be someone else for a few hours every other week.

Presently we were all in Archie's basement, spread around a large gaming table with a green velvet top. It was wonderful to be able to roll dice without them skittering off the edge of a wooden table if there wasn't enough room for dice trays. Overhead, the sound of tiny feet pitter-pattering—or more like thump-thumping—signaled that Archie's kids were having a fun night with their mom upstairs.

In my lap was my canine best friend, Antonio, a three-year-old Chihuahua with mostly black fur, though part of his chest, underbelly and three of his four paws were white, making it look like he'd lost a sock. He had the sweetest set of satellite dish ears that picked up on every tiny sound, and tan patches circled the black markings around his eyes, giving the distinct impression he had a bandit mask on.

And yes, he was totally named after Antonio Banderas, famous for playing Zorro, the charming masked vigilante.

"Trick, you get to the top of the stairs first," Sabrina said, looking to Matt. "There's a closed door."

"Right." Matt's Australian accent made it sound a little more like *roight*. "I will open—"

"Check for traps!" At least three of us all shouted at once, startling poor Antonio in my lap, who swung his little head around, miffed that he'd been woken up from a nice snooze. Ben leaned over and gave him a little pat, which mollified the small dog and sent him back to la-la land.

"Right, traps. Of course." Matt raked a hand through his shoulder-length blond hair and grinned. "I'll check for traps."

Sabrina nodded. "Make a perception check."

"Dude, that's your *main* job as a Rogue." Archie laughed.

"Nah, lock-picking and thieving is my main job." Matt wriggled his long, musician's fingers above a small cluster of dice. He selected a lime green d20—a twenty-sided die called an icosahedron—and rubbed it between his hands. "Come on, give us a good one."

He rolled the die onto the velvet, where it tumbled a few times before teetering on one edge and rocking to a stop. A groan from the other side of the table meant it was not good news.

"I'm putting that bloody thing in the dice jail," Matt said, waving his hand in frustration. Ben picked up the die and tossed it into a small box with an open top fashioned to look like a small jail cell. It contained three other dice, which had committed similar such sins of rolling poorly, including one which had delivered *two* natural ones in a row, aka the worst possible roll. "With my wisdom modifier that comes to a princely four."

Sabrina chuckled. "There are no traps that you can see."

"Maybe we should wait—" My cleric's cautious suggestion was cut off.

"I'm going to try the handle," Matt said boldly as I dropped my head into my hands. I had a feeling this door was bugged, and since his wisdom check hadn't revealed any traps, we could be in for a nasty surprise. It was a good thing I'd armed myself almost entirely with healing spells for this session, and I still had two slots free. "Does the door open?"

"You're surprised to find that the door is unlocked and the handle moves freely," Sabrina said.

"I open it."

"As you push the door open, you hear the faintest sound of something snapping on the other side."

"Oh no!" Erica's eyes went wide. "That's not good."

"There's a brief pause where you hear nothing and then *boom!* A large explosion of heat and sound knocks the door completely off the hinges and throws you back five feet down the stairs. You take . . ." She rolled some dice behind her DM screen, which kept our prying eyes away from all her plans and notes. "Seven points of bludgeoning damage as you hit the wall on the first staircase landing."

"Well, I guess I deserved that." Matt reached forward for a small tablet where he updated his character sheet to remove seven hit points from his total.

"Fire is now quickly catching on the wood building. Bright red and orange flames lick up the side of the doorframe and smoke begins to billow in the stairwell." Sabrina grinned. "And that's where we're going to finish tonight's session."

"No!" I groaned. "I want to know what's in the room!"

Cal reached out a big meaty bear paw to pat my shoulder. "My girlfriend is brutal with the cliff-hangers."

"So brutal," I agreed.

Everyone began to pack up their things. For some of us, it was a quick affair. I had a single set of the polyhedral dice required to play Dungeons and Dragons, made of clear plastic chock-full of pink and purple glitter, which had been a gift from Sabrina when I agreed to join her D&D group. They lived in a cute velvet pouch that also fit my iPad. Erica, on the other hand, was a self-confessed dice goblin who brought a huge leather pouch to every session, from which she tossed fistfuls of dice onto the table and was very superstitious about which ones to play and when. She was also the person most likely to toss a die into the dice jail. I'd grown to be comforted by the dull sound of the dice all clattering together inside the big pouch when she arrived at each session.

Just as I was gathering up my things, my phone pinged with an alert to say that the Baked by Chloe email inbox had received a new email. I had created an alert so I could respond to emails as quickly as possible, because I never wanted to keep a customer waiting longer than was necessary.

Since everyone was standing around chatting, I figured I could quickly tap out a response. But as soon as I opened the email, I knew it wasn't one I would be responding to. In fact, it wasn't something I wanted to read at all.

HOW DARE YOU PUT OUR TOWN INTO DISREPUTE.

The all-caps shouted at me from my phone screen and I could already guess who'd sent it and what the email contained before I opened it. But since I was a glutton for punishment, I opened it anyway.

> You have continued to ignore our requests. At some point we will be forced to take action. This is your last chance. Close your business or else face the wrath of the people who want this town to remain clean and whole-some. Your drug café is not welcome here.

It was the fourth email like it that I'd received in as many weeks—I had them all saved in a special folder. Weed might be legal but not everyone believed it should be, and some folks had *very* strong opinions about it. This was despite all the research that pointed to the benefits of cannabis, such as the positive impact on the economy and employment opportunities, *and* the fact that having production regulated protected people who chose to use it, like Grandma Rose and Aunt Dawn and—

if my café's continually full tables would indicate—lots of people from our town.

But rather than simply choosing to exercise their right not to patronize my café, those people anonymously vented their frustrations into my inbox.

This email, however, had a slightly different feeling to it. Other emails simply told me I was a bad person or immoral or that I should be ashamed of myself, but this one—and one other I'd received recently—posed the same vaguely worded threat.

> Or else face the wrath of the people who want this town to remain clean and wholesome.

What did that even mean? My café was clean and wholesome. Everything about my business was aboveboard and ethical. I had an accountant to ensure I paid the right taxes, I paid Erica much higher than minimum wage, and I sourced my ingredients (both of the weed and non-weed variety) from local farms. Heck, I even furnished the café with secondhand furniture salvaged from charity shops and garage sales up and down the coast.

What was more wholesome than helping the planet?

"Everything okay?" Sabrina came up beside me and I almost jumped a mile in the air, fumbling to fade the screen of my phone before she could see the vitriol typed across it.

"Absolutely. You know I can't stay away from work," I joked.

She slung an arm around my shoulders. "Are you ready to go? I know you've got an early start tomorrow."

I'd hitched a ride here with Sabrina and Cal earlier, and he was carrying all her DM stuff like a true gentleman. "Yep, ready to go."

I shoved my phone into my bag and pasted on my brightest

smile. I hadn't told anybody about the emails. Not Sabrina, nor Grandma Rose . . . not even Aunt Dawn. I wasn't going to be bullied out of my business by someone—I highly doubted there was a "collective" behind the emails—who wasn't brave enough to say it to my face. And I certainly wasn't going to worry anyone I cared about with something so ridiculous.

I doubted anything would come of these emails and if they continued to contact me, I'd simply block their email address. After all, some jerk hiding safely behind their keyboard wasn't anything to worry about . . . was it?

CHAPTER 3

One week later . . .

The Azalea Bay Ice Cream Festival was soon to be underway. Our town was a popular vacation destination and it boasted a large number of seasonal events that drew crowds to our small patch of the world. A pro surfing competition, which had occurred a few weeks back, officially kicked off our "silly season" of jam-packed events. The ice cream festival had been a personal favorite since I was a little kid because I'd always loved tasting the unique and flavorful creations of the artisans who took part.

And I'd learned over the years how to do it without getting brain freeze.

Azalea Bay really did have it all. But the high season came with a lot of pressure, as many of the tourism-focused businesses needed to cover the bulk of their earnings in the six-month period between May and October when people regularly flooded our shores. Festivals were a big help to that, and this one was no different. So to say I was thrilled about being on the other side of the vendor tables for the first time ever was an understatement.

"I'm so excited that you're going to be vending this year!" Grandma Rose said, echoing my thoughts as she clapped her hands, causing the balloon-like sleeves on her dusty pink blouse to flutter in the breeze. "Everyone is going to love your ice cream."

"Thanks for the vote of confidence." I grinned.

The festival was due to open at noon the following day and currently all vendors were gathered in Azalea Bay Park setting up their stalls. The festival committee had erected several large white marquee tents under which some of the vendors would operate, but there were also food trucks parked in two rows, one at either end of the festival. A dining area was created around the existing picnic tables, expanded with additional seating, including some Adirondack chairs painted in sorbet shades.

Grandma Rose had offered to assist me in setting up the stall, and Jake and Lawrence were due to arrive any moment to lend their helping hands as well, while Erica and Aunt Dawn held down the fort at Baked by Chloe. Over the weekend the café would be closed while the festival was in full swing, since I couldn't manage making food for both places. I'd been trying to find a junior baker to join our team for weeks now, but so far nobody had ticked all my boxes and I was determined to find the *right* person.

Aunt Dawn said I was being too picky, but I knew that relationships in the kitchen were vital to the success of any café or restaurant. I'd worked in places where people didn't click and it always created problems. So I was taking my time to get it right.

Grandma Rose's phone pinged with a text message.

"Looks like Lawrence is here," she said. "I'll go meet him and Jake and bring them over so they don't get lost."

It wouldn't be a long trek, since we—and therefore Jake, who was our neighbor—lived right across the road from the park. But I imagined Grandma Rose escorting them was more about her spending a few extra minutes with Lawrence than any genuine concerns about them getting lost.

"Sure thing." I nodded, stifling an amused smile.

The festival vendors consisted of a mix of local and non-local businesses. Our town ice creamery, Dripping Cones, had the biggest stall since they were one of the main attractions and had been for years. They were famous along the coast for their vanilla waffle cones—which were the best I'd ever tasted. Frankly, I wasn't even bothering with waffle cones for our stall because theirs were so good, there was no way I could compete!

And not every stall at the festival sold ice cream, either. Some had ice cream–themed items instead—which was good, because eating nothing but ice cream all day was an express ticket to a stomachache. The local cake store, Sweet Tooth, was selling several themed cupcake flavors including waffle cone, French vanilla ice cream and their adorable "ice cream sundae" cupcake, which had the frosting scooped to look like a ball of ice cream complete with chocolate fudge drizzle, crushed nuts and a cherry on top.

As I was kneeling and fiddling with our stall's banner, I sensed a presence behind me. "Chloe! Great to see you here."

I glanced over my shoulder, my eyes widening. It was Calista Bryant.

"Hi." I got to my feet and brushed my hands down the front of my jeans. "Great to see you, too."

Calista was taller than me by a good few inches, but her lanky limbs made that difference feel even more exaggerated. Her blond hair was shaved on one side, while the other side swooped across her forehead to finish at her chin. She had some piercings—two studs in each ear, plus a ring in her septum—and her dress sense was "goth Pippi Longstocking." Today she wore a short black dress with lime green patch pockets and a white shirt underneath, the sleeves rolled back to reveal tattoos decorating both arms. On her lower half, knee-high striped socks disappeared into a pair of bright green Doc Martens.

"Did you have a chance to listen to the episode yet?" she asked with a friendly smile.

"Are you kidding?" I laughed. "I had my entire family huddled around my phone the second it went live."

"That's awesome! I've eaten a lot of really average weed brownies in my time, and I was thoroughly impressed by what you made."

I flushed. Being praised by someone like her was a *huge* compliment. "I really appreciate you sharing that with your audience. It's already brought people into the café."

"Feel free to return the favor by sending some customers to my book signing tomorrow," she replied with a wink. I noticed people looking at her and whispering from the neighboring stall. They looked like fans who were a bit too starstruck to come over and say hello.

"I doubt you'll need my help to have a line running out of the festival, but I will absolutely send people your way," I promised. "In fact, I'll be in line myself."

"I was hoping you would be here, but I wasn't sure . . . what with this being a family event and all. I'm sure they had to jump through a ton of hoops for the licensing."

"They did." I nodded.

For a moment, it had looked like we might not be able to participate. The legalities around serving cannabis goods were tight, but knowing I was going to be on the *Starch Nemesis* podcast had certainly made the event organizers keen to have us included. They must have pulled some strings—even getting the mayor involved, I'd heard—because we'd gotten the go-ahead last minute.

"You're currently standing in the 'adults only' section of the festival." I gestured to the white tent enclosing the space where my stall sat along with several others. "They're going to have people posted at the entrance here who will be checking ID to make sure no minors come through."

Our tent also had its own seating area, since all the items purchased for immediate consumption would need to be consumed within the boundaries of the licensed area. The event organizers had done an amazing job with it, stringing fairy lights across the tables and chairs, and setting up some wine barrel standing tables and even had a few velvet love seats dotted around for festivalgoers to share a romantic moment.

Aside from me and my cannabis goods, there was a local brewery serving beer floats with their famous chocolate ale, as well as a company from the East Coast who made wine-flavored ice cream. I'd made a mental note to pick up a tub of their strawberries and champagne flavor to try out. We also had a mixologist making ice cream–themed cocktails, and a luxury lingerie company selling all manner of slinky bedroom things—including a lace-trimmed silk robe in a sweet lilac shade with sundaes on it, which was sorely tempting me.

"That's a smart move. Everyone is going to want to see what goodies are hidden away in here." She nodded her approval. "Well, I'll see you around tomorrow."

"Thanks for coming to say hi."

She waved and walked away, not getting more than a few feet from me before a curvaceous woman with dark skin and waist-length black braids came into the tent—the sides of which were rolled up since no products were allowed to be sold during the set-up period. I recognized the woman as Calista's assistant, Destiny. She was showing Calista something on her phone and they both had furrowed brows and tense expressions. I wondered what that was all about. But before I could ponder things further, someone else came into the tent.

It was Starr Bright.

She made a beeline for me, raising one hand in a wave. It occurred to me that she looked almost the polar opposite to Calista—with long platinum-blond hair, tanned skin, glitter lip gloss and a crochet maxi dress in baby pink that revealed a white bikini underneath. It was a cute look, but I dreaded to think what kind of crazy tan lines it would create.

"What are you doing talking to *that* witch?" she said as she approached, disdain dripping from her tone as Calista and Destiny disappeared out of the tent. "Although I guess you must love her since she gave your café the most glowing review."

I bristled at the jealousy in her tone. But fighting with Starr in public wouldn't be good for me or my business, so I swallowed back the urge to mention the accusatory Facebook post she'd written, even though it felt like pushing a boulder down my throat one gulp at a time.

"Hi, Starr," I said, completely ignoring her question. "Are you excited for the festival to begin?"

"Of course. With all this sugar around, people's digestive systems are going to need some reprieve." She shuddered as though even the mere mention of sugar might do something horrible to her. "I know that our coconut 'nice-cream' is going to be a huge hit!"

"I guess that makes mine naughty-cream," I joked.

"Hopefully Santa isn't watching."

"A guy who needs to be rewarded with cookies wherever he goes sounds like he has a bad case of the munchies, to me." I raised one shoulder into a shrug.

Starr snorted, but then her expression turned serious. "I guess you heard what Calista had to say about Sprout, then."

Looked like I wasn't going to get out of having this conversation whether I wanted to participate or not.

"I listened to the whole episode," I said carefully. "I'm sorry that she gave Sprout a bad rap. It's undeserved."

Starr blinked, as if surprised. "Thanks."

"I know you and I have very different philosophies about food. . . ." And life. And everything, really. Starr and I were as different as two humans could be, *except* where it came to passion for our business. "But her review was unfair."

"It absolutely was unfair. That's Calista Bryant for you," Starr said bitterly. "She takes joy in bringing other people down."

Was Starr simply referring to the podcast's use of snarky reviews to garner attention? Or was there something more to it? Starr's comment made me wonder if the review had been personal in some way. It certainly seemed vicious enough to be the case. Did they know each other?

"I, uh, I don't know if you saw my Facebook post." Starr fiddled with one of the many holes in her crochet dress, her eyes downcast. "I was angry after the episode came out and I might have implied that some people hadn't earned their reviews the right way."

"I *did* see it, actually," I replied, unable to keep a slight edge out of my tone.

"I don't think you did anything underhanded, for the record." Starr looked back up and met my eyes, a guilty flush spreading across her cheeks. "I felt like I needed to say that to you, face-to-face."

I was taken aback by the comment. Starr and I weren't friends at all, but we'd been in each other's orbit since I'd come home. I'd always gotten the impression she thought I was feeding Azalea Bay the devil's food, and not because of the cannabis, ironically. Starr thought butter and sugar were poison, and therefore I was dealing unhealthy substances to the people of our town.

Could she have sent the anonymous email?

The thought flittered across my mind, like a leaf carried on the wind. What would she have to gain by trying to intimidate me out of my business? Nothing. While we both owned cafés,

I don't think we were exactly serving the same customer base. It wasn't like running me out would make a massive difference to her bottom line.

I shoved the thought away—it was nothing but paranoia.

"I'm sure loads of people who come to the festival will love your nice-cream," I said, not even flinching at the cringeworthy term. Go me.

"And I'm sure loads of people will love your naughty cream," she replied. For a moment, it felt as though something like mutual respect passed between us.

We could coexist in this town, doing our individual things. We might not live by the same code or philosophy, but that didn't mean we couldn't respect one another. Starr waved goodbye just as Grandma Rose, Lawrence and Jake all turned up, faces full of smiles and hands ready to get to work.

The following morning, which was a Thursday, I was in the Baked by Chloe kitchen bright and early. The plan was to prepare everything here—enough for the full day of trade—and then transport it to our stall at the festival. Since it was my first time participating in the festival, we'd decided to keep the menu simple. I'd rather have a limited number of items for sale and ensure that I could make everything well enough to meet my high standards, than bite off more than I could chew and end up with either: A, a subpar product; or B, risk not finishing everything on time.

With input from Aunt Dawn, Erica, Grandma Rose, Jake and Sabrina, I'd decided on three menu items:

1. An ice cream sandwich using my "everything but the kitchen sink" cookies.
2. A lemon meringue sundae.
3. And for a drink option, blueberry ice cream floats.

Each menu item came with a choice of two cannabis-infused ice cream flavors: vanilla bean with blueberry swirl, or classic chocolate. It had been a challenge to come up with three menu items that would taste good with either ice cream option, but we'd gotten there in the end and I was happy with the result.

"Right, have we got everything?" I glanced at Aunt Dawn, Erica and Jake, who were stacking the containers of food and ingredients we needed for a day of selling.

The ice cream was stored in silver tubs with lids, which would fit into the mini freezers the festival organizers had supplied for each stall. As for serving, we had a huge box of specialty ice cream bowls and milkshake cups made from recycled materials, as well as compostable spoons, so I didn't have to feel too terrible about handing out single-use items.

"I've got the cookies, meringues and sundae toppers," Erica said, the boxes stacked so high in front of her on the prep table that she could barely see over the top.

"I've got the ice cream." Jake had carefully placed them all into a large plastic tub packed with ice blocks to ensure they didn't melt during transportation since it was already very warm outside, despite being barely nine a.m.

"I've got the berry syrup, soda waters, and fresh berries," Aunt Dawn chimed in.

"And I have all the cups, bowls, spoons, promotional pamphlets and our uniforms." I let out a breath, feeling a nervous jitter in my stomach. "I think we're good to go."

We hefted the containers up and Aunt Dawn and Erica led the way, out the back to where our cars were parked on the street. It would take two trips to get it all packed into the cars. Jake had come with me that morning, and I was happy for the company to keep my mind off the nerves of working my first festival.

"Thanks so much for offering to help," I said, looking up at him as we headed outside to load up the cars.

"It's fun." He grinned. There was already a band of pink across his cheeks and bridge of his nose from where he'd been working out in his backyard the previous day.

Jake had formerly been a Wall Street guy, where he'd ended up burned out and jaded about corporate life after his close friend had suffered a heart attack in his early thirties. Quitting and moving to the West Coast had been a huge adventure and exercise in freedom for him, and these days he worked for himself, providing financial coaching to young college graduates and early-stage entrepreneurs. The best thing about it was that he could completely set his own hours *and* he could work from anywhere . . . like out on his back deck with a beer in his hand.

It also meant that he'd been able to shuffle some of his appointments to help me with the Baked by Chloe stall today.

"It's great to see you in action." He bobbed his head. Out in the early morning light, I could easily see the warm highlights in his thick brown hair and the freckles scattered across his forearms, cheeks and forehead. "I love how creative you are with your work. If I had to come up with recipe ideas all the time like you do, I feel like my head would explode."

"And if I had to help people with spreadsheets all day like you do, I think *my* head would explode," I joked.

"That just means we make a good team. I can help you with your business finances and you keep me supplied in cookies." He beamed and I couldn't help but laugh. The man did love cookies, that was for sure! In fact, besides Grandma Rose and Aunt Dawn, Jake was fast becoming my go-to taste tester for new recipes.

"I like that arrangement."

Jake and I had been taking things slow on the "relationship" front, not even going so far as to define it or label it. When I'd come home to California to stay with Grandma Rose while she underwent her cancer treatments, I hadn't exactly been sad to leave Paris behind. My life there at one point had been dreamlike, as if I was the main character in a TV show about an American girl making it in the cutthroat world of fine dining, snagging a passionate and fiery French fiancé along the way.

But it had all come apart at the seams. And diving into another relationship had *not* been on my list of goals. Only Jake had popped into my life, and despite some hiccups in the beginning, I was really starting to feel something for him. He was kind, enthusiastic, always up for an adventure.

I liked him a heck of a lot.

But he could clearly sense I was still skittish about giving someone access to my heart, and he seemed happy to go at my pace. So we hadn't put a label on things, but with each week that passed we spent more and more time together. For now, I was happy with where we were at—somewhere in between friends and partners.

We headed over to the Jellybean, our nickname for the powder-blue Fiat 500 which had once belonged to my grandmother and was now my main mode of transportation. It was ridiculously small and anyone who drove it looked a bit like a circus bear riding a unicycle, but Grandma Rose had never been very confident behind the wheel and you could throw this thing sideways into a parking spot and it would still fit. Too bad the engine was flakier than a well-made croissant.

"Please don't give out on me today, old gal." I patted my hand on the roof as Jake started to pile everything into the back.

When it was clear the Jellybean wouldn't fit even half of what I thought it would, we distributed the remainder between Aunt Dawn's and Erica's cars, and then we all headed off to the festival.

We were arriving quite early—maybe even *too* early, since

there were not too many other people around. But I'd rather be set up ahead of schedule and twiddling my thumbs, than rushing to get everything done on time. The sound of birdsong highlighted how quiet the park was as we lugged the boxes to our stall.

"One day I want to be a headliner like that," I said with a decisive nod toward the big tent that Dripping Cones had all to themselves as we walked past.

"You will," Jake and Aunt Dawn replied at exactly the same time. Erica chuckled and nodded in agreement.

It would take more people becoming accepting of cannabis before that happened. My mind drifted to the nasty email from last week, but I quickly shoved the memory aside. No way was I going to let some anonymous email ruin my buzz about the festival.

We approached the "adults only" tent where we would be vending today, and all the sides were rolled down. The rest of the marquee-style tents for the festival had open sides, but since they had to ensure ID checks for our tent, ours were down. The organizers had placed large industrial fans in each corner to keep things cool and I could hear them whirring as we approached.

Nobody was yet stationed outside the tent checking ID, like they would be later on, so we headed straight through the tent's opening, looking around at all the other stalls, which were mostly set up and ready to serve the people of Azalea Bay and beyond come noon.

"It's so exciting to be behind the scenes," Erica said as she walked beside me. "I've been coming to the festival since I was a kid."

"Me too. It's one of my favorite events of the year."

Our booth was on the right-hand side of the tent, and we deposited the items we'd carried from the car. Since we hadn't been able to bring everything in one trip, Jake and I immediately turned tail to head back to the cars for the rest while Erica and Aunt Dawn began unpacking.

"Let's take the other path, I want to see where the food trucks are parked," he said as we headed out of the tent and into the morning sunshine.

"Sure. I heard there's an amazing truck that does all different types of fried ice cream. What's it called?" I racked my brain. "Sweet Crunch, I think."

"Oh yeah!" Jake's eyes lit up. "I saw them on a docuseries that followed four friends starting their own food truck businesses."

Ahead, six colorful food trucks were lined up like tin soldiers. There would be another six on the other side of the festival. Sweet Crunchy—I'd forgotten the Y—had a cool black-and-white truck with splashes of neon-green and yellow paint. A menu was pasted on their window. I grabbed Jake's hand and tugged him over so we could have a sneak peek at what they were selling.

"Oh, look! Tempura-battered matcha ice cream with crispy lotus and candied lemon. Yum!" I was practically salivating. "The cinnamon jam donut one sounds great, too."

"Apparently the jam is homemade by the owner's mother. I'm going to eat my body weight in ice cream this weekend." Jake patted his stomach, which didn't look like it had seen a lick of ice cream in its life.

Ugh, men. It was unfair how fast their metabolisms were.

We walked along, inspecting the trucks. Sweet Crunchy was on the end. Next to it was a business that specialized in dairy-free ice creams, using things like coconut, almond and soy as alternatives. The third truck had the name "Hong Kong Creamery" emblazoned across the front and they had yummy ice cream flavors like milk tea and taro, which you could have topped with the fun add-ons often used for bubble tea, like tapioca pearls and grass jelly. Next to that was a food truck business that made cones out of donut batter topped with soft-serve ice cream. As we were walking past the truck, my foot hit something and I stumbled.

"Whoa!" Jake shot a hand out to steady me and we both looked down to see what had tripped me up.

It was a foot. Two feet.

I stumbled back, shrieking as I caught sight of two feet sticking out from under the donut-cone food truck, the bright green Doc Martens boots almost the exact color of the grass, which explained why we hadn't seen them from a distance. Above the boots were two legs covered in black-and-white striped socks.

"It's Calista." I dropped to my knees. "Call for help. She needs medical attention."

I heard Jake's voice bellow out to a festival staff member walking nearby. But as my eyes adjusted to the darkly shaded patch under the food truck, Calista stared unblinkingly into space, her mouth frozen open into an O of surprise and her face mottled purple and red from where a thick, glossy peach ribbon was tied tightly around her neck. Her body was bent at a weird angle, almost like someone had tried unsuccessfully to push her further under the truck. A couple of yellow rose petals were scattered by her legs and feet, almost like someone had applauded her death.

Unfortunately, no amount of medical attention was going to help her now. Calista Bryant was dead.

CHAPTER 4

"You have a knack for finding dead bodies, Ms. Barnes." Chief Theodore Gladwell had brought Jake and I to the festival's outdoor eating area to ask us some questions.

The area where we'd found Calista's body had been secured with yellow tape and the truck covering her body had been rolled back so the EMTs could get to her, but it was pretty clear that no amount of lifesaving activities would have any effect. I knotted my hands in my lap, squeezing my eyes shut for a moment to try to block out the image of Calista's lifeless expression.

I'd seen her just yesterday, so vibrant and alive . . . wearing those green boots and stripy socks. She must not have made it back to her accommodation.

"I have a knack for baking, Chief," I corrected him. "I have the *misfortune* of finding dead bodies."

He nodded, his expression difficult to read. The chief was in his mid-fifties and I hadn't always been his biggest fan, truth be told. He was as uptight and as straitlaced as they came. A real stickler, which served his job but had always made it feel like he was judging anyone who didn't color inside the lines. At one point he'd been convinced that my aunt was a murderer.

Unfairly so, I might add. He also thought I was nosy and reckless.

Only one of those was true.

Usually the chief could be seen around town in his official uniform, but today he was dressed casually. A checked shirt was tucked neatly into tan pants and a black belt dug into his slightly protruding belly. He was a big man, tall with broad shoulders and hands like dinner plates. While age had softened him some, he still carried himself with a foreboding physical presence.

"How do you know Calista Bryant?" he asked. He had a pen and a notepad in hand.

"She runs a podcast and I'd recently met her in a professional capacity when she featured my business on one of her episodes."

"Your cannabis bakery," the chief said, and I detected a slight note of distaste in his voice.

"That's right." I held my head high. "My perfectly legal, super *popular* cannabis bakery."

Under the table, Jake squeezed my knee, though I wasn't sure if it was a show of support or a warning for me not to poke at the chief. What if Chief Gladwell sent the emails? I dismissed the idea as quickly as it popped into my head. That was ridiculous. Why would the chief of police send anonymous emails threatening a civilian?

"And she spoke highly of your business?" the chief asked. Tiny pinpricks of stubble dotted his jaw, like he hadn't had the chance to shave before he'd been called to the scene. Either that or he hadn't been planning to shave. Like most folks around town, he probably had visions of spending the weekend eating a load of ice cream with his loved ones.

"She did."

"Had you had any subsequent dealings with her?"

"I saw her yesterday as I was setting up my stall for the festival. She came over to say hello and see if I'd listened to the podcast episode. We chatted for a few minutes and I told her I was planning to come by her book-signing today. That was it. We spoke for maybe five minutes."

The chief bobbed his head, his pen scratching across the pages of his notepad. "Can you give me the details of her podcast?"

I relayed the name and specific episode I was featured in, already cringing at the thought that he might listen to it. Not because I was worried about how I might come across, but I immediately thought of Starr and the verbal lashing Calista had given her.

But then something cold slid down my spine.

Hadn't Starr called her the Wicked Witch of the West Coast in her ranting Facebook diatribe? The image of Calista's stripy legs and boots sticking out from under the food truck was burned into my brain. It was almost an exact re-creation of that scene in *The Wizard of Oz* movie where the Wicked Witch of the West had the house fall on her.

That must be a coincidence . . . right?

"Do you know of anyone who might have reason to harm Ms. Bryant?" The chief's question yanked me out of my thoughts.

I gulped. *Oh boy.*

"Ms. Barnes." The chief raised an eyebrow. "If you know something, you're obligated by law to tell me."

"It's just that Calista was . . ." I didn't want to speak ill of the dead, especially when I personally had no gripes, but I had to be truthful. "If you listen to the podcast, you'll see. She could be very harsh in her reviews. I imagine that upset a lot of business owners."

I didn't call Starr out by name because I didn't think it was necessary. If the chief did his job and listened to the episode we were featured in, he would hear it for himself. I'd rather he come to any conclusions on his own than to have me point the finger at someone when they might very well be innocent.

I'd learned that lesson before.

"Anything else that you think we should know?" he asked.

"I don't think so." I knotted my hands in my lap. "I saw some rose petals by the body."

I'm not sure why, but that detail was stuck in my head. It was odd. Odd details usually meant something.

"I mean about your dealings with Ms. Bryant," he said, sounding impatient. "We have the crime scene investigation covered."

I shrugged. "I didn't know her well. I spoke with her twice and we got along fine. She certainly didn't confide anything personal to me, if that's what you're asking."

"What about you?" The chief looked at Jake, who was sitting very close to me, as if feeling protective. I was grateful to have him by my side.

"I never actually met Calista," he said. "I listened to the podcast to support Chloe but that was it."

The chief nodded. "Okay. That will be all for now."

"What do you think is going to happen with the festival?" I asked. We were due to open in two hours. "Obviously I don't want to be disrespectful of the fact that someone has died. . . ."

"TBD." The chief let out a long breath and raked a hand through his hair. For a moment I saw the stress of his job etched onto his face, lines deepening across his forehead and his mouth turning downward as though someone were tugging strings attached to each corner. "The mayor is going to be breathing down my neck about getting this all wrapped up so we can keep the festival going as planned, but there are procedures and rules to follow."

Out of the corner of my eye I spotted a woman approaching. It was Detective Alvarez. She had long dark brown hair pulled back into a ponytail and wide brown eyes blinking almost owlishly behind a pair of perfectly circular silver glasses. She was dressed in her usual white shirt, slacks and sensible loafers.

"Sorry, Chief," she said, her gaze flicking to me as she nodded in acknowledgment. "I need to borrow you for a minute."

"That's okay, we were done here anyway." The chief pushed himself to a standing position and Jake and I followed. "If you remember anything else, please contact me."

I nodded. "Of course."

"And please, Ms. Barnes, don't go actively *seeking* out information, okay? This is not a request for you to conduct your own investigation." He raised an eyebrow at me and I felt my face warm from the admonishment. But there was no point arguing with him, because it would be like arguing with a brick wall.

"Of course not, Chief Gladwell. I just want to get back to my vending duties."

Jake slung an arm around my shoulder as we walked back to the tent, my feet feeling heavier than usual. The festival might not go ahead at all, if police procedures dictated that everything be shut down. And poor Calista. She was barely ten years older than me and her life had been cut tragically short. It was so sad. Likely, she'd also been looking forward to a fun weekend, and had no idea it would be her last.

Three hours later, all the vendors and festival staff were still milling about waiting for updates about whether the festival was going to go ahead as planned. The crime scene had been cordoned off and there was a buzz of activity with police, medical and forensic personnel on site. Evidence markers were placed on the ground, photos were taken and the police were currently in the process of collecting every little thing that could be part of the crime.

They were doing their best to keep people away, but there

were plenty of local workers looking on, worried that yet another murder had taken place in our idyllic little town.

"Are you okay, girlie?" Aunt Dawn gave me a squeeze, her brow furrowed. After she released me, she pressed a water bottle into my hand. "You should drink something. I don't want you fainting in this heat."

"I'm okay," I promised. "But hydration is always a good idea."

The seal on the water bottle cracked as I twisted the cap and opened it, taking a hearty glug and relishing the cool liquid going down my throat. Sweat was already beading along my hairline and gathering in the small of my back. It would be cooler inside the tent, but I couldn't seem to drag my eyes away from the investigation.

"I wonder when they're going to tell us what's going on," Aunt Dawn mused. She pulled a velvet scrunchie from her wrist and dragged her frizzy dark purple hair back into a ponytail to get it off her neck. "I dread to think of all this food spoiling if we don't open today. Especially ours, since it's not like we can donate a bunch of weed products to the local shelter."

"Don't worry." I screwed the water bottle lid back on. "If they shut us down we'll just take everything back to the café and sell it there, at cost if we have to."

"That's a good idea." Aunt Dawn hated food wastage as much as I did.

I glanced around the area. There were dozens of business owners standing around outside the various tents, talking in low tones and constantly glancing in the direction of the crime scene. I'm sure people would be respectful if the police told us to go home because we weren't going to be able to open today, but the uncertainty of not knowing seemed to be getting to everyone. Not to mention that a murder had taken place only a few feet away.

There was a jittery, frenetic energy to the air and it was making me antsy.

"I'm going to go for a walk," I announced. "Maybe there are updates starting to circulate."

Aunt Dawn nodded. "I'll keep watch over the stall with Erica. Is Jake coming back?"

I'd told him to head home rather than stand around and wait. I felt bad that he'd taken the day off work to help me and now there was nothing to do, so we'd agreed that he would pop home until we knew more. Luckily he was so close that he could be back here in five minutes should we need the extra hands.

"Not unless I text him," I said. "But I'll report back if I hear anything."

I wandered away from the crime scene, further into the festival area. Some stalls looked ready to serve customers while others were in mid setup, as though abandoned halfway through the task. I saw people huddled in groups, talking. There was a "green room" set up for event staff and vendors to take breaks and have refreshments away from customers throughout the festival. I figured if there was any information going around, that would probably be where people would head to share it.

The tent for the green room was literally green—smart, because it stood out from the other tents making it easy to find, even if there would be a crowd to get through. During the event it would be staffed, but there was no one at the door currently since customers had not yet been let into the park. Inside were a couple of sets of chairs and tables, a few scattered bean bags, and a long trestle table with a few pitchers of ice water with fruit, packaged snacks like granola bars and small bags of chips, as well as bowls of fresh fruit and mints.

I saw some familiar faces, including Destiny Johnson, Calista's podcast assistant. Her long black braids were pulled up

into a large bun on top of her head, with a few small braids left
to hang free around her face. She wore a sleeveless dress with a
full skirt, featuring a print of brightly colored flamingoes and
frangipani flowers. With her were a man and a woman, both
dressed in vaguely nautical outfits in white and navy. Destiny
looked over at me as I came inside the tent.

"Hi." I raised a hand in greeting. "I'm so sorry for your
loss."

Destiny looked rather unmoved by my comment. "Well . . .
it's a shock."

It was then I noticed that she didn't appear to show any visible signs of grief or distress—no red-rimmed eyes, no tear
tracks on her cheeks, no smudged mascara. Not everyone out-
wardly emoted in times of stress, but if I didn't know any better, it looked like any other day for Destiny Johnson.

"Chloe, this is Tristan Patrick and Anouk De Vries." She
gestured to the man and woman.

"Hello." My attention was momentarily diverted from Destiny's strangely subdued reaction to her boss's death to the
people standing in front of me. "It's nice to meet you both."

"Call me Annie," the woman said with a polite smile as we
shook hands.

"You probably heard about Chloe's cannabis café on *Starch
Nemesis*," Destiny added.

"Oh, that's right." Tristan nodded, recognition flashing
across his face.

Tristan Patrick was not your average festival vendor. He was
an international restaurateur, award-winning chef and something of a food industry heartthrob. At over six feet tall with
sun-bleached blond hair, tanned skin and a square jaw, he gave
off strong Ken doll vibes. Not my type, admittedly. There was
something a little artificial about his appearance, like maybe
that his tan was fake or that his teeth were slightly too white. I
wondered if that's how all celebrities looked in real life—like

their appearance was designed for a television screen and not for the in-person experience.

Anouk—or rather, Annie—was the polar opposite. She had mousy brown hair cut into a blunt bob, small eyes, and a slim figure dressed in a starched buttoned-up white shirt, a navy pencil skirt that fell below her knees and chunky brown loafers. Her face appeared young but the outfit . . . well, it was a bit old-fashioned and made it difficult to guess how old she actually was. Thirties? Forties? I couldn't tell. Her only adornments were a pair of simple gold stud earrings, a small vintage-style cameo brooch pinned to the pocket at her chest and a *huge* glittering diamond ring that seemed completely at odds with the rest of her unassuming appearance.

The rock was beaming so much I wished I'd brought my sunglasses. Seriously, that thing was the size of a river pebble.

The way she hovered next to Tristan I had to imagine he was the one who'd put the ring on her finger. They struck me as an odd couple—he seemed to thrive on the spotlight and she looked like she would shy away from it.

"A glowing review from Calista is not something to be taken lightly. You studied at Le Cordon Bleu, correct?" Tristan asked.

"That's right." I nodded, still having trouble getting my tongue working properly. Was this what it felt like to be star-struck?

"Who did you work for in Paris? I know a lot of people in the scene there."

I mentioned a few of my bosses and it turned out we had some mutual connections—well, by mutual connections I mean that I'd worked in the kitchens owned by some of his friends, though I had been too far down the pecking order at the time for my name to have stuck in their minds. But still, knowing there was a crossover in the Venn diagram of our lives, even if it was only a sliver, was pretty darn cool.

"It's terrible what happened to Calista," he said after we moved on from the industry chitchat, his voice smooth as though he was giving an interview. "Such a bright light in our industry snuffed out all too soon. It's tragic, I tell you. *Tragic.*"

Annie nodded but didn't contribute anything. Destiny's eyes wandered to the opening of the tent, as though she was waiting for someone to arrive.

"She would want the show to go on, you know," he continued, nodding. "There is great food to be eaten and I have no doubt she would wish for this event to take place as planned. No doubt at all."

It sounded like Tristan knew Calista beyond being a listener of her podcast. Perhaps she'd interviewed him at some point. Or maybe they'd worked together. I knew Calista had worked in the food industry for many years *before* her podcast blew up. It was part of how she'd become famous—lots of industry contacts.

"It shouldn't be taking so long," he finished with a huff.

"The police have to do their job, Tris." Annie curled one hand protectively around his arm, her body almost melding with his, she was standing so close to him. "It's a crime scene now."

Well, *part* of the event was a crime scene. But maybe they could just block that bit off and let everything else go. Was that wishful thinking? Maybe.

"The poor owners of that food truck," I said. "Even if we get started I doubt they'll be able to join in. The police probably have to check the vehicle to see if it was involved with the murder."

"Murder." Destiny shuddered. It was the first time I'd seen any kind of emotional reaction from her. "Of course Calista would go out with something as dramatic as a public murder."

I frowned. What an odd thing to say.

"I always knew she would get herself in trouble," Tristan said, his voice losing its interview-ready polish for a moment as a slight crack split the word *trouble* in two. Something flashed across his face—something that felt real and a little raw—but it was gone before I could fully read him. "Calista didn't know when to stop. Sometimes she just went too far and . . ."

"She went too far, how?" I asked. Was he talking about her snarky interviews or had something else happened in the past?

"There was this guy," Annie said, shaking her head and making a clucking sound. "He was interested in her."

"*Stalking* her," Destiny muttered.

"She rejected him in a very public way," Annie explained. "Made a big, ranting post on her socials about how she was sick of some men not taking no for an answer."

Tristan frowned. "I didn't mean—"

"Hello! Hello, everyone!" Before Tristan could finish answering, a tall man with a beet-red face burst into the tent, his voice loud and desperate. He wore a suit, with the jacket slung over his arm and sweat patches gathering at the armpits of his shirt, which I saw when he raised his free hand to get everyone's attention. It was the event organizer—Miles O'Meara.

"Everybody, the police have informed me that we *will* be able to open the festival today albeit in a modified capacity. Gates will open by two p.m. I suggest you all head back to your stalls and get prepared. Thank you for your patience and please spread the word."

He hurried out of the green room tent before anyone could even think about asking questions. Tristan and Annie followed after Miles, leaving Destiny and I standing together. For a moment everyone stood around, exchanging glances as the news sunk in, then there was a flurry of activity as we all poured out of the tent.

It looked like the show would go on after all.

CHAPTER 5

Based on his earlier comments, I suspected that the chief had been pushed into letting the event go ahead by the mayor. Thankfully, because the food trucks were parked off to the side of all the tents and not in the middle of the action, the event organizers were able to separate things. Crime scenes took quite a long time to clear, I'd learned recently. A single hotel room had been cordoned off for more than twenty-four hours . . . and that was when the police weren't even sure a murder had occurred.

This time there was no ambiguity—ribbons didn't simply tie themselves around a person's neck.

As I walked back to my stall, I noticed there were now large tarps hanging up, blocking the view of the crime scene. Probably best not to have festivalgoers watching real-life CSI while they ate their ice cream.

"We heard the news!" Erica waved with both hands as I made my way over to our stall. She was in her pink uniform apron, which had our initials, BbC, embroidered in a scrolling font with a little cannabis leaf accent on the chest pocket. "Looks like we're opening after all."

"We sure are."

Erica handed me an apron and I slipped it over my head. Our stall was pretty much ready to go, since Aunt Dawn and Erica had unpacked and set up our recipe components, printed materials and serving utensils earlier, while Jake and I had been waiting around for Chief Gladwell.

"Any updates on Calista?" Aunt Dawn asked.

She was neatening our stand of pamphlets about how to consume cannabis responsibly, dosage information, differences between THC and CBD, and potential medicinal benefits. Not only was I passionate about destigmatization *and* creating the best treats possible, but I was also passionate about making sure people knew how to consume safely.

"I bumped into her assistant, Destiny," I said. "She, uh . . . didn't seem all that shaken up by the fact that her boss was found dead."

"I'm not surprised," Aunt Dawn replied, which to me *was* a surprise. She'd met Calista and Destiny the day they came for a private tasting at Baked by Chloe.

"Why do you say that?" I asked.

"I got a weird vibe when they came to visit." She lifted one shoulder into a shrug. "I don't think they liked each other much."

I thought back to their visit, but nothing jumped out in my mind to corroborate my aunt's observation. It was all a bit of a blur and I'd been so anxious I wasn't my usual observant self. I always trusted Aunt Dawn's opinion on stuff like that, however. She was good at reading people.

"I guess lots of people don't like their boss," I said with a shrug. "That's nothing too unusual."

"So you don't think she did it?" Erica asked.

"That's not for me to find out," I replied, remembering the earlier warning I'd received. "Chief Gladwell asked if I had

any idea who might have killed her and I said that she's probably pissed off *a lot* of people with her podcast. That's an almost
endless supply of suspects."

"Not endless," mused Aunt Dawn. "They have to be *here*."

That was an unsettling thought.

"Well, I don't want to have murderers on my mind today," I
said. "I'm very sad that Calista is gone, of course. It's absolutely awful that someone would do that to her and I'm sorry
her family is going to have such tragic news."

"What a call to receive." Erica clucked her tongue and
shook her head. "Those poor people."

"I know," I said with a sigh. "It's the call absolutely nobody
would ever want or could ever be prepared for."

But as much empathy as I had for Calista's family, I was also
determined to follow the chief's instruction not to go out "actively seeking" information. I was just a bystander like everyone else.

*A bystander who found the body and has solved two murders
previously.*

There was no time like the present to start following the
rules, right? I could keep my nose clean for once.

"But I want us to have fun and I want our customers to be
delighted and to have a great day." I nodded, trying to pick my
mood up and stop thinking about the murder. The police
would do their job and I would do mine. "Sound good?"

"Sounds excellent, girlie." Aunt Dawn gave me a squeeze
and Erica nodded her enthusiastic agreement. "Let's get this
show on the road."

The first couple of hours of the annual Azalea Bay Ice
Cream Festival were, in a word, bonkers. I don't think Aunt
Dawn, Erica or I stopped to catch our breath as soon as people
flooded into the tent, and there seemed to be a line at every
stall. I'd hurriedly sent an SOS text to Jake about half an hour

in and he'd come rushing over to help out. There was barely enough room for all four of us behind the stall, so we had to be clear about who was doing what.

Jake was on drinks duty, making the ice cream floats. Erica was on sundaes and ice cream sandwiches, and Aunt Dawn was on quality control and handing over the orders once they were made, along with napkins, spoons, straws, pamphlets, etc. I was on the register, being the face of the business. It wasn't my usual role, I had to admit. I was at my best in the background—creating in the kitchen and getting lost in ideas for new recipes. But I was excited to meet customers new and old for the four days of the festival, and it seemed a *lot* of people had heard about me from *Starch Nemesis*, and wanted to say hello.

"I was practically drooling the *entire* episode." A bubbly woman with a curvy figure in her late twenties stood in front of me, eyes sparkling with excitement. "I will literally eat anything that Calista recommends. I was a bit of a pothead back in my college days, but I like edibles way more now. Doesn't make the smell hang around in my hair and I appreciate that."

As if to emphasize her point she tossed her rather impressive mane of natural copper hair over one shoulder in a way that made it look like she'd spent her entire life practicing being in a shampoo commercial. And with glorious hair like that, she probably could!

"I'm so happy you stopped by today. I'm sure you'll *love* the sundae," I replied with a friendly smile. "Just head down to the end of the stall and your name will be called when your order is ready."

I scrawled her name on the receipt and placed it next in line behind four others that were waiting to be picked up.

"Hi there," I said to the next customer in line. "Welcome to Baked by Chloe, where we give your baked goods a higher purpose."

A woman in her fifties walked forward, hand stuck out on a ramrod straight arm. "Deirdre Niece. My friends call me Dee. I'm a podcaster."

"Hello." I shook her hand. "Great to meet you."

Deirdre was shorter than me, with a large bosom that swayed heavily under a loose maxi print dress. The fabric was so heavily patterned I felt my eyes go a bit crossed, almost like I was trying to solve one of those Magic Eye things. She wore a set of earrings with a matching necklace and bracelets from which dangled an array of colorful sailboat charms. The whole effect was a little gaudy, but weirdly, it suited her.

"What can we tempt you with today?" I asked.

I gestured to the small printed sign that Jake had helped me design in Photoshop. It showed all three of our menu items with a cute border made of Eiffel Towers, macarons and cannabis leaves all in pretty shades of sage green and pink.

"I'll take one of each." It was so loud in the tent I had struggled to hear some customers, but I had no trouble hearing Deirdre. Her voice boomed loud as though she knew exactly how to project it. Theatre training perhaps? Or maybe she was a teacher or presenter of some kind? "I'd love to interview you for my podcast. My show is *very* popular. No doubt you've heard of it. *Cheesed Off.*"

She looked at me expectantly. I had not, in fact, heard of *Cheesed Off.* But something about the woman's aggressive assurance that her podcast was popular made me suspect that if I admitted I didn't know of it, I probably would offend her.

"Of course," I said with a smile, biting back a small surge of guilt at telling a lie. "I *love* listening to food podcasts. It's wonderful to meet you in person."

She beamed and I had a feeling that I'd given the correct response, even if it wasn't a truthful one. "Well, about that interview? Maybe we could go now?"

I glanced at the line snaking away from our stall and cringed. "I'm sorry, we're super busy right now. The delayed opening meant there was quite a rush and I don't want to leave my team to manage it without me."

"What about this evening? The festival doesn't close too late, right? We could meet after." Her smile was determined. This woman would not take no for an answer. "What do you say?"

"Sure," I relented. I would probably be exhausted by then, but promotion was a good thing if I wanted my business to grow. And what harm could a podcast interview do? "Why don't you come by the stall here around closing time and we'll find somewhere to talk?"

"Excellent." She nodded and pulled a wallet out of a small bag that was clipped around her waist. "I look forward to it."

I rang up her purchase and she headed down to the waiting area, where I could hear her telling the other waiting customers that she ran a podcast. Well, she seemed to have the self-promotion thing down pat. I made a mental note to look up her show before the meeting since I had lied about knowing it.

"She seems pushy," Erica said with a wrinkled nose as she came up beside me to grab the next lot of orders. "Fancy pressuring you into an interview in front of all your customers. So rude!"

I chuckled. Erica was protective of those in her circle, and I was proud to be there as both her boss and her friend.

"I'm sure she's harmless," I replied. "Some people just don't really get the whole social etiquette thing."

"Or they choose to ignore it," Erica muttered. "But I guess all publicity is good publicity, as they say."

"True."

By hour four, I needed to trade jobs to give my voice a break. Eventually, the initial rush died down as some folks headed off to the beach with full bellies. It meant there was less noise in the tent and we could work at a bit of a slower pace, at least for the moment. There were also regular showcases and presentations happening at a makeshift stage in the middle of the festival that would also draw people away from the stalls a few times a day.

Currently, a manufacturer of ice cream machines was doing a demo of how to make ice cream at home. Tomorrow and the day after, the organizers were having a fun competition to make the best sundae possible in under a minute, as well as a few bigger-name guests doing individual presentations. That's why Tristan Patrick was here. He was one of the headliners. Tomorrow afternoon he would be showing people how he created his world-famous dessert—"Joys of Nature."

Yes, it was a rather ostentatious name for a dessert. But Tristan Patrick was a rather ostentatious man *and* he'd twice been nominated for the James Beard Award for Outstanding Pastry Chef, so he'd earned the right to give his desserts over-the-top names. I wondered how much he was getting paid to attend the festival—probably a lot. Hopefully I'd be able to duck away for a break when his session was on so I could watch for a few minutes. Nothing inspired me more than watching a high-caliber chef at work.

"Chloe, that's two more sundaes. Both with vanilla and blueberry," Erica said, bringing me back to the task at hand. "And, Jake, one ice cream float with chocolate."

My sundae was no "Joys of Nature" but it was a delicious dessert, in my humble opinion. To start, I spooned tart lemon curd into the bottom of a bowl. That was followed with the cannabis-infused ice cream—two small scoops per sundae, which I measured out precisely to ensure the dosage was as correct as possible. We were purposely going with a smaller serving size than I would use in the café. This was for two reasons. One, because people at the festival often wanted to try multiple dishes and a smaller serving meant they could have more variety. Two, because the strain of cannabis I had used for the ice cream was fairly potent.

The strain was from a small local grower and it was called Christmas Morning. The flavor profile was deliciously sweet—with notes of lemon and blueberry and a gentle grassy greenness that provided a fresh balance. Since this strain didn't have anywhere near as much of the earthy, funky (or skunky) scent that some people found off-putting, I'd reserved it for the ice cream festival because A, it would pair great with the sweet desserts we were serving; and B, it was a good "starter" strain for edibles, so long as I kept the dosage on the lower side to account for the high potency.

After the ice cream went into the bowl over the curd, I snapped two thin lemon cookies in half, carefully arranging the shards in the bowl so they stuck out at interesting angles. I then tucked three small meringues around the ice cream, nestling them down into the curd on the bottom. With a spoon I drizzled some more lemon curd over the ice cream, creating a pretty splash of vibrant yellow against the creamy white ice cream with rich blueberry swirls. To garnish I used a wheel of candied lemon, which had been lightly scorched with a kitchen blowtorch, and sprinkled some crushed salted macadamia nuts on top for crunch and a delicious saltiness to contrast and brighten the citrus and vanilla.

"Two sundaes, ready to go!" I brought the bowls to the serving area and placed them down so Aunt Dawn could call out the customer's name.

I was about to head back to collect the next order when something caught my eye—a thick, glossy peach ribbon. It formed the handle of a beautiful peach, white, and powder-blue striped bag, the kind that you might receive for your purchase at an upmarket retail store. I'd looked at getting similar bags for Baked by Chloe, with those luxurious ribbons, but they had been out of my price range.

This time, however, I wasn't struck by the beauty of the ribbon so much as the familiarity of it. It looked identical to the ribbon I'd seen tied around Calista Bryant's neck. The ribbon that had most certainly cut off her airway and caused her to expire.

"Excuse me." I stepped around Aunt Dawn and leaned over the table we were using as a serving counter, waving to get the customer's attention. She smiled in response. "Hi, I . . . this might be silly, but that bag you're carrying is so pretty. Where did you get it?"

"It's nice, isn't it?" She turned the bag around to show me the logo printed on the front. At the sight of it—so very familiar—my blood ran cold. "It's from this cool organic café called Sprout."

Also known as the organic café owned by none other than Starr Bright.

CHAPTER 6

"Do you think you could hold down the fort for a bit?" I asked Aunt Dawn.

Her eyebrows immediately shot up in concern. It wasn't like me to leave the business when there was work to be done. Most days she practically had to shoo me out with a broom to take my lunch break. But the line was manageable, only one to two customers deep and it had been like that for the last twenty minutes while the demonstrations were going on.

"Sure." She nodded. "Is everything okay?"

I debated whether to tell her about the ribbon, but I figured I could catch her up tonight. At the very least I could hear what Starr had to say rather than accidentally starting a rumor. But things were not looking good here—first Calista publicly trashed Starr on her podcast, then Starr retaliated by calling her the Wicked Witch of the West Coast, then Calista's dead body was found with two stripy legs sticking out from under a food truck with Starr's ribbon tied around her neck.

Could Starr be a killer?

There was part of me that just couldn't see it. Sure, she could be gossipy and judgmental, but who wasn't from time to time? As much as folks liked to think of themselves as being above such behaviors, everyone could have a bad day here and there and make a snide comment or say something they shouldn't. It was human. It didn't make her—or anyone else—a fundamentally bad person. It certainly didn't make them a killer.

"I'm just going to grab something to eat and stretch my legs," I said, which wasn't untrue. I planned to pop into the green room and grab a drink and a granola bar and some fruit, but first I had a stop to make.

I slipped off my apron and slung my bag over one shoulder, before heading outside. I wasn't exactly sure where Sprout's stall was located within the festival, so I headed toward the front entrance where a board showcased the layout of the festival. All the business names were listed with a grid ID to show where they were on the map.

"Sprout, Sprout, Sprout . . ." I ran my finger down the list. "A2."

That was on the westernmost side of the festival, toward the top of the park.

The festival was absolutely buzzing with activity. Families wandered around, wrangling excited children and coaxing smiles from sullen teenagers. There were couples hand in hand, groups of friends laughing and sharing their purchases, and solo ice cream lovers all indulging their tastebuds. I walked past a small seating area and saw a group of young women with their phones out, their collection of elaborately topped ice cream cups all pushed together to make for a sugary sweet Instagram-worthy picture.

It warmed my heart. Food, I had always believed, brought people together.

I scanned the stalls as I crossed over to the other side of the festival. Each marquee held stalls of a similar theme, like how Baked by Chloe was in the "adults only" marquee. Sprout had been grouped with other wellness and health-focused businesses in the "happy healthy ice cream" marquee. The businesses here had a variety of health and dietary focuses including a business called Co-co Cones which specialized in vegan desserts, another which made low-sugar and diabetes-friendly ice creams, a gluten- and nut-free dessert bar, and a place which specialized in avocado-based desserts called Avo Good Day. Their menu featured a large picture of what appeared to be a frozen chocolate mousse and rich chocolate ice cream. I made a mental note to check them out in more detail later.

That was intriguing to me, since I loved avocados.

Yes, I was a Millennial cliché.

Sprout had a large stall at the back of the marquee, and several people milled around, some carrying the bags with the telltale peach ribbons. The stall itself was beautifully decorated, just like the permanent café on Azalea Bay's main strip. There was a large board with a neon-pink sign which said "yum" in scrolling letters, the edge of which was covered in trailing white flowers—fake, I suspected, both for practicality and cost—but the effect was visually stunning and very on-brand for Starr.

I rose up onto my tiptoes to look over the crowd to see if I could spot Starr serving customers. But there were three people on duty, not one of them her. Maybe she'd gone for a break.

I skirted around the people lining up, ignoring the dirty look one older man shot me. I wasn't queue-jumping, though.

"Hi, Chloe!" One of the girls smiled brightly at me as she spooned fruit salad over a large scoop of yellow ice cream that looked like it could be mango-flavored. I'd seen her a few times working at Sprout and she'd come into Baked by Chloe once or twice. I knew her to be Mei Lin, a college student who was home for the summer.

"Hey, is Starr around? I was hoping to catch her."

Mei Lin's expression immediately turned wary. "She's not here right now."

I could see that with my own eyes, but something about Mei Lin's change of mood made something strange settle in my stomach. "Do you know where I can find her?"

"Um . . ." Her eyes darted over to her colleague, a blond woman of around thirty, but the woman was engaged in chatting with a customer while she processed their purchase. "I don't know."

"You don't know or you can't tell me?" I asked gently. I didn't want to stress the poor girl out, but I had a horrible feeling that something bad was going on.

"I really don't know." The wariness slipped away to reveal genuine worry underneath. "I had ducked off to use the restroom and when I came back she was gone. That was more than *four* hours ago."

That was right around the time the festival opened, perhaps slightly before. It seemed odd that Starr would vanish at such a critical time. I know she was as excited about vending at the festival as I was.

"I called Rhea to come and help me when Starr didn't come back and Liz only just started her shift an hour ago." Mei Lin nodded toward the blond woman. "We've all tried contacting Starr to see what's going on, but she won't pick up or answer our texts."

I frowned. "That's odd."

Mei Lin bit down on her lip. "I'm supposed to go home in an hour and I promised my mom I'd help her with some stuff. She's going to be upset if I don't show up."

"Starr will turn up," I said, reassuringly. "But if I hear anything at all, I'll make sure to come tell you."

"Thanks." Mei Lin nodded. "We haven't stopped all afternoon."

I decided to head to the green room and grab a few water bottles to bring back for the workers at Sprout. The temperature was still rising and even though there was a lovely ocean breeze rolling through, when it died down the heat could feel oppressive.

Where could Starr have gotten to?

I spotted the green room tent and headed toward it, passing by another marquee—this one was specifically aimed at kids with its brightly colored stalls and mascot walking around in a large ice-cream-cone outfit. Massive props to whoever that was, because it had to be *scorching hot* inside a costume on a day like this. I skirted around the kids' tent, dodging a boy and girl of about ten who were racing around, faces sticky with ice cream and their parents looking more than a little harried. I imagined there would be some very tired moms and dads in Azalea Bay tonight!

Past the kids' tent was the open stage, where it looked like the "making ice cream at home" demonstration was ending. I picked up my pace, because once the audience dispersed, we might find ourselves with a busier stall again.

I hurried toward the green room tent where there were fewer people milling about—due to both its slightly out-of-the-way location and the fact that it was only meant for festival staff and vendors. I raised my lanyard up to the woman checking names at the tent's entrance and she waved me through with a bored expression. This might be the least fun job at the festival . . . well, aside from the people who have to install and remove the portable toilets!

Inside, it was cooler and I welcomed the shade and fans with a contented sigh. My uniform T-shirt was clinging to my lower back and my ponytail felt sticky against the back of my neck. I lifted it up and used my other hand to fan my overheated skin. Glancing around the tent, it was clear that Starr wasn't here.

There were only five people in the tent—two older women

wearing matching candy-stripe shirts, a man eating a sandwich and watching something on his phone with earbuds in, a woman hunched over a book, and the owner of Dripping Cones, who was talking softly into her phone. She caught my eye and smiled, raising a hand in a friendly wave. All of us local business owners tended to know one another, but her phone call continued and I didn't want to interrupt to see if she'd seen Starr about.

I was about to grab the water bottles and head back out when I heard sniffling near me. The woman who was hunched over the book wasn't actually reading—she was crying. It was the kind of crying where it was clear she was trying not to draw attention to herself. Soft sniffles, a covert wipe of her eyes. I didn't recognize her, so she was likely from out of town.

I hovered for a minute—fighting between my desire to see if she was okay and my desire to figure out what had happened to Starr. But in the end, I couldn't leave the poor crying woman without at least seeing if she was okay or if she needed anything.

"Excuse me?" I asked as I stood by her table, bending down slightly to catch her eye. "Are you okay?"

She lifted her head, revealing two red and watery eyes, a runny nose and tear-tracked cheeks covered in a heavy smattering of cinnamon freckles. Her skin was a light brown color and she had a gap between her front teeth that made her look younger than I suspected she was. For a moment I thought she was going to tell me to get lost—there was a sharp defensive air around her, despite the tears. But all of a sudden, her eyes dropped to the logo on my shirt and recognition flashed across her face like lightning.

"Are you Chloe?" she asked.

"I am." It was strange to be recognized, although I'm not sure it would have happened if I was out of uniform.

"I heard all about your cannabis café on the *Starch Nemesis* podcast," she said, her eyes watering again as her voice cracked. "I was going to come visit your stall on my break, but then I heard . . ."

I lowered myself into the seat next to her. "Were you friends with Calista?"

"Not friends, exactly." She shook her head. "But she came out to visit my first business a few years back, gave us a glowing review. It really put us on the map."

She reached into a small bag that was hanging off the side of her chair and pulled out her wallet. She fished out a business card and handed it to me—*desserts for the soul, inspired by soulful Southern cooking.* Her name was Tamika.

"She would come and visit us from time to time. I was always struck by how passionate she was about food. My mama raised me just like that." Tamika sniffled. "Food is how you show others you care."

I felt that in my heart. "I'm really sorry for your loss."

"I told her she was digging where she shouldn't be digging." Tamika shook her head and let out a heavy sigh.

"What do you mean?"

"She was working on some big exposé thing. Last time she visited me, she hinted that it was going to blow *Starch Nemesis*'s success out of the water."

"Another podcast?"

Tamika nodded. "Yeah, but kind of an investigative show with a limited run. Not a big ongoing thing like what she was already doing. But she said if it went well, she might do another season. There were plenty of scandals in the food world. Her words, not mine."

Interesting. A big exposé from the food world that she was going to share with her million-plus audience. That could make someone pretty mad. After all, there had to be people involved . . . otherwise what would be the point of producing a show exposing something if there were no consequences?

"Do you know what it was about?" I asked.

Tamika shook her head. "She didn't say. Only that it was something to do with a person she'd previously respected and worked with . . . but that could be anyone. She was in the industry a long dang time."

I nodded. "True."

"I told her to be careful." Her breath hitched as she fought back a small sob. "I said people get really protective when you go digging around their patch. She didn't listen. Calista never listened to anyone."

The list of possible reasons that Calista Bryant might have been killed seemed to be growing faster than kudzu. There were all the business owners she'd ticked off with her blunt reviews, a potential stalker she'd publicly rejected, and now a possible exposé podcast that was sure to ruffle feathers. I wondered if that was what Tristan Patrick had been about to mention when we got interrupted in the green room, earlier. Maybe Destiny Johnson would know about the exposé, given she was working for Calista.

This is not your investigation. Leave it to the police.

I would. But I had promised the chief if I heard anything—*without* soliciting—then I would pass it on.

From what I could tell there seemed to be people who loved and hated Calista in equal quantities. That was her in a nutshell: polarizing. But which one of these things was responsible for her death?

It could be any of them.

The rest of the day was a blur. After dropping some water off to the employees of Sprout—who still had not heard from Starr—I headed back to my stall to find Aunt Dawn, Erica and Jake swamped with customers. We were busy until about forty-five minutes before closing, when we ran out of some ingredients. The cookies, for example, needed to be baked fresh each day for the ice-cream sandwiches and the sundaes, so I would be back in the café's kitchen before opening tomorrow to whip up that day's batch.

"Wow, that was nuts." Jake raked a hand through his hair and let out a long sigh.

"Wall Street here has clearly never worked in food service before." Erica chuckled as she moved past him to tidy up all our serving bowls and cutlery for the next day. Since we could only make the ice cream floats with what we had left, most customers were deciding to come back tomorrow instead. "Bit different to working in a suit and tie, eh?"

Jake chuckled good-naturedly. "Uh, just a little. But I'll take being run off my feet over having some number cruncher breathing down my neck all day long."

It was hard to imagine Jake in an expensive suit, with his hair gelled and game face on. Especially looking at him right now, wearing Converse high-tops and shorts that had little flamingos embroidered on them and the braided leather bracelet he always wore on one wrist. He didn't have that cutthroat corporate vibe, because his personality was so laid-back and easygoing.

"Thanks for helping out." I placed a hand on his arm and smiled. "It was a lifesaver having that extra pair of hands today."

"Any time." He nodded. "I was going to be all chivalrous and offer to make you dinner tonight, but would it be terrible to suggest we order pizza instead? I'm exhausted."

My stomach growled loudly at the mention of pizza. "Count me in for the minimal effort option."

"I know you said you only wanted me to work the first day to help make sure everything was going smoothly, but something tells me tomorrow is going to be just as busy," he said. "I can help you out all weekend if you want. Being summer, my workload is pretty quiet anyway."

"Really?" I let out a sigh of relief. "That would be amazing."

We started preparing the stall for the next day's trade and I served the last-minute customers who came by, letting them know we only had the ice cream floats left for today. Some were simply happy to have a cold drink, and I had one couple tell me about how they had a small grow-op just for family and friends on the property where they'd built a tree-house-inspired tiny home. The self-described "legit stoners" were super friendly and I loved seeing the pictures of their adorable home.

I even had time to look up the *Cheesed Off* podcast in preparation for my meeting with Deirdre Niece. One thing I could immediately tell was that this production was nowhere near as professional as *Starch Nemesis*. For starters, the podcast's logo was a little . . . budget. The slice of Swiss cheese on a serving plate looked like a DIY job, rather than something done by a graphic designer. I also noticed that the episodes weren't released in a consistent fashion. There would be episodes weekly for a month or two, and then there would be a several-month break, then a single episode and another break, then another smattering before it petered off again.

Perhaps this was more of a hobby for Deirdre rather than a job?

I switched with Aunt Dawn for the last fifteen minutes, leaving her to chat with customers while I popped my AirPods in and quickly took stock of what we had left, what I needed to make the following morning, and whether we were likely to run out of any of the serving items or things I had made in advance, like the lemon curd and ice cream, etc.

While I scribbled in my notebook, the podcast played into my ears.

"This is Dee and you're listening to Cheesed Off, *a podcast for food lovers where I tell you what and where to*

eat, and which places you should avoid. So grab a cup of
coffee and don't let your delicate sensibilities lead you to
be . . . Cheesed Off."

I winced at the cringe-worthy delivery. Jamming the podcast
title into the opening spiel sounded forced and unnatural, like
Deirdre had been determined to make it fit even when it didn't.
Okay, so it definitely wasn't as polished as *Starch Nemesis*, with
its quality writing and high-level production. But I wasn't about
to cancel the interview simply because the podcast didn't appear to be a big one—after all, I believed in supporting small
businesses, so that should probably cross over into media businesses, too, right?

"In today's episode I'm going to take you on a tour of
food trucks in an unlikely food mecca: Indianapolis."

The wording made me hit pause on my phone. An "unlikely
food mecca" was exactly how Calista had described Azalea
Bay in her latest podcast. It was a specific turn of phrase that
jumped out at me. Frowning, I hit play again.

"Now I know some of you still listen to Starch Nemesis,
even after I told you about my history with . . . well, I try
to keep it PG13, so I won't use the word I'd like to use.
And I know *they did an episode recently on this. Do you*
know how Calista Bryant even heard of Indianapolis
being a great spot for food trucks in the first place? Uh,
that would be me. I told her I was going to record this
episode and yeah . . . that was a year ago. But still, it was
my idea and she stole it. Just like she stole Starch Nemesis
for her title. I came up with that name!
"Anyway, today we're not talking about back-stabbing
former friends. We're talking about portable restaurants."

I was startled by a nudge in the ribs and when I looked up, I saw Aunt Dawn gesturing to a woman standing in front of the register. It was Deirdre Niece and she was waving at me enthusiastically.

It looked like she was yet another person with a grudge against Calista Bryant.

CHAPTER 7

Since the festival was closing and we all needed to vacate until the following day, Deirdre and I decided to have the interview at Baked by Chloe because it would be quiet and we could talk uninterrupted. I drove us over in the Jellybean and she spent the entire trip name-dropping people in the food industry.

"I met Guy Fieri once, great guy. Ha! No pun intended." We were almost at the café and she'd been prattling on without taking a breath. I hadn't even gotten a word in. "I think he might have had a bit of a crush on me, you know. And then there was Adriano Zumbo, who I met when he was filming in LA. I spotted him at a restaurant and just walked right over. Some people are too shy to do that, but not me. They're always happy to hear from someone who appreciates their work and they all love talking to me."

I knew having worked with some very successful chefs—one who did a brief stint on a French reality cooking show—that this was not necessarily the case.

"Christina Tosi and I hit it off big-time. She thought I was absolutely hilarious." She let out a deep, raspy laugh as if to back up her point. "You know, I guess I just have one of those magnetic personalities. I'm a real extrovert, ya know. Life of the party."

I was already regretting my decision to do this interview. Not only was the name-dropping a massive cringe, but someone dominating the conversation with how "hilarious" and "magnetic" they were was a big turnoff. Nothing wrong with being confident, but this was a bit much.

I pulled into one of the parking spots outside the café. "Well, Deirdre, let's head inside and talk some more."

"Call me Dee, all my friends do. And I feel like we could be great friends! You know, I have the sense I'm winning you over." She got out of the car and bustled up to the front of the shop ahead of me, her maxi skirt dusting the ground like she was a living broom. "You might be quiet, but I can tell when someone likes me."

My quietness was simply a lack of opportunity to participate in the conversation, but I didn't voice that out loud. Instead I walked up to the door and cleared my throat so she would move aside to let me unlock it.

"Welcome to Baked by Chloe," I said as I opened the door and held it for her. "Azalea Bay's premiere cannabis café."

"It's real cute," she said, nodding her head as she walked inside. "I like the Paris theme. Have you visited?"

I blinked in surprise. I'd expected that Dee might have done *some* research if she'd wanted to interview me for her podcast, and the fact that I'd studied and trained in Paris for years before coming back to America was right at the top of the "about" page on the company website. Not exactly information that was hard to gather.

"Uh, yeah," I said, motioning for her to take a seat at one of the tables. "After I finished college here I went to Paris and trained at Le Cordon Bleu. I then worked under several fine dining chefs around Paris before making the move back to California and opening this café."

"Right, right."

"So you run the podcast by yourself?" I asked. "That must be a lot of work."

"Oh, it is." She nodded vigorously. "I even learned Photoshop to make the logo myself. You know, that's what it's like when you run a small business. You have to wear all the hats!"

I understood the sentiment, although I didn't necessarily agree. I'd hired a graphic designer to do the Baked by Chloe logo because if I tried to do it . . . well, I would also have ended up with something that looked like it was made with clip art. Running a small business meant doing a lot of things by yourself, but it also meant outsourcing to experts sometimes, too.

Dee pulled out a microphone with a stand and put it on the table in front of me. Then she clipped a smaller microphone to her chest and set her phone down between us. "Ready to get started?"

I mustered a smile and hoped it would be over quickly. I was dying for some of that pizza Jake had mentioned earlier. "Yes, I'm ready."

"I'll record the interview, and it will be edited into my regular show. You see, my listeners prefer to hear *me* do most of the talking—that's why they subscribe. For me. I'll cut your answers up and pepper them through the episode so as I'm talking about your desserts, they can hear a bit from you as well. Sound good?"

"Sure." I had no idea that was how things normally worked, since I'd only done one podcast before. "It's your show, so you just tell me what to do, Deir—uh, Dee."

"So tell me, Chloe. What brought you to baking with cannabis?"

I launched into a story I'd told dozens of times in the last few months about how I was disillusioned in Paris after my life began to fall apart.

"On top of all that, my grandmother was diagnosed with

breast cancer, so I decided to come home to Azalea Bay. The oncologist had suggested cannabis might help with the nausea and pain she was experiencing, but she didn't like the taste of the gummies so I started making her weed brownies . . . and the rest is history."

"I'm curious, have you had anyone *not* be supportive of this venture?" she asked. "Cannabis is still a controversial topic."

My mind flashed to the nasty anonymous emails I'd received in the Baked by Chloe inbox. I still had no idea who sent them or if they had any plans to make good on their threats. But I didn't want to give people like that any airtime.

"My family and friends have all been incredibly supportive," I replied. "My aunt is my business partner and the café was her idea, originally. I've been lucky to have so many people rally around me."

"But how about other people in the town or beyond?" She leaned forward and looked at me in a conspiratorial way, like we were two best friends having a gossip session. It immediately made me lean further back in my seat to get some distance from her. "Have there been any protests about the café or about what you sell from local folks?"

"Not particularly."

"Oh come on, you must have had *some* controversy?"

Was this a food podcast or a tabloid show? I felt my hackles raise, but I forced myself to keep my demeanor relaxed. I wasn't going to give her the satisfaction of getting me frazzled on tape.

"Cannabis isn't universally accepted," I admitted. "But all businesses have to know and understand their market. I'm not out here trying to convert anyone. I'm simply providing a high-quality experience for people who *do* want to consume edibles and I educate the customers who want to know more or who are unsure how they feel. But my job, ultimately, is to bake incredible treats. It's not to convince anyone what they should or shouldn't put into their bodies."

Dee seemed wholly dissatisfied with my answer. But if she was hoping to get a rise out of me, then she would be left wanting.

"That's a very politically correct answer," she said, sounding skeptical. I tried not to bristle.

"Perhaps, but it's also the truth," I replied with a shrug. "There are people who banned *The Hunger Games* because they disagree with the content. Some countries banned the *Fifty Shades of Grey* movies. It happens in *all* creative industries. In fact, the Theodore Roosevelt speech about the 'man in the arena' is pretty apt. If you're doing anything with your life there will be people who criticize you, but that shouldn't stop you or me or anyone else from celebrating the value of trying to achieve a dream."

It was a topic I felt passionately about. Whatever people's views on cannabis, the fact was Aunt Dawn and I were putting ourselves out into the world. There would be people who loved us and those who loathed us. It was simply the way things were. I couldn't waste my time worrying about people who thought cannabis shouldn't have been legalized in the first place. Ultimately, their beef was with legislators. Not me.

Baked by Chloe was a legal business, end of story.

"And what *are* you trying to achieve with Baked by Chloe?" Dee asked. She was sitting properly back in her seat now, the edges of her mouth a little downturned at the fact that she hadn't been able to lure me into some juicy tidbits for her podcast.

"A safe and welcoming experience for people who use cannabis, great quality edibles, and destigmatizing the use of cannabis locally and beyond." I smiled. "If I can help some folks feel more comfortable about accessing the benefits they get from THC and CBD, then I'm calling it a win."

The interview went on for another half hour while Deirdre

asked me about my process for baking with cannabis, how I came up with the recipes for the ice cream festival and any tips and tricks for first-time consumers. She concluded the interview by telling me that my business wasn't guaranteed a positive review, because she had to keep her integrity for the sake of her audience's trust.

"I understand," I replied as she packed up her recording equipment. "I believe my food speaks for itself and I respect that you have to be authentic in your reviews."

"You must be feeling pretty good getting such high praise from *Starch Nemesis*," she said, looking up from her tote bag where the microphones were now packed away. "Calista doesn't hand out glowing reviews very often."

I found it interesting that even though Dee clearly disliked the woman, she paid such close attention to her work. It smacked of jealousy. I knew from my time working with a few top chefs in Paris that success could be like that—the higher you climbed, the more people wanted to take what you had.

Could professional jealousy have played a part in Calista's death?

"It was a big confidence boost, for sure." I nodded, the questions still swirling in my brain.

"Too bad for her audience that she won't be around to make any more episodes." Dee lifted one shoulder in a nonchalant shrug, and her tone was as even as if she'd simply commented on the weather.

I was disliking this woman more and more by the minute.

"It's terrible that a young woman lost her life in such a violent manner," I said. There was some ice to my tone, and while I knew it was stupid to get snippy with someone reviewing my business, I couldn't help it. "Murder is always a tragedy."

"So is theft." Dee slung the tote bag over one shoulder. Her short, spiky hair was looking a little limp from the hot day and she fanned herself. But she didn't seem even the slightest bit ashamed of her callousness. "Did you know that Calista and I used to be friends? We met at a conference and I thought we were going to be best buds for life. Then her podcast took off and suddenly I was a nobody to her. She acted like she was too cool for school. And *then* she stole my ideas! I had a whole episode planned for food trucks in Indianapolis and she totally made the episode without even giving me credit."

I somehow doubted that Dee was the first person to have discovered that there were good food trucks in Indianapolis and it wasn't like those businesses were a secret. If what she'd said on her podcast was true, she'd had the idea and then never did anything about it anyway.

"Who does that to a friend, huh?" Dee huffed. "Then she started dating Tristan Patrick and well . . . that was it. I was officially out of her circle. She didn't even invite me to his restaurant opening—that new five-star place in Manhattan. I really wanted to go. I could have made so many connections and she couldn't do me the courtesy of getting me an invite."

From my experience, those types of opening events were usually restricted to celebrities, important folks in the industry, critics with big publications and traditional media. Not podcast hosts with a thousand or so followers. But I could imagine how upset Dee would have been—she seemed to be someone who thought she should have a higher station in life.

Frankly, I didn't miss the social politics of that life *at all*. There was always drama over who was invited and who wasn't. Hurt feelings and retaliation. I hated it.

Then something else clicked in my brain—an important piece of information.

"Wait, Calista and Tristan were dating?" I raised an eyebrow.

I hadn't gotten that impression from him this morning. Even if they clearly were no longer together when she died, surely he would have seemed a little more cut up about her death. Although, to be fair, his new fiancée was standing right there. Perhaps that would have caused issues between them and maybe he'd held it in.

"They were keeping it hush-hush because she'd reviewed his restaurants and some pop-up event he did in Boston. It would look bad if it came out they were sleeping together when she told everyone to go eat there. But *I* knew something was going on because she cancelled on me when I said I was going to be in town, and then I saw him at her apartment!"

"How did you see him at her apartment if she cancelled on you?" I asked, confused.

Dee's face flushed. "She said she was sick and I was doing the best friend thing by taking over some chicken soup. But turns out she wasn't sick . . . just a back-stabbing non-friend."

Yikes. It sounded like whatever friendship Calista and Dee had at one point, it had really deteriorated. Given Dee's completely unemotional reaction to talking about her former friend's death, it really made me wonder if she had something to do with it. Jealousy was a heck of a motive.

"How long are you in town for?" I asked, trying to sound smooth and not *too* interested, just like I was making regular old small talk. "I assume you got in yesterday in time for the festival."

"Actually, I got in the night before and I'm heading home on Monday. I'm here all weekend."

"Did you manage to get out to any of the local spots last night?" I asked casually, pushing up from my chair. "We have some really great restaurants in town."

"Nah, I spent the night in my room at the Azalea Bay Bed and Breakfast. They have a great restaurant on site."

Hmm, so potentially no alibi for the murder if she was staying there alone. But that was if Calista had been murdered last night, and not early this morning? That was information I didn't have. Luckily for me, I happened to have a solid connection with the Azalea Bay Bed and Breakfast—my best friend, Sabrina! Maybe she could corroborate Dee's comings and goings.

This isn't for you to investigate.

The feeling was like summer mosquito bites that only got angrier the more you scratched. I knew I should leave it alone. I *would* leave it alone.

I bid Dee farewell through the front door and locked it behind her. Before heading off to have pizza with Jake, I wanted to write myself a plan for the following morning so I knew exactly what I had to prepare for day two of the festival. I'd barely made it across the café when I heard a loud banging at the back door.

I froze on the spot, heart pounding. Silence settled like softly drifting snow around me, quieting the world. My ears almost rang from how hard I was trying to listen. Maybe it was just kids running along the alley, playing ding-dong ditch. Or had the anonymous email sender come to make good on their threats? It wouldn't be the first time someone had attacked me in my own café.

The pounding started again, and with a shaking hand, I pulled my phone up and typed 911 without hitting the dial button. I wouldn't be caught unawares by a killer *twice* in my own café. If I saw someone menacing at my back door, then I'd hide myself in the office and call for help.

Slowly, with my heart in my mouth, I ventured into the kitchen to see who was banging on my back door.

CHAPTER 8

Boom. Boom. Boom.

"Chloe! Open up!" a high-pitched voice demanded through the door. "It's me, Starr."

"What the heck?" I deleted the numbers from my dial screen and pocketed my phone as I rushed over to the door. When I opened it, Starr all but tumbled into my kitchen looking more disheveled than I had ever seen her.

Her cheeks were flushed red and it looked like she had been crying—the redness making her blue eyes appear even brighter than normal. Her waist-length platinum blond hair was a mess, strands of it twisted and kinked as though she'd spent the whole day wrapping it around her finger. The usually sleek ends were frayed and frazzled. She was wearing a cream-colored linen slip dress which was deeply wrinkled and one of the straps had slipped off her shoulder. There was a brown stain in the fabric, too.

"Where have you *been*?" I shut the door and turned to her, shaking my head. "I came looking for you earlier and your poor staff were stressed out trying to manage the crowd."

"At the freaking police station." Her eyes were wild and she slumped back against my prep table. "The chief cornered me this morning and said I had to come with him. Then they kept me in an interrogation room for, like, an hour before they even came to talk to me. Then it was question after question after question."

Her voice wobbled and her eyes filled with tears.

"They think I killed Calista." Her hand fluttered at the base of her neck and I could see her whole body was shaking. She probably hadn't eaten for hours and her blood sugar might be dipping.

"Here, come and sit out in front. I'll get you a glass of juice." I took her by the elbow but she shook her head.

"I can't be seen, like, cavorting with a competitor." She sniffed and I had to resist the urge to roll my eyes. I'd been to her café plenty of times and it wasn't an issue. "Anyone could walk past and look in the front window."

I brought my hand up to my temple and massaged. "Fine. Stay here a second."

I went out to the front to fetch a glass from behind the serving counter. Then I brought it back into the kitchen and grabbed some orange juice from the fridge that we kept on hand for our canna-gria.

"Is it one hundred percent juice?" she asked. "I usually only drink fresh-pressed."

"I promise it's one hundred percent juice," I said, too tired to buck against her antics. I poured her the glass and handed it to her. "Now tell me, what happened? Why do they think you killed her?"

I mean, I could *easily* guess. But I was curious about what the police had said to her.

"They found one of my ribbons around her neck." She sipped and then, likely determining that I wasn't feeding her some artificial juice concentrate poison, she took a few big gulps. "Plus her bad review of my business apparently gives me motive. I don't know if they saw my Facebook post yet but . . ."

"That probably doesn't help your case." I frowned.

"You *have* to help me." Starr plunked the now empty glass down on my silver prep table and grabbed me by the shoulders. "I can't go to prison. I'm too pretty! And I've never lifted weights before because I get bulky if I do too much resistance training. I bet they don't even make sure the food is organic, either. It's probably"—she shuddered—"from a can."

Starr was right—she was *not* cut out for prison. That much was plainly obvious.

"You should get a lawyer, Starr." I shook my head. "I'm not qualified to help you."

"Oh, my dad's a lawyer." She waved a hand. "I have the whole legal representation thing on lock. I'm sure he'll help me . . . I think."

"Then why do you need *my* help?"

"You're a murder solver. Like that guy, Hercules Pirate."

I shuddered at the butchering of one of my most beloved fictional characters—Hercule Poirot.

"It was all over town how that newspaper called you Murder She Baked after Brendan Chalmers died. The wrong person would totally have been thrown in jail if not for you." She clasped her hands together in a begging position. "If that happens to me it will *ruin* my reputation in this town. Even if my dad makes sure that I don't get convicted, the damage will already be done. People will talk about *me* instead of the other way around!"

On one hand, the panic in her voice made me feel sorry for her. On the other hand, maybe a little taste of her own gossiping medicine wouldn't be the worst thing in the world.

"If you didn't do it, then you have nothing to worry about," I said gently. "You have your dad to help. The police will check all angles and they'll figure out who the real killer is. You just have to be cooperative, answer their questions and don't say anything publicly about Calista. Not even on Facebook."

"I think it's going to take more than that"—she hung her head—"if they start digging into my past. . . ."

I blinked. "What do you mean?"

"Calista and I . . . we were friends. Best friends. We grew up together in Idaho." The word "Idaho" was barely above a whisper, almost like she hated to admit she'd spent time there rather than being LA born and raised like she preferred people to believe. "Then we went off to college together. We were roommates for the first year until it all fell apart. She stole my boyfriend, so I got revenge. Then she got revenge back. If they talk to *anybody* who knew us back then, they're going to hear about how much we hated one another and all the cruel things we did."

Oh. Boy.

"I didn't do it, Chloe. You have to believe me." She looked at me imploringly. "Like, I'm a pescatarian. I don't believe in killing animals, and humans are, like, totally animals."

I wanted to ask why fish weren't considered animals, but I didn't think that would be helpful to the conversation.

"Do you have an alibi? Do the police even know *when* Calista died exactly?" I asked.

"They need to do the autopsy, but the detective was very concerned about my movements last night, specifically after midnight." She sighed. Okay, so the medical examiner must have given them a rough window for the time of death. "But I was at home, sleeping. Sleep is *so* important. Did you know a single night of bad sleep can make your cells age? I'm going to be forty next year. I can't have more wrinkles than nature is already trying to foist on me."

I looked at her face, where there was not a single wrinkle to be seen. "So that's a no to the alibi, then?"

"It's a big old nope to the alibi." She covered her face with her hands. "I'm doomed."

"Look, you don't need to pick out jumpsuit sizes yet, okay?

Give the police a chance to do their job. Call your dad and we can keep an ear out for any information that might help the detective find the killer."

Starr looked up at me. "Do you really think they'll find the right person when they're busy looking at me?"

An uncomfortable sensation settled in my gut. I had seen firsthand how the police could be diverted away from the killer when they were focused on the wrong thing. Murder was complicated. Evidence could lead people down the wrong path. People lied, even when they hadn't killed anyone. It wasn't easy to catch a murderer.

"Starr, you're going to be fine." I laid a hand on her shoulder. "From what I can tell, there are plenty of people who had some kind of a grudge against Calista and I have a sneaking suspicion the police are going to be talking to *a lot* of people over the next two days. You're just one person on the list, okay? Not the whole list. Try not to panic. Maybe try . . . meditation?"

That seemed like something she would gravitate to.

She let out a long breath and nodded. "You're right. The power of breath is what I need right now. Thanks for listening to me."

"Hey, we're kind of like colleagues, right?" I smiled. It would be a lie to say we were friends, but clearly she viewed me as someone she could trust since she'd turned up on my doorstep asking for help. That counted for something.

"Yeah, I guess we are." She smiled.

"Call your dad," I urged. "It can't hurt to have the support of family."

I saw Starr out of my kitchen and slumped back against the door, simultaneously exhausted *and* wired. Another murder in Azalea Bay? Who could have seen that coming?

* * *

Before heading to Jake's place for a much-needed meal and debrief, I went home to shower the day from my skin and pop on some fresh clothes. We were still in that early phase of a maybe-relationship where I changed my outfit a half dozen times before settling on the right balance of casual and cute to boost my confidence but also feel comfy enough for sitting and chatting on the couch. Tonight that meant a blue dress with little yellow flowers that I'd bought at a market while living in Paris, and some tan leather slide sandals. My first California summer back home was barely halfway through, and my hair was already looking blonder than ever. I pulled it back into a claw clip and pulled a few strands free around my face.

There, cute but comfortable.

Downstairs I was greeted by a very excitable Antonio, who danced around my feet, tail wagging and buggy eyes staring luminously up at me with love.

"He missed you today," Grandma Rose said. She was seated on the couch with a silk scarf around her head, a breezy floral tunic and loose white pants on, and a book open on the coffee table, spine up. It was a good thing Lawrence wasn't around as, being a retired author, he always promoted the use of bookmarks rather than leaving a book open upside down where it would create a crack in the spine. "The little thing was hovering by the front door from about six p.m. onwards, just waiting for you to get home."

"Awww." Guilt stabbed me in the gut. It was almost eight p.m. and this was much later than I normally returned home. I scooped the dog up and cuddled him to my chest. "Sorry, bud. It was a busy day. I missed you, too."

He burrowed into my neck, curling up on my chest and rubbing his nose against my skin. I wasn't sure I had ever known such unconditional love as I had from this fella.

"Maybe I should bring him to Jake's place," I said. "I can't bear the thought of leaving him behind again."

"Tsk tsk. Two men at the same time?" Grandma Rose teased and I laughed. "I think that's a great idea. I'm sure Antonio would appreciate the change of scenery, too. I didn't take him for a walk today because it was so hot and he was tuckered out after the one we had yesterday."

Sadly, the little dog's legs couldn't always keep up with his desire to get out and about.

"And how are you feeling after today? That must have been a nasty surprise finding that poor woman," Grandma Rose said. Aunt Dawn had called her with the news after I found the body and finally made it back to the stall.

"It was a nasty surprise." I nodded, stroking the little patch between Antonio's eyes. He sighed in contentment and I felt some of the stress from the day melt away. Dogs really were a cure for everything. "But I'm okay. Honestly, a nice evening chilling on the couch with Jake is exactly what I need."

Antonio let out a snort as if to say, *What am I? Chopped liver?*

"And you too, bud." I scratched between his ears and he settled back down. *That's better.*

"Good. Well, you two have fun." Grandma Rose picked her book back up, looking rather pleased to have an evening with nothing more to do than some reading. "I'm going to have fish for dinner, but I was wondering if you had plans for those herb scones I saw in the kitchen?"

"Have them." I put Antonio down and grabbed his harness from the hook by the front door. It was such a short walk to Jake's it felt almost silly to have him on a leash, but I had this terrible fear of him running into the road. "The cannabis ones are marked with a bit of sharpie on the container so you know which is which. One of those will be enough, dosage wise."

"Perfect."

I looked at my grandmother closely as I helped Antonio's little legs through the chest harness. He was practically vibrating with excitement at the possibility of an outing. Grandma Rose, on the other hand, seemed like she was having a low energy day. I'd expected her to pop by the festival to see our stall, but she'd told Aunt Dawn that she was going to stay home, instead.

I knew she often felt tired and queasy during her chemo treatments, and we were in the middle of one batch right now. Then she would have another break. Her oncologist was due to check the status of the cancer soon, and we were all desperate for good news. It was hard seeing my grandmother—who was one of the strongest, most active seniors I knew—slowing down and struggling to get off the couch.

"How are *you* feeling?" I asked, trying to hide the worry from my voice. I had learned that although my grandmother liked to know I cared, she *hated* when I went into helicopter mode. I think it made her worry more about her condition.

"I'm okay, Chloe," she said in a tone that told me not to fuss.

"If you're allowed to ask me then I'm allowed to ask you," I said more than a little defensively.

She chuckled. "That's fair. Although as your elder, I have more rights to be protective over you."

"False. We're equals where that's concerned." I left Antonio doing excited and impatient tippy taps by the door to go and hug Grandma Rose. I noticed she was still sporting some bruises from her latest lot of blood tests. The nurses sometimes had trouble finding her veins. "I love you, that's all."

"I love you too, Chloe." She squeezed me back and her arms felt a little weak. I bit down on my lip. "I'll be fine. The treatments are tough but I'm hopeful the outcome will be good. And look at the bright side; now I have a valid reason to add to my silk scarf collection."

She patted the one currently wrapped around her head, which was a deep clay pink with some soft yellow flowers on it. Her hair was almost totally gone now and she'd finally asked me to shave what was left, because seeing the fragile, wispy strands made her feel worse about the whole thing. Most days if she was staying around the house or not seeing people, she wore a scarf. But she'd recently bought a wig made of silver hair that was cut into a nice shapely bob, which she wore out and about.

"You have a valid reason to buy whatever you want whenever you want," I said.

"Is that because life's short?" she asked with a raised eyebrow.

"No, it's because life is for living, regardless of time."

She nodded thoughtfully. "I like that sentiment."

"Me too." I glanced over to where Antonio was now spinning in circles by the front door, desperate to get going, and steadily getting his leash tangled around his legs. "Okay, okay. We're going. Sheesh!"

"Don't come home too early," Grandma Rose said with a cheeky smile.

"How the times have changed," I muttered as I scooped up Antonio and untangled his leash. "I remember when you used to threaten to ground me if I broke curfew."

"That was before I was ready for great grandkids," she replied cheerily and without any remorse at all.

Shaking my head, I walked Antonio outside and blew her a kiss before I closed the door. Grandma Rose was totally unabashed in her desire for me to have children. As for what *I* wanted? Eh, I was on the fence. All I knew was that my career and my business were too important right now to even *think* about the possibility of children. And I didn't believe becoming a mother was a requirement for a woman to live a happy and fulfilling life, either.

But in any case, at twenty-eight I still had time to decide what I wanted in life.

Jake opened the front door before we'd even gotten halfway

up his driveway, because he'd seen us coming through the window. Antonio's tail wagged with vigor.

"Hey, you brought the little man." His face lit up.

The dog tugged so hard on the leash I gave up and let it go, and Antonio raced forward, straight into Jake's arms.

"Who's chopped liver now, huh?" I muttered with an indulgent smile. Watching Jake scoop Antonio up and roar with laughter as the dog tried to lick his face was pretty much the most heartwarming thing ever.

I was a sucker for a cute man and cuter dog.

"I hope you don't mind, but I've already ordered the pizzas. I'm so hungry," Jake said as he held the door for me and placed Antonio down so I could help him out of his harness. The dog did a happy little shake and immediately trotted off to go and inspect the unfamiliar territory, nose to the ground, question mark tail up in the air. "They got here a few minutes ago."

I sniffed the air. "Oh, that smells incredible."

I followed Jake into the kitchen where the pizza boxes containing wood-fired pizzas from La Bella Cucina were sitting on his countertop. He flipped the lids open. There was one with prosciutto, pear and arugula topped with wafer-thin shavings of parmesan cheese, and another with the restaurant's beloved homemade pork and fennel sausage along with caramelized onions, fior di latte, and fresh basil. My mouth immediately began to water.

Jake had the plates waiting for us and I grabbed a slice of each. He'd even put a jug of water with some lemon slices and ice out with glasses. Ordering pizza in was the easy option, but he still made an effort with the little things. I appreciated that.

We carried our meal into the living room and settled on the couch, which was a basic dark gray but had a cozy-looking blanket in gray and white checks thrown over the back. Jake's house was sparsely furnished in that typical bachelor-pad way. But the items he owned had personality—there was a gorgeous abstract painting in shades of sky blue, gray and olive green on the wall, which was signed in the bottom corner by the artist. He also had a collection of crystal scotch decanters sitting on a mid-century sideboard, all of which I believe had belonged to his grandfather, who had heavily inspired his love of vintage things.

"How did the podcast interview go?" he asked.

"It was . . . okay," I replied. "The podcast host is a bit strange. Turns out she is *not* a fan of Calista Bryant. Like many people, I'm discovering."

"What did she say?" He picked up a slice of pizza and took a bite, making a small moan of pleasure in the back of his throat. La Bella Cucina tended to have that effect on people.

"That she and Calista used to be friends but they drifted apart when *Starch Nemesis* blew up." I filled Jake in on more of the details, including the alleged theft of ideas and what I'd heard on Dee's podcast. "The list of people who have a grudge against Calista is *long*. She's reviewed hundreds of food businesses over the last few years."

"How many per episode, do you think?" Jake asked. I could tell his mind was ticking over.

"From the ones I've listened to, between two and four. Occasionally she'll do a full episode on one place, but that's rare."

"And she's up to . . ." Jake pulled out his phone and looked at his podcast app. "Episode 143. So, if we averaged out the businesses mentioned per episode to three, that's four hundred and twenty-nine businesses reviewed in the five-ish years the podcast had been around."

Of *course* Jake jumped straight into the numbers. You could take the guy out of Wall Street, but you couldn't take Wall Street out of the guy.

"Right." I nodded and took a bite of my pizza.

"If, on average, she gave one good review, one middling review and one bad review for every episode, that's *a lot* of pissed-off business owners."

Antonio trotted up to the coffee table and started sniffing around for scraps, and I passed him a small piece of sausage, which he happily gobbled up.

"Could be anyone," he said.

"Exactly. Not to mention people in the podcasting world she might have ticked off, like Dee. Or that superfan stalker guy she rejected. I personally liked Calista. But she was a very . . ." I scratched my head and tried to think of the right word. "Unapologetic in her criticism."

Sadly, I knew as well as any woman that those of us who were seen as aggressive or opinionated or take-charge often ended up with more than a handful of detractors. While those qualities might come across as "leadership material" or "a sign of ambition" in men, for women they were often checks in the negative column. I hated that society was this way, but I'd seen it firsthand in kitchens. The female chefs were often labelled as bitchy or volatile, while the men were no-nonsense or passionate.

"The cops have been looking at Starr," I said and Jake nodded, unsurprised. He knew about the ribbon and the podcast episode, already.

Then I filled him in on Starr's visit to the café.

"Yikes." Jake cringed. "Do you think she did it?"

Despite there being a definitely healthy pile of indicators pointing to Starr being the murderer, my gut told me otherwise. "Honestly, I don't think so. She's very self-assured about her business. The bad review upset her, obviously. But I doubt it's shaken her belief in what she's doing, and I know she has a super loyal customer-base here."

Sprout was one business that probably didn't need to rely

on tourism, since her café was packed with regulars even during the down season.

"But she *did* tell me they have history going all the way back to college, so"—I shrugged—"I guess it's possible. She came to me for help."

Jake raised an eyebrow. "And what did you say?"

"That she should call a lawyer."

"But you've got the itch to investigate, right?" Jake looked at me with amusement in his eyes. We might not have known each other long in the grand scheme of things—only a few months—but he knew enough to know when something was demanding my interest.

"Maybe just a little," I admitted. "But I have so many other things to worry about, like getting through the rest of the festival *and* trying to hire a junior baker to help me in the kitchen. I need to focus on those things."

"Mmm-hmm." Jake nodded as he took another bite of pizza, not looking like he believed me. Even Antonio was giving me the side eye from where he sat on the floor, looking up. Or maybe that was simply me projecting and all he wanted was another bite of sausage.

"Don't say it like that, I'm serious," I insisted as I fed him another small morsel.

"I think the lady doth protest too much," Jake said, barely able to conceal his grin.

"Whatever," I grumbled as I got off the couch to grab myself some more pizza. "Just you see, I'm going to be on my best behavior."

Something told me that neither Jake nor Antonio was buying what I was selling. Sadly, that made three of us.

CHAPTER 9

After we'd eaten our pizza, I suggested we go for a walk. The sun was still out, though it had dipped on the horizon, and the evening had that wonderful gold-bathed quality to it that I always thought made everything look just a hair more beautiful. After a long, hot day, the air was balmy, cooled by a gentle breeze blowing off the ocean.

We made our way down to the beach and I let Antonio off his leash so he could run around on the hard-packed sand by the water's edge. Jake and I strolled side by side. Though the beach was somewhat crowded with tourists, the water lapping at my bare feet while my sandals dangled from my fingertips made it feel like we were the only two people in the world.

It was corny and romantic and I started to wonder if this was what my life could look like—a thriving business, a smart, funny and kind man by my side, a fur-baby scampering on ahead. It sounded pretty darn good to me.

"You know, if we were older and wearing more white linen, we could totally look like we were in a commercial for some vague medication right now," Jake said out of nowhere. "Ask your doctor about Snerflederp."

"Snerflederp?" I laughed so hard at the combination of the ridiculous made-up name and his OTT commercial voice-over tone that I almost choked on my own spit. Here I was thinking about how my life could be full and happy, and he was imagining us in a medication commercial. "What the heck?"

Jake looked at me and cringed. "I just ruined the moment, didn't I?"

I wiped a tear away from the corner of my eye, still laughing. "I mean . . . yeah, kinda."

"It's my MO. I'm not a hearts and roses kinda guy, I guess." He raked a hand through his hair. "Sorry."

"Don't apologize. Honestly, I'm at the stage of life where I'd rather witness the creative genius of the guy who comes up with the name 'Snerflederp' than be with someone who brings me roses instead of actually talking about our problems." The words spilled out and now it was my turn to cringe. "And if you hadn't already ruined the moment, I totally would have just then."

"I'm glad it's not just me." He looked down at me and there was so much warmth in his eyes that I immediately let go of the mortification of bringing up my ex. Again.

I'd moved on from Jules. Quickly. That was probably due to both the manner of our breakup and the timing—right when Grandma Rose had received her cancer diagnosis. The perfect storm of events had brought so much clarity that I think on some level I'd felt an ounce of relief that I wasn't going to marry the temperamental French chef after all. We were all wrong for each other, but I'd gotten caught up in the dream of not being alone in Paris anymore.

But that did not a stable relationship make.

Communication made a relationship. Humor made a relationship. Respect made a relationship. And it felt like for the first time, I might have found those things with someone.

"Frankly, I never thought I would find someone as socially

awkward as me," I teased and Jake laughed good-naturedly. "It's a relief."

"Glad to be of service." He bowed and then reached for my hand. I gulped.

Up until now, I'd been a bit gun-shy. Worried about repeating my mistakes. Worried about falling flat on my face in front of people I cared about.

But all of a sudden those things didn't feel so scary anymore . . . not so scary that I would avoid holding hands with Jake in public in case anyone saw us. Who cared if people knew we were kind of an item?

Antonio scampered ahead, catching the attention of a little girl of about five with hair the color of a shiny copper penny. Her eyes lit up in delight as she watched him trot about, reveling in the attention. As we got closer, we saw her mother approach just as the little girl reached out to pet him.

"Stacy, you know better than that. What should we do if we see a cute dog?" the mother admonished. She was tall and slim, with the same copper-colored hair as her daughter. But whereas the little girl had a mini lion's mane, the mother wore her hair cut into a sleek bob.

"Ask permission to pet them," the little girl replied, her voice slightly sing-songy, as if she had repeated those words dozens of times before. I had to stifle a laugh.

"That's right." The mother looked to me and then back down at the little girl.

"Can I pet your dog?" she asked, her eyes shiny and full of hope.

The mother cleared her throat.

"Please," the little girl added.

"Sure." I bent down to scoop Antonio up so I could hold him while she had a pat, just in case she was rough. I was an overprotective dog mama, that was for sure. "Just be gentle because he's very small. But he's friendly."

Her chubby little hand immediately shot out and went straight for the soft patch between Antonio's ears. The dog, bless him, leaned right in and let his eyes flutter closed with happiness. I knew some small dogs got nervous around strangers, but my little guy was friendly as friendly could be. He'd never make a guard dog, because if a burglar broke into the place he'd probably beg for scratches.

"Thank you," the mother said, stroking her girl's hair. "She wants to be a vet when she grows up. This week, at least."

I chuckled. "I'm pretty sure vet was on my list, too. Along with princess, ballerina, astronaut and cupcake taster."

"Cupcake taster is *still* on my list," the woman joked.

"Are you in town for the ice cream festival?" I asked. Stacy was making funny faces at Antonio, who yipped happily in response, his tail batting against my arm as it wagged. It seemed like she was gentle and respectful of the dog's personal space, so I put him down to let them play for a minute.

"I am." Her smile dimmed for a moment. "I was actually here to see Calista Bryant. I'm her literary agent."

"Oh. I'm so sorry for your loss." I shook my head. "I was looking forward to picking up a copy of her book and getting her to sign it."

"She was a great writer, you know. The podcast is wonderful, of course, but her voice really shone while she was writing this book. It pushed her to a whole new level. She was bold, acerbic. I've seen a lot of people try to write nonfiction and none of them had the storytelling skill that she did."

"She *was* very good at telling stories," I said. "She came to visit my café for the podcast and we were laughing the whole time while she told me all the crazy things that had happened to her over the years. It was so fun it didn't even feel like work."

Well, except for the heart-gripping anxiety that she was

going to publicly shred my business, of course. But Calista had made me want to open up, unlike the podcast episode with Deirdre Niece earlier, where it felt like I was nothing but potential gossip fodder.

"What's your café's name?" the woman asked.

"Baked by Chloe. It's a cannabis café."

"Oh!" Recognition flashed in her eyes. "I thought you looked familiar. I came by your stall today but the line was so long I didn't get a chance to buy anything. Calista had told me I *must* stop by." She smiled. "I'm Penelope Hendriks, by the way."

"Nice to meet you." I indicated Jake. "This is Jake. My . . ."

Oh god. What was I supposed to say now? How was I supposed to introduce him? We'd been holding hands and that felt safe. But sticking a label on it? Calling him a friend might give him the idea that I didn't want something more with him, which wasn't true.

"My boyfriend," I squeaked.

"It's great to meet you." Jake stuck his hand out, his voice smooth and even like I hadn't just made a social fumble. But if I listened closely, did I detect a hint of satisfaction in his tone or was that just me getting up in my own head? "I'm sorry for your loss as well."

"I really hope they find who did it." Her eyes misted over and her lower lip wobbled. "It's so senseless. She was such an intelligent person with big ideas and a zest for life. I can't understand how someone could just snuff that out."

"Do you have any idea who did it?" I asked.

I know, I know. I wasn't supposed to be soliciting information. But what was the harm in one teensy little question? I caught Jake looking at me pointedly from the side with a distinct air of "I told you so."

"Someone without a heart, that's for sure." She sniffed. "I honestly don't know much about what happened to her. Her sister called me a few hours ago to let me know Calista had passed, and by then it was all over social media. They're saying it's murder. I can't even fathom."

"I can't either." I sighed. "But the police will do their best to catch the person who did this to her."

Penelope snorted. "I'm from New York, okay. I know not all murders get solved."

I hadn't detected a New York accent until just then, almost as if when she talked about her home state her accent suddenly came to life. Was it common to assume a murder wouldn't be solved? If anything, I'd have thought the opposite . . . but I guess that said more about my sheltered upbringing than anything else.

"There was an incident a while back, now that I think about it," Penelope said, her brow furrowing as she looked out at the ocean as if there were answers bobbing in the waves. "A guy turned up at an event and she became uncomfortable. Calista had come to visit me and we were doing an early press preview of her book at this cool place in Brooklyn. Somehow this guy snuck into the venue and she freaked out."

"Do you know who he was?" Jake asked, and now it was my turn to give him a pointed look. Turned out I wasn't the only one struggling not to snoop.

"I don't." Penelope shook her head. "He cornered Calista when she went to the bathroom, and the bookstore manager threw him out. I never saw him."

It sounded like it could be the overzealous fan I'd heard about. But nobody seemed to know who he was. I wonder if Calista had mentioned him by name when she put him on blast on her socials.

The police will find that name if she did. Let it go.

"Anyway, I'll definitely come by your stall tomorrow," Penelope said, pulling her shoulders back and giving herself a little shake. Her eyes flicked down to where her daughter was still petting Antonio. That was probably enough morbid talk around the youngster.

"Please do! I hope you're still able to enjoy some nice family time," I said.

We gave Stacy the chance to give Antonio a little goodbye hug before Jake and I headed back along the beach. We made it all the way around to where the sand ran out as the ocean lapped directly against a wall of rock that jutted up into the sky, forming part of a steep walking trail up to the lookout. I'd always loved this area of the beach because it was where hard and soft met, a perfect intersection of opposing things that somehow made both seem even more beautiful than they were on their own.

The sun was getting low and now the fat, glowing orb sat half-descended against the horizon and the beach had started clearing out, leaving behind a handful of surfers chasing the last of the dying light. There were a scant few clusters of teenagers and couples about, too. But most of the young families and older folks had retired for the evening.

Jake, Antonio and I took our time walking back, mostly in contemplative silence. Eventually we made our way back toward the stairs leading up to the boardwalk, where we stopped to brush the sand from our feet and I took a moment to clip Antonio back onto his leash.

"Oh crap," I said, slapping a palm to my forehead as a memory jolted me. "I have a horrible feeling I forgot to lock the back door at the café. Starr's visit totally rattled me."

I tried to think hard about what I'd done. I remembered seeing Starr out and closing the door, but when I tried to recall an image of myself locking up . . . I was drawing a blank. I knew I wouldn't sleep a wink tonight if I didn't check.

"Do you mind if we go past so I can make sure it's secure?" I asked. "Ugh, I'm so annoyed at myself."

"Of course we can," Jake replied with an easygoing shrug. "I'm in no rush."

"Thanks. We'll probably get there and the door will be properly locked like usual, but I *hate* the feeling I might have left it open."

"It's like when you go out and you think you've left the stove on," Jake said, nodding. "Can't shake the feeling even though every time I've gone back home to check, it's always been turned off."

"Exactly! Why do humans do that? I always stress myself that the house is burning down and I invent all these terrible scenarios in my head, when really the stove can be on for eight hours if I'm slow-cooking a stew and nothing bad happens."

Jake chuckled. "Humans are weird."

Antonio swung his little head back to look at us as if to say, *No kidding.*

When we made it to Baked by Chloe, the door was, indeed, locked. It was simply my own paranoia that had made me desperate to check, but Jake and I had a good laugh about it. After giving the handle a rattle for good measure, we turned back around to walk home. It was quiet out—with only La Bella Cucina still open and a lone couple sitting in the window table surrounded by fairy lights. The sun was rapidly setting now and the streetlights flicked on one by one.

As we strolled down the street, I caught sight of Sprout, dark and empty. Or, at least, it *should* have been empty. There was a flicker of movement inside and I froze outside the large street-facing window.

"Did you see that?" I peered inside through the glass, but now all I could see were tables with the chairs stacked upside down on top and the long glass cabinet at the front empty and gleaming. At the back of the café, the usually hot pink neon lights spelling out "joy" were turned off, which felt strangely ominous.

"See what?" Jake frowned.

"I thought I saw . . ." I shook my head, about to walk away when I caught sight of something.

A slight movement of shadows, intentional. Not just a shifting of the light. I squinted.

Someone was crouched behind the main counter, almost out of sight. All I could see was the slight outline of a dark figure distorted through the layers of glass, now empty with no food to fill it. I blinked. Was I imagining things? For a moment, there was no movement and I wondered if it *was* nothing more than the long day and tiredness making me see things.

But then the shadow moved. "Someone's hiding in there!"

The figure suddenly popped up and darted into the kitchen as if realizing they had been spotted. But they moved so fast I wasn't able to see whether it was a man or a woman, or even if it was an adult or someone younger. What I did know, however, was that Sprout had a back entrance into a small alley, just the same as we had at Baked by Chloe.

"Hold this." I shoved Antonio's leash into Jake's hand and made a dash for the corner of the street, where the alley could be accessed, my sandals slapping against my feet. I wasn't going to try to apprehend the person—let's be real, a hero I was not—but I wanted to see if I could tell *who* had been skulking around in Starr's café. Because if they had any legitimate reason to be there, they would not have been hiding.

Or running.

I skidded around the corner of the street and ran toward the alley, but when I went to turn down it, my foot caught hard on something. I pitched forward, shrieking as I went over, landing fast and hard on all fours, my palms and knees crying out with the pain at the impact and the scrape of hard concrete roughing up my skin.

I looked up, but the figure was already moving fast, racing down the alley so quickly all I could see was that they were wearing jeans and sneakers and a navy and white striped sweatshirt, their hair covered by a baseball cap. I hadn't even seen their face because they'd tripped me before I even realized someone was standing there.

And who even wore a sweatshirt on a ninety-something-degree day?

"Chloe!" Jake raced around the corner with Antonio tucked under one arm. "What happened? Are you okay?"

I glanced down at my palms, which were grazed with pinpricks of blood blooming. "I'm fine. I just . . ."

What *had* happened, exactly?

"I think I ran into the person who was hiding in Sprout." I shook my head. "Or maybe they ran into me. They tripped me and I fell backwards, then they turned around and ran. . . ."

I pointed to the alley and Jake jogged forward to look down it. "I can't see anyone. But there's a door swinging open."

He helped me up and I winced as I tried to brush the dirt from my palms. I would need to wash them and get some antiseptic on to make sure nothing got infected. Antonio whined as if he could sense something was wrong and Jake tried to soothe him with a gentle pat on the head.

We walked slowly and cautiously down the one-way alley that all the restaurants, cafés and other retail businesses backed onto. This area was most often used for deliveries and for trash collection, and also for staff and business owners to come and go without using the front entrances. It wasn't a wide street, just big enough that a small truck could go through and the dumpsters could be wheeled out to the street.

The door swinging open was indeed to the back of Sprout.

"I don't think we should go inside," Jake said. "We don't know what they were doing in there *or* if they've gone back in to hide."

"Agree. How about I call Starr and tell her what happened and you call the police to report suspicious activity?" I suggested.

"Deal."

Whoever was sneaking around in Sprout was *not* supposed to be there—of that, I was sure. But was it connected to Calista's murder or was something else going on in Azalea Bay?

CHAPTER 10

Starr arrived on the scene so quickly she couldn't have come from far away. Like earlier when she'd come to my café, she didn't seem her usual self. In fact, I'd wager she hadn't made it home yet because her hair was still wildly out of place and her mascara was still smudged. Not to mention, she wore the same outfit and the fabric seemed even more crinkled than before.

What had she been doing all evening?

"You didn't see *any* details about the person who was inside?" she asked, continuing the conversation from when she'd hung up on me mid-sentence to come meet Jake and me. "Not even hair color or skin tone?"

I shook my head. "It's like they were hiding around the corner of the alley, waiting for me. Then they tripped me when I tried to turn, so I never even had the chance to see their face. I only saw the back of them as they ran away. I *think* they were white . . . but I'm not one hundred percent sure."

"Were they tall or short?" Starr prodded.

"Average?" I cringed at her frustrated huff. "It was hard to tell because I was on the ground. They didn't seem particularly large or small."

"Were they carrying anything? Like, do you think they were

trying to *rob* me?" Starr was almost vibrating with stress. "The gall."

I tried to slow the memory down in my head to see if there was anything that grabbed my attention, but the details were blurry. "I didn't see them carrying anything. Not in their hands, at least."

The only thing of real value in a café aside from expensive kitchen equipment—which I definitely would have noticed the person carrying—would be money. But many hospitality businesses didn't even deal with much cash these days. In fact, there had been a bit of an uproar from some older locals about one of the coffee shops switching to card only in the last few months. But for a place like Sprout, which had a clientele that skewed younger, most customers would be paying by card or with the digital wallet on their phones or smart watches. Which means the cash register and the safe out back wouldn't exactly have a huge yield.

Unless Starr kept other valuable things there . . . but I couldn't see anyone going to such lengths to steal the semiprecious crystals she charged her smoothie bowls with, when you could buy something equivalent on Etsy for a couple of bucks.

"I'm going to check it out," she announced, stepping past me toward the open door that Jake and I had been guarding. So far, there had been no movement inside, but we couldn't be sure that the person who'd pushed me over—or an accomplice—wasn't waiting inside.

"I don't know if that's a good idea." Jake looked to me, worried. "We should wait for the police, right?"

"Screw the police," Starr spat. "This is my business and I'm allowed inside."

She marched into Sprout through the back door and Jake and I exchanged glances. "Stay with Antonio and keep a lookout for the detective. I'll go with her."

If anyone dangerous *was* inside, I didn't want Starr to be by herself. Especially not if they had a bone to pick with her personally. There was a murderer running around loose in Azalea Bay, after all.

"Who's in here?" Starr called out as she walked through the kitchen and into the area behind the counter that looked out over the café's seating area. It was strange to see Sprout from this angle, almost like I was viewing it backwards. "Show yourself!"

Silence was the only response. I came up behind Starr and looked around. The place was empty. Whoever had snuck in here was long gone.

"What do you think they wanted?" I asked as Starr ventured out into the seating area to look under the tables. Although it was no use, we could see the whole space. There was no one here.

"How would *I* know?" She shook her head. "Like, I'm the victim here."

"I wonder how they got in." I went to the café's front door—which was made of glass and framed in steel—and tested the lock. It was firmly in place and there was no other way in through the front. "They must have come from the back."

"Makes sense." Starr nodded. "Less people likely to see you breaking in."

I had flashbacks to a time when a killer had broken into my café and conked me on the head with my own kitchen utensils. They'd come through the back, too.

"Thank goodness you weren't here," I said.

"Thank goodness? What do you mean? If I was here I could have chased them down and found out what was going on!" Starr looked slightly wild in the eyes. She was jittering as though she'd had several cups of very strong coffee. "I wouldn't have let them get away."

I wasn't sure if she meant that as a dig at me or if she was just frustrated that we didn't have answers. Either way, I wasn't going to get my nose bent out of joint. She was stressed out and I understood that feeling. Starr checked everything she could think to check—the cash register, the safe out in the back, her supply cupboard. Nothing appeared out of place.

Her café was similarly laid out to mine, with most of the space being dedicated to the front of the house and the kitchen, and only a scant little single-person space allotted to an office out back. She had a tiny desk with a laptop on it, the small safe underneath pushed into a corner to give as much leg room as possible. A framed watercolor print hung on the wall above the desk with the words "Do what you love and you'll never work a day in your life" written in curling script.

Look, I wasn't above a little Instagram wisdom here and there, myself. But this one never failed to grind my gears. I loved running Baked by Chloe, but trying to claim running a small business wasn't work simply because I was passionate about it . . . complete crap. Getting up at the butt-crack of dawn every day and hauling myself to the kitchen—that was work, no matter which way you spun it.

Before I could roll my eyes, I noticed something on Starr's desk—a vase of yellow roses.

My brain immediately flashed up the image of Calista's dead body, her neck tied with one of Sprout's peach satin ribbons and yellow rose petals scattered on the ground.

That seemed like a big coincidence.

"Pretty flowers," I said, almost to myself.

"The roses? They're cute, I guess. I'm not really into yellow. It clashes with my hair." She lifted one shoulder into a shrug. "And roses are a bit old-fashioned, if you ask me. I prefer something more natural, like wildflowers."

I wasn't sure what was *unnatural* about roses, exactly. I mean, they all grew from the same dirt, right?

"Did someone send them to you?" I asked.

To my surprise, she flushed. I'd never known Starr to be

connected with anyone in town, so if she had a romantic partner of any kind then it was a well-guarded secret. I glanced
down to a small wastebasket shoved against the wall. Clear cel-
lophane and pink tissue paper decorated with a fine pattern of
white flowers and silver polka dots was wadded up and shoved
inside. I recognized it as coming from a local florist—Heavy
Petal.

"Have you got a secret admirer?" I asked and she raised an
eyebrow like she might find the question suspicious, so I quickly
turned on my "girl club" mode. "Starr! You dark horse."

"Eye on the prize, Chloe," she admonished, although I
could tell she wasn't annoyed so much as deflecting. "Someone
broke into my café and I want to know what they were doing.
Ugh, there's *nothing* here that gives me even a single freaking
clue. It's totally bogus."

Just as I was about to head outside to check on Jake, the
back door opened and Detective Alvarez stood there. She was
wearing the same outfit I'd seen her in at the crime scene earlier today, although her dark ponytail had lost a few strands of
hair, which floated around her face, and her large circular silver glasses were sitting slightly lopsided, giving her the appearance of a slightly frazzled but studious owl.

Looked like we'd *all* had a long day.

"Jake has given me the main details, but let's go over what
happened, okay?" she said. I noticed her eyes strayed to Starr
more than me, almost like she was observing her very closely.

The four of us—and Antonio—trooped into the main seating area and I noticed that Detective Alvarez had a quick look
inside the office as we walked past. Her shoulders almost
seemed to stiffen at something. Had she seen the roses? Was
she connecting them to the petals found at the scene?

Or was there something else that seemed to have the detective on edge?

*   *   *

Half an hour later Detective Alvarez had taken a thorough look around the inside of Sprout, recorded statements from Jake and I, and had assured Starr that if she happened to notice anything out of place that the police would want to hear about it. Sadly, there were no security cameras in Sprout—not unusual for a small business that didn't deal in much cash. But that might change now. As we wrapped up, Starr insisted on staying at Sprout and giving a friend a call to come get her. Since Jake and I had walked here, we couldn't offer her a lift and she lived on the other side of town.

The offer of a ride from Detective Alvarez had been met with an immediate refusal, unsurprisingly.

The three of us walked outside, leaving Starr to wait for her friend with the doors locked. I'd offered to stay with her until her friend arrived but she'd refused. I got the impression she wanted a moment alone. As we made it out of the alleyway and onto the street, after showing the detective which way the maybe-burglar had run, she paused. Jake had put Antonio onto the ground and he sniffed around the detective's feet. A smile flickered over her face and I got the impression she was resisting the urge to bend down and pat him.

"He's friendly. You can give him a pat if you want," I offered.

Her face brightened and for a second I got a glimpse of the person behind the badge—Adriana Alvarez, rather than Detective Alvarez. She bent down and gave Antonio a scratch behind the ears, which the dog liked so much it made his back leg shake with pleasure.

"My abuela had Chihuahuas when I was young," she said, smiling. "Like, five of them. They were all yippy and demanding, but my gosh she loved them."

I laughed. "Chihuahuas get a bad rap, but they really are the most loving, snuggly little dogs. All this guy wants is to be fed and then to curl up on someone's lap. *Anyone's* lap, really. He's not fussy."

"He's a cutie, for sure." She stood and brushed her hands on her thighs and Antonio looked a little disappointed that the pats were over. "How long after you called Starr did she turn up here?"

The change in conversation—and Detective Alvarez's tone—felt like whiplash.

"Uh, not long," I replied. "Maybe five minutes. Possibly less."

"Less," Jake confirmed. "Probably closer to three and a half minutes."

That was Jake to a tee—precise, down to the thirty-second increment.

The detective nodded and I could see something was churning in her brain. "Are either of you close with Starr?"

Jake shook his head.

"Not really . . ." I pressed my lips together, trying to think about how to answer the question. "She and I are in one another's orbits professionally, I guess you could say. There's a local 'women in business' networking group I joined recently that she's very active in. It's how I have her phone number, actually. She coordinates the meetings and then texts everyone the details."

I'd only been to one meeting so far and I'd quite enjoyed getting to know other female business owners and entrepreneurs around town. It was great to swap stories and tips, and learn from the more experienced women who'd been doing this a lot longer than I had.

I contemplated telling the detective that Starr had come to me after she met with the police, but something in my gut told me that would only paint her in a bad light. And really, why did they need to know that piece of information? Starr had asked for my help and I'd told her it would be best to call a lawyer. It wouldn't help solve the mystery of Calista's death *or* of the break-in at Sprout.

I decided to keep my mouth shut.

"Has she mentioned anything about money troubles in relation to her business during these meetings?" the detective asked.

My eyebrows shot up so hard it was a miracle they didn't launch themselves into space. "Money troubles with Sprout? Uh, no. Seems like business is thriving. They're always full."

The detective nodded. I was desperate to ask for more information but I knew that was useless—Detective Alvarez was a vault. She gave away nothing.

"You two okay to get home?" she asked.

Despite the fact that she was only about six or seven years older than me—at my best guess—she had a big sister vibe about her. Protective. Alert. I got the impression she really cared about Azalea Bay, even though she hadn't been here that long since moving up from LA.

"We're fine." I looked to Jake, who nodded his agreement.

"I'll make sure I get these two home safely," he said, still holding on to Antonio's leash. "Scout's honor."

The detective gave us a nod and a tight smile before she headed off to where her car was parked on the main road. Jake and I headed in the other direction toward home.

"What do you think that was all about?" he asked. "Money troubles? I don't know how there could be money troubles when she charges nearly ten dollars for a smoothie simply because she waved a crystal near it."

"I've never gotten that impression at *all*." I shook my head. "And the question about how quickly she turned up when I called her . . . so strange."

"I wonder if the detective thinks she snuck into her own café," Jake mused. "But why on earth would she do that?"

"No clue." I looked down at my grazed palms. I'd given them a wash in Sprout's kitchen while we gave a statement to the detective, and thankfully nothing seemed to be lodged under the skin. It was just raw and I'd likely be in for a rough time in the kitchen tomorrow trying to work with bandages and gloves. "But I did notice something. . . ."

"Yeah?"

"She had yellow roses in her office—from Heavy Petal," I said. "And there were yellow rose petals near Calista's body."

"That could totally be a coincidence," Jake said. "Lots of people like roses."

"Yeah, I guess you're right." I nodded, trying to brush off the feeling that the flowers were somehow connected to the murder. "But between that and the ribbon used to strangle Calista, it seems like a *big* coincidence."

Jake nodded. "True."

Something weird was going on with Starr Bright . . . and I wanted to find out what it was.

CHAPTER 11

The following morning was, as I predicted, rough. I got up early to head to the Baked by Chloe kitchen to get everything ready for another day of trade at the ice cream festival and it was a real pain in the you-know-where to do my job with injured hands. Thankfully the grazes didn't appear infected, but I still had to keep them bandaged up with a pair of food-safe gloves over the top. That was a nonnegotiable rule of the kitchen!

Since we were only transporting the stuff that needed to be baked fresh, Aunt Dawn and I handled it on our own. Erica met us at the stall about half an hour before the festival was due to open, and Jake would come at lunchtime to cover breaks. Since my hands were not working at full capacity, I would work the register most of the day. Thankfully, I had already trained the others on how to assemble the dishes.

With ten minutes to go before opening, I was fussing with our menu board, trying to make it sit perfectly straight on the stand, when a familiar figure hustled over to our stall.

"Chloe, I need to talk to you." It was Starr and she looked wired, the bags under her eyes so large she could have used them to pack for a round-the-world trip. Had she even slept last night?

I glanced at Aunt Dawn, who looked on with concern. "Is everything okay?"

Starr shifted her weight from one foot to another, looking like a deer about to flee. She had on a floor-sweeping maxi dress in pale blue and a pair of Birkenstocks. Over one arm was a rough-textured tote bag. It was a typical outfit for her, but the dress was creased and she was missing one of her fake nails. Her usually glossy platinum-blond hair looked greasy and un-kempt in a messy low bun, and she had smudges of black under her eyes that indicated she might have slept in her makeup.

"I, uh, just need to borrow you." She tried to muster a smile, but it fell.

"I'll be back in a minute," I said to Aunt Dawn and Erica, who both hovered nearby, sensing that something weird was going on.

As I exited my stall, Starr grabbed my hand and practically dragged me outside and around the back of the marquee, where it was empty and quiet.

"Someone is trying to *frame* me," she said before I even had the chance to ask what was going on. Her eyes welled with tears. I was shocked by the emotional display—this was not like Starr at all. "I know you have no reason to help me, but I'm desperate."

"What do you mean someone is trying to frame you? How are they doing that?"

Her eyes darted furtively around. "Last night when you called me to say someone had broken into Sprout, we couldn't find anything amiss, right?"

"Right."

"Well, there *was* something. You were looking at the lock on the back door and . . ." She swallowed. "I found this sitting on my desk in plain sight. I hid it before the detective arrived."

She dug into the tote bag hanging off her shoulder and pulled out a black leather notebook. The front was embossed with the initials: CB.

I gasped in recognition. "Is that . . . ?"

"Yeah." Starr nodded. "It's Calista's notebook."

I'd seen her using it at Baked by Chloe. She'd even told me that she always took her notes by hand, a habit she'd had since the beginning. A way of keeping her grounded and connected to her work. She was a writer at heart—just like her literary agent had told me.

I shook my head. "How—"

"That person who you saw lurking? They weren't trying to rob me. They snuck in to leave *this*! And I would bet my last dollar that they were planning to call the cops to make sure they found it."

It seemed preposterous. Outrageous. Like something out of a movie.

I didn't dare touch the notebook.

"You *have* to believe me," Starr begged.

"Why didn't you tell the detective?" I asked, frowning.

"Are you freaking kidding me?" Starr gaped at me. "They already think I killed Calista. If I turn up and show them that I have her private notebook with all kinds of trade secrets written inside, that's only going to make them suspect me *more*."

"But someone else planted it," I protested.

"And you think they'll believe that? Puh-lease. I *know* you're not that naïve."

I thought back to the questions that Detective Alvarez asked me last night about how quickly Starr turned up after I called her. Clearly there was some suspicion that she was the one sneaking around. It wasn't a stretch to imagine the detective assuming Starr had gone to grab the notebook out of hiding in order to destroy evidence, and then claim it was planted after her plan was foiled.

"Did you read it?" I asked, keeping my voice low.

"Yeah. It's juicy. Like, *super* juicy." Usually gossip like this would cause Starr's eyes to sparkle. Right now, however, it made her skin turn a sickly shade of green, almost like she was about to toss the contents of her stomach all over the grass.

"Like, juicy enough that someone would kill her over it?"

Starr nodded gravely.

"Wow." I shook my head, feeling totally at a loss on what to say. "Did you call your dad?"

A strange expression flittered over Starr's face, like my question had prompted something painful. "Yeah."

"And what did he say?"

"That he, like, wouldn't represent me." Her lower lip wobbled. "I thought he might put our differences aside, but I assumed wrong."

I reeled as if slapped. What kind of a father refused to help their daughter in a moment of crisis?

"We have a complicated relationship." She huffed a stray piece of hair out of her eyes. For a moment, Starr looked utterly exhausted. Her skin was sallow, her eyes unfocused and teary. "I'm not the supersmart lawyer daughter that he'd hoped for. Let's just put it that way."

I felt a deep pang of empathy for her that made my chest ache, because I understood what it was like to be abandoned by a parent. It was the deepest cut in the world.

"I don't have anyone to turn to," she said, her voice shaking as she tucked the notebook away. "I know *everyone* in this town and people always come to me when they want information. But the truth is . . . I don't have any real friends. I'm just the gossip girl."

Part of me wanted to point out that maybe her lack of friendships was *because* she was the gossip queen of Azalea Bay. It was hard to trust someone who dealt in secrets. But saying that would only upset her more and I didn't want to kick the woman when she was already down. That wasn't cool.

Besides, maybe it was a chicken and an egg situation. Starr had no friends *so* she dealt in gossip in the hopes of proving herself valuable, rather than the friendlessness being a consequence of her actions? I couldn't say for sure.

"When your aunt was a suspect in Brendan Chalmers's murder, you got involved because you knew they were looking at the wrong person," she said, her eyes pleading with me. "It's happening again. I'm innocent, Chloe. I didn't kill her."

I felt like I was being pulled in two directions at once. On one hand, I wanted to be the "good girl" who did what the police told her to do and kept her nose clean and out of their business. But on the other hand . . . I never could say no to someone desperately in need. I could never leave someone to suffer by themselves. Because in *my* darkest moments, I'd had family and friends rally around me.

And I believed that everyone deserved that.

The question was, could I trust that Starr was telling the truth? My mind flashed back to the roses sitting in her office. First the ribbon, then the roses, then Calista's notebook. It would absolutely look suspicious to the police if they knew about it, because that was now *three* key pieces of evidence pointing to Starr.

Which, if she didn't kill Calista, meant someone was hell-bent on framing her. But that was a big "if."

"Meet me after the festival tonight." The words tumbled out of me, curiosity taking over my need to follow the rules.

I wanted to know what was in that notebook *and* I wanted Calista to have justice. Besides, if I refused to help Starr then there was every chance she would simply destroy the notebook to stop it being used against her. If that happened, nobody would ever know if the key to this murder was written inside.

And given this vital piece of evidence was potentially being withheld from the police, then they weren't operating with the full picture.

I knew in my heart no amount of convincing would get Starr to hand it over to the detective. It was too risky for her. So the only option left was for me to see what was inside.

"Let's meet at my café," I said. "We can go over everything together."

To my surprise, Starr threw her arms around my neck and squeezed. "Thank you."

I walked back to the stall with an uneasy feeling in my gut but my heart full of resolve—I would help find Calista's killer.

Whoever it might be.

"I heard about you from *Starch Nemesis*." The woman in front of me sniffled. She was short and full-figured, with green-tipped hair and a purple T-shirt that said *mince meat, not words*—the podcast's catchphrase. "I can't believe Calista is gone."

I'd heard these same two sentences over and over during the morning's trade as news of Calista's death spread. Yesterday, it had mostly been the vendors talking about it, but today was supposed to be Calista's book signing, and the stall they had set up sat eerily vacant. Now that people knew why, piles of flowers and teddy bears and other trinkets of appreciation had started to be placed there, a memorial growing organically as if from the earth. The festival organizers had decided to leave it there, since they didn't want to curb people's need to mourn.

Having a murder take place during the festival was bad enough; they didn't want to get cancelled on social media as well.

Boxes of books, the sides stamped with Calista's publisher's logo, sat unopened behind the table where she was supposed to sit and greet her fans. I saw her agent milling around earlier in the day, talking on the phone and looking sad and harried. Likely the publisher was trying to figure out what to do with the books—did they sell them to honor Calista's memory or would that seem callous?

"It's really a huge loss," I said, offering a sympathetic nod. "I was a big fan, too."

"She would want us to enjoy this, right? Food was her life." The woman whisked away her tears with the back of her hand. Her pale skin was turning pink and splotchy. I felt so bad for all the people grieving today. "Sorry. I'm just really emotional right now. I've listened to every single episode of the podcast and I feel like I knew her."

"I totally understand."

Behind the woman, a line had formed while she figured out what to order, still sniffling. The man standing behind her huffed impatiently. The inside of the marquee was getting full and tension buzzed in the air. Or maybe that was simply me projecting because I was feeling rattled about what Starr had shown me earlier.

"You know what, I'll go with the blueberry ice cream float," the woman said eventually, pulling a wallet out of her bag.

"Great choice," I replied. "Now, we have two options for the ice cream—chocolate or vanilla with blueberry swirl."

She looked panicked, as though the thought of yet another choice was simply too much to handle. Behind her, the man who'd huffed rolled his eyes.

"I would personally suggest the vanilla and blueberry swirl," I said gently. "The flavors are really harmonious and we use a very high-quality vanilla bean for the ice cream. It's very delicious."

The woman let out a relieved sigh. "That sounds great."

I processed the sale and directed her to wait at the other end of the stall where Jake was gathering the orders and calling out names. He was smiling and chatting with people, his chill, friendly energy helping with the tension. Behind me, Erica and Aunt Dawn were working at full pace, almost dancing around one another like ballerinas sharing a stage. Our team worked so well together. Even when the rest of the world felt stressful and unpredictable, I knew I could rely on these people.

It was a good feeling.

The festival seemed even busier today than it had yesterday, possibly because not everybody could take a random Thursday off to go and eat ice cream. But being Friday it seemed like lots of folks had decided to have a long weekend and locals and tourists alike were ready to nosh their way through the park, trying not to get brain freeze. By two o'clock, I was desperate for a break. I'd sent Aunt Dawn first, since she tended to get hangry if she didn't eat lunch close to twelve. Then I'd told Erica to take hers next, because she was a hard worker and would easily forget to take a break if I didn't remind her.

Now it was *my* turn to step away from the hustle and bustle for a half hour. I ditched my uniform apron and hurried out of the marquee tent before anyone could stop me. The sheer number of people who'd come by the stall to say they'd heard about me on *Starch Nemesis* was amazing, but it also meant I could easily get distracted talking to people and right now I was on a mission.

Rather than using my break to relax, I had to visit the florist. I'd have to get something to eat on the walk back, because I was a busy business owner *and* an amateur sleuth. There were not enough hours in the day to do things separately.

Thankfully, Heavy Petal, Azalea Bay's premiere florist, wasn't far from the park where the festival was being held. In fact, once I exited the park on the north side I found myself immediately behind a familiar strip of shops. Sabrina and I did a yoga class once a week in this part of town, so I was here often. Heavy Petal was four doors down from the yoga studio.

I hustled over and pushed open the glass door, above which

a bell tinkled announcing my arrival. AC/DC played from hidden speakers, the sound of which created a fun juxtaposition with the beautiful display of summery bouquets in all shades— from vibrant red, to sprays of white and pink, to sunny cheerful yellow.

Behind the front counter, a familiar face looked up and broke into a smile. Heavy Petal's owner, Caterina Flores, beckoned me over with one heavily tattooed arm. "Chloe! Nice to see you. I thought you'd be busy with all things frozen and sweet today."

"I'm on my lunch break," I replied.

Caterina was part of the women in business group I'd joined and I liked her a lot. She'd been in business a long time, was savvy, had a great sense of humor and wasn't afraid to tell it like it was. Because of this, sometimes she and Starr butted heads on small things.

"What can I help you with?" she asked, leaning forward on the counter. Behind her, there were two orders lined up—a box of pink peonies with silvery green eucalyptus that had a pink teddy bear nestled inside, and another arrangement with long stems of grass and flowers in earthy shades of blush, rust and a deep brownish red.

"This might seem like a weird question, but do you remember if you sold a bouquet of yellow roses recently?" I asked.

Caterina clucked her tongue. "Several. Yellow is always a popular color for summer."

"Do you manage the deliveries of flowers to people yourself, or is that something you outsource?"

Her lips curved up into an amused smile. "Have you got a secret crush, Chloe? Are you worried I'm going to find out who it is?"

"No, no. Nothing like that." I shook my head. My crush was fast becoming very *un*-secret. "It's . . . well, it's kind of related to the murder of the podcaster at the ice cream festival."

"I heard about that." Caterina's eyes widened. "You think my flowers killed someone?"

I contemplated how much I should say—I didn't want to be spreading details about the murder beyond what the police wanted to share, and they hadn't yet made a statement about there being rose petals near the body.

"I don't even know that *your* flowers were involved, specifically. Just some flowers." I cringed at how vague that sounded. "I can't really say more than that without potentially starting a rumor and I don't want to do that. It's just . . . a hunch."

"You're just like that *Murder She Wrote* lady!" Caterina chuckled. "She was always having hunches."

She crouched down behind her counter for a moment and pulled out a thick book. Caterina seemed wary of technology. She used an old flip-style phone, refused to be on social media, and ran as much of her business as possible with pen and paper. That included all her orders, which were documented in a large order book and her receipts, handwritten using carbon paper to make copies.

I wasn't sure if it was because of her age—being that she was in her mid-fifties—or if it was a personal choice, since she seemed to prefer things of another time. Whatever the reason, it gave Heavy Petal a nostalgic feeling, which combined with Caterina's old school rock aesthetic, made for a unique and memorable vibe.

"I'm only doing this because I like you, Chloe. And you have me intrigued." She flipped the heavy cover of the order book open. "Now, I can't give you any confidential information, of course, but if you happen to see what is written in the pages of my order book, then I guess that can't be helped."

I grinned. "You're the best."

"How long ago were the flowers ordered?"

I gave a furtive glance around to make sure no one was eavesdropping, but we were the only two people in here. "I don't know exactly. They looked fresh, though. Maybe within the last three-ish days."

She licked her forefinger and began flipping the pages. There were *a lot* of orders.

"Holy moly, Caterina. Business is good, huh?" I blinked. "Wow. That's amazing."

"Lots of summer weddings this year. In fact, I'm going to be working until at least midnight tonight playing catchup because we've been so busy." She flicked a few more pages. "Yellow roses, you said?"

"That's right."

"We had an order for a bouquet of yellow roses with some mimosa and sunflowers." She tapped one finger to her chin. I noticed her hand had a few scratches and calluses on it, likely from all the hard work she put into making her beautiful floral creations. "And another with yellow and white roses."

"This one was *only* yellow roses."

She flicked through some more pages and my eyes drifted to a little pamphlet that sat on the counter. The heading at the top read, "Rose colors and their meanings." Curious, I picked it up and took a closer look. Apparently red roses were for passion and romance, bright pink was for gratitude and celebration, white was for innocence, pale pink was for sympathy, deep pink was for admiration and yellow was for friendship.

"Are these true?" I asked, holding up the flyer. "Is that really how people pick their roses?"

"It's just marketing." She waved a hand and made a snorting noise. "Flowers are flowers. They are all beautiful, but some people want to find meaning in every little thing. Okay, so we had three bouquets of *only* yellow roses ordered in the last few days. Two on Thursday and one yesterday. All three were for delivery."

"What's the delivery window?" I asked.

"Flowers have to be ordered before eleven a.m. if they want

same-day delivery, because my guy comes at two p.m. for the pickup. Since we only do delivery to the local area, that usually means all the deliveries get made between two and five unless something unusual happens," Caterina replied. "Bridal deliveries are different, of course. But none of these orders were for weddings."

Given Starr's flowers were looking very healthy and perky in this summer heat, it was highly likely she was *one* of those orders.

"Do you ever sell bouquets of roses without an order?" I gestured to the area behind me, which had several pink buckets filled with bouquets of flowers. Most of them were mixed-floral bouquets, with Caterina's signature quirky combination of colors and textures. She even had some "rock and roll" bouquets which had silver plastic stems topped with skulls interspersed between the flowers. "Would it be possible that someone just walked in and bought a bunch of yellow roses without the purchase making it into your order book?"

"Unless we're about to hit Valentine's Day or Mother's Day, I don't keep many bouquets that are just roses. It can be more expensive and, honestly, I find most people are attracted to the more creative, textured designs that feature a variety of flowers and grasses, anyway. They're also less of a financial risk for me, because I can use three or four expensive flowers and create the rest of the bouquet with more affordable options. And some people find roses a bit . . . traditional."

I nodded. Personally I'd always loved roses, but that was because my grandmother had such an affinity for them. But Starr had said something similar when I asked about her roses, so there must be something to it. *Were* roses traditional and old-fashioned? Perhaps.

"Did any of those orders happen to be delivered to a business address?" I asked, hoping I wasn't totally pushing my luck.

But Caterina seemed intrigued by the whole thing and she looked down at her book again. "Just one. Ordered on Thursday and delivered to . . . oh. Delivered to Sprout. I wonder who was sending Starr flowers."

I leaned forward to get a closer look at the order page.

"Interesting, this one was paid with cash. No customer name." She cocked her head. "There was a card included."

The block handwriting of the card's message stood out nice and clear, obviously to make sure there were no errors when Caterina or one of her staff members was writing it out while fulfilling the order.

Losing is not in my vocabulary.

"Cryptic much?" I scrunched up my nose. "What an odd message to send with flowers."

Was it a threat? A promise? If it meant something bad then surely Starr wouldn't have kept the flowers. Were they referring to losing *her*? She had certainly blushed when I'd suggested the roses might have a romantic connection.

Caterina rolled her eyes. "That's nothing. You should see some of the weird stuff people ask me to write. I had a guy come in here just last week and ask me to include some of his 'erotic poetry' in the card."

"Yikes." I cringed. "Do you remember who placed the order?"

"I didn't take this one. We had a big wedding that day and I had to drive some of the table arrangements to the venue myself, since they didn't all fit in our delivery guy's truck. Marty took the order, but he's gone somewhere up north hiking with his girlfriend. Won't be back in cell phone range until Sunday."

Crap.

"That's about all I can tell you, sorry." Caterina flipped the book closed. "Do you think Starr is involved with the murder?"

Did I? Clearly I had *some* suspicion, since I was here wanting to know about how she came into possession of the same flowers I'd seen at the murder scene. But my gut was still pointing to the negative when I thought about her as a suspect, even with a potential mountain of evidence against her. Maybe that's *why* I felt suspicious—it seemed like too much. Like someone really wanted her to be the main suspect.

"Not Starr, but I'd be very curious to know who sent her those flowers." I chewed on the inside of my cheek for a moment. "Like I said, it's just a hunch. Nothing concrete. The police haven't come to speak to you, have they?"

Caterina shook her head. "No."

"They might."

She tapped the side of her nose, winking conspiratorially. "And if they do, you were never here."

"Thanks, Caterina."

"See you at the next meeting?" she asked as the bell tinkled over the door, indicating that a new customer had entered the shop.

"Sure thing! Thanks again." I gave a wave before I headed out of Heavy Petal and into the bright afternoon sunshine.

The details of the murder swirled in my head. Calista was strangled with one of Starr's ribbons, and yellow rose petals were found by the body. Someone then sent yellow roses to Starr with a cryptic note—like, what the heck did that even mean??—and they didn't leave their name on the card that went with the flowers. Did she know who sent them to her? Was it all a big coincidence?

Or was someone really trying to set Starr up to take the fall, like she thought?

That last question circled in my mind as I walked back to the ice cream festival. What if the murderer had purposely sent Starr the flowers in the hopes that the police would find them? Then that person broke into Sprout to plant Calista's diary as extra evidence. Were they planning to call the cops themselves after they snuck back out and I'd interrupted their scheme before they could finish the job? That's what Starr seemed to think.

But it wasn't exactly an airtight plan. So many things could go wrong: A, what if the police didn't follow up the lead? B, what if the person got caught red-handed breaking in with the journal? C, what if Starr destroyed the evidence before anyone could see it?

As I was walking, I decided to Google the phrase from the card that had been sent with the roses to Sprout.

Losing is not in my vocabulary.

The Google results showed it was a quote from some famous Dutch soccer player. But there were also very similar quotes from Venus Williams and Cristiano Rinaldo and some random businessman I'd never heard of who'd funded a load of important tech startups. It was also generic enough that the person who left the message with the florist might not have intended to use someone else's quote.

There were too many pieces of the puzzle still missing.

Thankfully we still had more opportunities to find answers. If there was anything in Calista's journal pointing to the murderer, then I would do my best to find it.

CHAPTER 12

Feeling like I had no better handle on this mystery than when I'd set off, I headed back toward the festival in the hopes I might be able to catch part of Tristan's demonstration. My stomach growled angrily, so I made a quick stop at one of the quieter cafés off the main strip and got myself a sandwich and an orange juice to go, which I scarfed down on the walk over. By the time I made it to the festival and wove my way through the crowd to the center where the demonstration stage was set up, Tristan was already underway.

From a distance, with the sunshine beaming down on him, he looked every bit the burgeoning celebrity chef. His white teeth almost sparkled in the bright light and his hair looked even more golden than it had when I'd met him yesterday in the green room tent.

"Joys of Nature is more than a dessert," he was saying. His voice came clearly through a microphone mounted somewhere near him. "It's an experience. Anyone can make a dessert that tastes good. I want to create experiences that transport people to a mystical world of flavor, texture and of sensory explosion."

The audience was abuzz with anticipation. I noticed it was

mostly women, though ages ranged from teenagers all the way to silver-haired ladies in their sixties and seventies. Almost all of them seemed absolutely awestruck. Annie was poised at the side of the stage, pride shining out of her face. I also saw Destiny standing in the crowd, watching with an intense expression. I decided to make my way over.

It wasn't easy to wade through the densely packed crowd and I murmured *excuse me* and *sorry* as I went, earning myself a few dirty looks, until I found a spot next to Destiny. She glanced over at me coolly at first, but then her eyes warmed with recognition.

"Taking a break from serving customers?" she asked.

"Yeah, it's *packed* today."

"Mmm-hmm. Woulda had a *long* line at Calista's signing table." Destiny's accent had a soft Southern sound to it. "It's too bad."

I still didn't detect any regret or sadness in her voice, nor in her expression. Her eyes were trained on the stage, watching as Tristan explained how he created the sweet-grass lemon curd that formed the bottom layer of the dish—a vibrant yellow smear against the black plates they used exclusively in his restaurant for maximum visual impact.

"Any updates from the police?" I asked, watching Tristan work deftly, his long-fingered hands shot from a camera above and magnified on two screens, one on either side of the stage.

"They came by last night to ask some questions, but I had nothing to tell them." She lifted one shoulder into a shrug. Today she was dressed in a '50s-style full-skirted dress in a vibrant yellow, patterned with images of citruses, including wheels of orange and wedges of lime and whole lemons. Her black braids hung loose around her shoulders.

"What did they want to know?" I asked.

"They seem hung up on the fact that I was in the Airbnb Calista rented for us while she was out being murdered, but what else was I supposed to do in this small-ass town except work in my room?" Destiny glanced at me. "Sorry, I know this is your hometown and all. But nothing is open past eight p.m."

"No offense taken." I shook my head. But I noted that meant she didn't have an alibi. "Small towns aren't for everyone."

"Amen to that." Destiny chuckled and she had a delightfully raspy laugh. It occurred to me this was the first time I'd heard her laugh, since she'd been all-business when she and Calista had visited Baked by Chloe. I got the impression she was someone who took a while to warm up to people. "And like I said to the detective, I've only been working for Calista for the last six months. In that time I met a bunch of people who'd wish her ill. But I don't know anything about her murder."

My eyebrows shot up in surprise. "Oh. I assumed you'd been working with her for a lot longer than that."

"Calista didn't hang on to her assistants very long. As my mama would say, she changed them more often than she changed her underwear."

"How come?"

"Her personality on the podcast wasn't for show, if you know what I mean. That whole"—Destiny made a gesture with her hand—"attitude . . . it was *really* her. And she was like that with everyone. She always acted like nobody was on her side when really, she never gave anyone a chance to be on her side because she pissed them off so quickly."

"Except Tristan," I said, watching for Destiny's reaction.

"*Even* Tristan." Destiny made a soft snorting sound. "That man woulda done anything for her and she treated him like a dog on the street."

Interesting. So Destiny knew about Calista and Tristan being together. Maybe that wasn't as much of a secret as Dee had made it out to be.

"Well, he moved on pretty quickly," I mused.

"To Little Miss Plain Jane?" Destiny shot me an amused

look. "She has a big ol' pile of cash from her daddy, which will do him a world of good when he opens his next restaurant. And who says love is dead?"

Destiny didn't even try to hide the sarcasm in her voice. Up on stage, Tristan had moved on to his pandan-infused creme and was telling a story about the experience he'd gained working for one of Singapore's top chefs. Pandan was a fragrant tropical plant known for its naturally sweet aroma, the leaves of which were popular for flavoring desserts and drinks in Southeast Asia. I'd tried a pandan milk-based custard once before and it was delicious.

"Don't mind me," she said. "I just resent people who can buy their way to the top while the rest of us have to break our backs for it. Tristan was always a social climber like that. But it's one thing I can say about Calista—she worked hard. Harder than most. Nobody got her to the top 'cept herself."

"Were you planning to stick it out with Calista?" I asked. "Seems like you could handle her attitude even if the other assistants couldn't."

"Darn right, I'm no pushover. In fact, I had all these ideas for the podcast and was ready to become her coproducer. I have no idea what happens now that she's dead. I *want* to keep the show going, of course, but . . . I need to speak with a lawyer and see if a verbal agreement means anything even though we hadn't signed a contract yet."

Interesting. That made it sound like Destiny didn't really stand to benefit from Calista's death, especially if she wasn't aware of whether she would have any claim on the podcast. Not that I'd thought of her as a suspect, really, other than her unemotional response to the death. But perhaps that was just how she was dealing with it, on the inside only. Or maybe their relationship was so focused on business that they had no personal connection at all.

"I hope you sort it out," I said. "It would be a shame for

Starch Nemesis to go away. It really helps small businesses like mine. Dozens of people have told me in the last two days that they found out about me from the podcast."

Destiny nodded, her attention drawn back to the stage. Tristan was piping the pandan creme into perfect little mounds on the black plate. He then placed shards of pistachio brittle into the creme piles, carefully standing them so the sharp pieces glowed amber in the afternoon sun, like crystals jutting out of a rock. I watched enraptured as he made flowers from candied paper-thin curls of lemon rind and moss from matcha white chocolate. The dish evolved into this strange almost-alien eco-system of sweetness, with colors natural to earth, only dialed up to eleven.

"And the pièce de résistance," he said with near-perfect French pronunciation, "the tapioca tadpoles."

He spooned small, dark green pearls covered in something jellylike into the "pond," an area encircled by the matcha white chocolate moss, which was filled with edible foam. It was border-line culinary trompe-l'oeil—a visual illusion to trick you into seeing a slice of nature, rather than food.

"Wow," I breathed as the camera zoomed out a little to capture the dish in all its glory.

I know some people—*many* people—scoffed at fine dining, with its tweezer-applied garnishes and fuss. But this was art.

"Thank you all for coming to my demonstration today," he said warmly, smiling out into the crowd as he stepped back and spread his arms wide, almost as if embracing the admiration of the crowd. "It's been a pleasure."

As the festival crew began to help corral people who wanted to meet the man behind the dessert, I turned to Destiny. "I can't even imagine how much they must have paid him to come here. I mean, this is a great festival but . . . like you said before, it's a small-ass town."

"I don't think he came for the money," Destiny said cryptically. "He doesn't need that anymore."

Before I could respond, she lifted her hand into a wave and was swept along by the crowd. I glanced down at my watch and almost yelped. I'd been gone for forty minutes—a good ten minutes longer than I'd intended. I turned on my heel and hustled back to the Baked by Chloe stall, my head full of questions and not nearly enough answers.

Right before closing, as the crowd finally died down, I sent Jake and Erica home for the day. Then it was just Aunt Dawn and I, and as we were chatting, a familiar face approached the booth. It was my aunt's girlfriend, Maisey.

"Hello!" I said, smiling. "You look lovely."

"Thanks." Maisey twirled. She was wearing a floor-sweeping blue skirt with a subtle floral print with a crisp white shirt on top, tied at the waist.

It was adorable to see my aunt's influence on Maisey's fashion sense. The two were like chalk and cheese where that was concerned—Aunt Dawn was boho to the max with loud prints, bright colors, and big billowing silhouettes. In contrast, Maisey was more polished and preppy. The patterned maxi skirt was a new look for her.

"I don't know how you swan around in these things all day." Maisey looked at my aunt. "I've nearly tripped over my own feet half a dozen times already."

"The hazards of looking fabulous." Aunt Dawn grinned. "What are you doing here? I thought we were meeting at home."

Home? I busied myself cleaning up, pretending like I wasn't going to listen in on their conversation. Grandma Rose had speculated that Maisey might move in with Aunt Dawn, given she was currently going through a nasty divorce and didn't want to stay in the marital house, even though it was her name on the deed, not his. *And* he'd already moved in with his brother. But I could understand not wanting to be in a space filled with bad memories.

"I can hear you listening, Chloe," Aunt Dawn said, shooting me a knowing look. Maisey covered her mouth with her hand and stifled a laugh. "Don't pretend like you're not."

"There's hardly anywhere else for me to go," I groused. "And you're not exactly quiet."

"We've got nothing to hide." Maisey ran a hand through her short blond hair. "I'm going to stay with your aunt for a while."

She sounded nervous. And excited.

"It seemed silly for her to be paying rent on a new place when I have so much room," Aunt Dawn added. "It's financially responsible."

"Sure it is," I said, not even trying to keep the amusement out of my voice.

I looked over at the two women as they exchanged sparkling glances. They were like two young kids in love and I was thrilled to see it. With my mom skipping out on me when I was still a kid, my aunt had stepped up in the biggest way. Grandma Rose had taken me in and Aunt Dawn had rallied around me—often playing the role of protective big sister, taking me shopping for prom dresses and teaching me to do my makeup and making sure I knew about safe sex. She'd been at every birthday, every Christmas, every life milestone, always with a proud smile on her face like I was her own child, rather than her niece.

Seeing her happy was important to me. And Maisey made her happier than anything.

"Where are you two going tonight?" I asked.

"Some hoity-toity country club thing." Aunt Dawn pulled a

face and Maisey swatted at her. "Can you think of a place *less* appropriate for me?"

"Buckingham Palace?" I suggested and Aunt Dawn tossed a biodegradable spoon at me.

"It'll be nice," Maisey said, although I detected some doubt in her tone. "It's a charity dinner thing and my sister is organizing it. Okay, look, it'll probably be boring, but it's for a good cause."

I laughed. "Ahh, the truth comes out."

"What are you doing tonight?" Maisey asked.

"Jake and I are going on a double date," I replied. Aunt Dawn's eyebrows raised in interest, but I waved a hand to let her know not to get too excited. "Well, we're having dinner with Grandma Rose and Lawrence at his house."

"I'm not sure that counts as a double date," she replied with a laugh. "And what twenty-something goes on a double date with her grandmother? Good lord, girlie. You should be out doing young people things."

"I *like* hanging out with Grandma Rose." I frowned. "What's so bad about that?"

"So long as you're doing it because you want to and not because you're . . . hovering."

Ever since Grandma Rose had been diagnosed with breast cancer, I had certainly been wanting to spend as much time with her as possible. And yes, okay, maybe I had been "hovering" a little because I was worried, especially after the chemo infusions knocked her around. And sure, Grandma Rose had told me on more than one occasion—okay, close to ten or twelve—that I wasn't going to change anything by watching her like a hawk.

But seeing her go through cancer treatment was scary and hard, even if she was the strongest woman I knew and the toughest grandma in the world. I couldn't *not* hover just a little.

"Firstly," I said, feeling more than a little indignant, "Lawrence *invited* me and told me to bring Jake. Now, I suspect that's because he needs help with his computer and since he has no grandkids of his own, we're the closest thing to biological tech support he's going to get. But I still like to think it was a genuine invitation."

It was the curse of every Millennial—you were signed up for a lifetime of "fixing" computers and printers and cell phones, even if you had no real aptitude for it. Because, at a minimum, you'd been Googling almost as long as you'd been alive, so therefore you had one up on the older generations.

"I think it's sweet," Maisey said.

"Thank you." I tossed my hands in the air. "Most grandparents feel like their grandkids don't call enough. I'm the opposite of that."

"Hey, before you start throwing pitchforks at me, I was simply saying that it's important for you to get out and do young people things, too," Aunt Dawn said, holding both hands up. "You work so hard, Chloe. You need to have a life as well."

Balance—the elusive skill that most businesspeople failed to cultivate until after they'd retired. I'd worked for several high-level chefs and restaurateurs back in Paris. Not one of them had any semblance of a personal life.

"I do young people things," I protested. "I play Dungeons and Dragons."

I made the error of starting to tick the list off on my fingers before realizing that it was a very short list.

"Hmm?" Aunt Dawn looked at me expectantly, a smug expression settling into her features the longer my silence went on.

"I go to yoga with Sabrina," I added.

End of list.

"And I walk Antonio," I tried meekly.

"Walking the dog does *not* count." Aunt Dawn rolled her eyes. "Cute as he is. That's responsible pet ownership, not a hobby. Every time I've come over when the café has been closed, I've found you in the kitchen working on new recipes."

Baked by Chloe was open Wednesday through Sunday, and was closed Monday and Tuesday since those days tended to be the quietest around town. And yeah, I could often be found in the kitchen—whether at home or in the café while it was closed—working on new recipes. Wasn't that a good thing?

"As my business partner, aren't you *happy* that I'm a workaholic?" I asked.

Aunt Dawn came over and pulled me into a hug, extinguishing my annoyance like it was a candle flame she was snuffing out. "As your business partner, yes. As your aunt, no. It's my job to make sure you have good influences around you and that you lead a fulfilling life. That includes passion for your work, of course, but it also has to include other things. Life can't *ever* just be about work. And it can't only be about family obligation, either."

If my aunt had her way, I'd be like her with a string of hobbies and social engagements and travel plans crammed into my calendar like toys overflowing from a Christmas stocking. Lord knew how she fit so much into her life. But if I was honest, it was the thing I admired *most* about Aunt Dawn—her zest for life. Her passion for having fun. She'd dabbled in everything from tarot reading to tree shaping to canine freestyle dancing to competitive aerobics to glass blowing. The list went on.

"Just make sure you don't neglect the other areas, okay?" She squeezed my shoulders.

"I promise."

Aunt Dawn and Maisey continued to chat about their plans for her moving in, which was aided by the fact that Maisey's family business was a furniture removal company. I smiled listening to them make plans for the future—even if it was a near-future—and served the slow trickle of customers who were coming through in the last hour of the festival.

My hands were feeling okay enough for me to make a few items here, especially since most folks were ordering the ice cream float. As I was making the drink for two men who appeared to be in their fifties, I let my gaze roam around the marquee. One or two of the other stalls were already packing up for the day, having been quiet for a while now. Unsurprisingly, the stall with the adult "toys" was doing a bustling business. I caught sight of Dee the podcaster standing there, jiggling something fluffy and pink while her deep, raucous laugh boomed through the quiet space. Beside her a man stood at least a foot taller than her and rail thin, his cheeks flaming and a hand scrubbing over his face. He had thin reddish hair pulled back into a ponytail and a straggly red beard. A scar cut into one cheek, making a divot in his pockmarked skin.

Dee reached down and squeezed the guy's backside right there in the open for all to see. Was that her husband? Boyfriend? I couldn't remember if she'd told me she was travelling with anyone. But whoever he was, it looked like he might be getting lucky tonight.

"Here you go." I slid the two ice cream floats over to my waiting customer, who reached for them eagerly. His companion had gone to secure a table.

"Thanks." He bobbed his head. Long hair hung around his face, past his chin. He had an aging surfer-dude look about him—tanned, fit, wrinkles from years out in the sun and eyes not quite fixed on anything, almost as if his mind were already on the waves. "It's, like, so rad to see that weed isn't frowned upon anymore. When I was in high school, people thought I was just a stoner. But now I run my own tech company and I still smoke weed every day. So I'm, like, a successful stoner."

He chuckled to himself and gave me a friendly smile before walking off. I wasn't surprised by the admission, I could smell it on him. Literally. But I loved hearing about stories of people who'd bucked societal constraints to rise up in life.

Personally, I preferred baking with weed rather than smoking it. Of course I'd dabbled a bit after recreational use became legal in California, but I craved control too much to get high on the regular—it was the very reason the technical aspects of baking suited me so well. These days, I opted for one of our signature CBD chai lattes when I was stressed, because I loved the soothing and calming effect that the mixture of CBD and spiced milk had on me.

Plus it didn't make my hair smell the way smoking did. Win, win.

Regardless of my own preferences, I was happy to do my part in helping to change the tide of opinions about cannabis, so that other people who used it, like this customer, wouldn't feel judged. As the thought swirled in my head, I found myself reaching for my phone, a strange tingle of intuition prickling along the back of my neck. Opening up the inbox for Baked by Chloe, I saw we had a rush of new emails. The one sitting at the top made a sick sensation settle in the pit of my stomach.

The subject read: You'll be sorry.

CHAPTER 13

With a shaking hand I clicked on the email, but there was no message inside. Only an attachment. A photo. I wasn't sure whether I wanted to see what this person was sending but curiosity got the better of me. I clicked.

It was a familiar image—the front of Baked by Chloe. But the window was smashed.

I gasped and Aunt Dawn came rushing over.

"What's wrong?" Her usually jovial, joking spirit turned worried in an instant. I wordlessly handed her the phone and the breath rushed out of her, followed by a low-uttered curse. "Who sent this?"

Oh boy. I knew keeping the threatening emails a secret was going to come back to bite me.

"It's an anonymous email. I have to get to the café." I ripped my apron over my head and tossed it down. "Can you finish up here?"

I tried to grab my phone from Aunt Dawn's hand but she held it out of my reach. "You are *not* going there by yourself, young lady."

"But—"

"I'll go," she said. Great. There was no budging Aunt Dawn when she went into full mama-bear mode.

"This isn't the first email." I hung my head.

"What?" My aunt sounded like her head was going to explode. Uh-oh. As much as she was a chill hippie most of the time, I also knew she had a temper when someone pushed her buttons. And finding out I had been keeping this secret was *definitely* going to push her buttons. "Why didn't you tell me?"

"I thought it was a hoax," I said meekly. "You know what people are like on the internet."

"Not really," she muttered.

"They say whatever they want because they're shielded by anonymity. It doesn't usually mean anything in the real world." I bit down on my lip. "I thought it was just some jerk spouting off for no reason."

"Chloe, god help me—"

"I'll take her to the café," Maisey said, her voice gentle. She was still standing by the register and a worried look that matched my aunt's had made a line form between her brows. "We'll drive over and check it out together. We can call the police when we get there and you can give them the whole picture."

I shot her a look of gratitude and then turned to Aunt Dawn. "Are you okay with that?"

"Fine, but be careful. Don't even *think* about going inside unless a police officer is there with you, okay?" She shook her head. "I don't want a repeat of what happened last time."

And by "last time" she meant that time an intruder whacked me over the head with my own cooking utensil. "I promise."

"We're going to talk about this," she said, her mouth setting into a grim line. It felt like I was a teenager again, about to be grounded. "I don't want you keeping secrets from me, *ever*. Especially not if someone is threatening you or our business."

I hadn't wanted to worry her. Aunt Dawn had a lot on her plate what with coming out and starting a relationship with Maisey, and supporting Maisey through her much gossiped-about divorce. I hadn't wanted to pile on.

"I'm sorry," I said. "I should have told you."

"We'll talk later. I mean it." She made a shooing motion with her hands and went to go serve a customer who'd approached the stall. The festival was due to close in the next half hour anyway, so it wasn't likely that she would struggle to manage the stall on her own.

"You're in big trouble, huh?" Maisey asked as we hurried through the festival, which was far emptier than the last time I'd ventured out of the marquee.

"Yup," I replied miserably. "I thought I was doing the right thing not adding any more stress to her plate."

"Your aunt is made of tough stuff. She can handle it." There was a genuine warmth and admiration in Maisey's voice when she talked about my aunt.

"I know." I nodded.

"And don't you worry," Maisey reassured me. "Whoever did this, we'll find out. No one is going to get away with hurting my new family."

Despite the worry and anger coursing through my veins, I felt a surge of happiness at hearing those words come out of Maisey's mouth. Grandma Rose and I had tried to make her feel welcome and part of our family unit from the beginning, so knowing she felt the same about us made me feel warm and fuzzy inside.

Well, underneath the burning need to throttle whoever had damaged my café!

In ten minutes we arrived at Baked by Chloe and the mystery of the anonymous threatening emails took an even stranger turn. . . .

There were no broken windows on the café.

"What the heck is going on?" I shook my head.

Maisey and I stood outside the café, with its pristine and untouched windows, while I pulled out my phone and brought up the picture from the email. Pinching my fingers against the screen and widening them to zoom into the photo, I noticed something that had escaped my attention in the moment of panic earlier.

"It's photoshopped!"

Now that I had zoomed in, I could see where some of the edges of the image of broken glass didn't perfectly line up with the window of the café. There were some pixelated spots and even a weird reflection in the window—a building of some kind—that wasn't possible to have come from anything that existed outside the café.

"That's truly bizarre." Maisey massaged her fingers into her hairline, ruffling her short strands of sun-streaked blond hair. "Why on earth would anyone do that?"

I whirled around, suddenly seized by the feeling that I was being watched. The sensation prickled along my skin and I gave a little shake. But it didn't budge. Nobody looked out of place, however. I didn't recognize most of the faces, of course, since there were so many tourists here at the moment. But most folks looked as though they had come from the beach, skin crusted with sand and salt, pink bands of sunburn across their noses, dreamy smiles on their relaxed faces. Not a single person gave off a "I send threatening emails" vibe.

"I have no idea why someone would do this. If people have a problem with cannabis, why don't they take it up with their local representative or something? Our business is legal."

Frustration made my voice shake and I balled my hands into fists, trying to keep the emotion inside. If someone *was* watching, I didn't want to give them the satisfaction of seeing me rattled. None of the restaurants that served wine were targeted like this. And alcohol had been illegal during prohibition!

I took a deep breath and then let it out slowly.

"If there's one thing I've learned since coming out as bisexual, it's that some folks are so blinded by their own judgment that they never even consider there are real humans involved in these issues," Maisey said darkly. "It's almost like they think their opinions matter more than actual people."

"I don't think it's *almost* like that. I think it's *exactly* like that."

"How long have these emails been coming?" Maisey asked. She stood close to me, almost protectively, like she was ready to put her hands up if anyone came to do me harm.

I could see what my aunt liked about her—she was good. Honest. Authentic.

"Negative emails have trickled in since we opened," I admitted. "Most of them were from people telling me I'd brought sin to our town and I should be ashamed of myself, but they didn't make any threats. The ones from this email address, however, only started very recently. I don't know if they're trying to mess with me or if they really *do* have plans to make good on their threats. It's so stupid. If you don't like weed, then don't come into the café. Problem solved."

"Ah, but you're applying logic where no logic exists." Maisey rolled her eyes. "Some people love to police the behaviors of others. It's not enough for them to not engage in the activity themselves, they get power from trying to stop other people doing it."

"I will *never* understand that," I muttered.

"Me either, Chloe. Me either."

At that moment, the sensation of being watched started up again, but this time the source was clear. In my peripheral vision, I saw Starr approaching us. It was time to dig into Calista's journal.

"I'll stop by the police station tomorrow before the festival opens and let them know about the emails, I promise," I said to Maisey. "But there's no need to do anything right now. You've got your charity thing tonight and I don't want to hold you up."

"Are you sure?" Maisey asked, looking uncertain.

"Absolutely. I'm having a quick catchup with a friend now, anyway. Then I'll head home to get ready for tonight."

"Maybe you should ask Jake to come get you," she suggested. Even though the Jellybean was parked at home and Grandma Rose *could* drive it, she didn't like to be on the roads later in the day on account of her bad eyesight. "Just to be safe."

"If I feel like it's unsafe, I'll call for backup. Scout's honor." I wasn't exactly sure what the proper hand signal for Scouts was, so I made the Vulcan salute instead, which made Maisey laugh.

"Well, okay. You be safe." Maisey lifted her hand in a friendly wave as she departed, and Starr walked over.

I partially expected Starr to make some comment, since she had been one of the people gossiping about the divorce, but it was almost like she hadn't even noticed Maisey's presence. Her eyes had a slightly unfocused quality to them and she almost seemed to be vibrating with nervous energy.

"Come on," I said, motioning. "Let's go inside."

I opened the front door to the café and let Starr in, locking it behind us and making sure the CLOSED sign was fully visible.

"Let's go out back," I suggested. "We don't want anyone seeing potential evidence from a murder investigation in broad daylight."

Even saying it out loud made me queasy. I *knew* we should be taking this to the police, but Starr wouldn't agree to it, and if I called the cops then I would be casting even more suspicion on her. Both options—keeping evidence from the police and ratting out Starr—felt wrong. Talk about being stuck between a rock and a hard place! But I figured taking a look at the journal now was the lesser of two evils, and if I found something important that might help clear Starr, *then* I could call it in.

"Do you want a drink or anything? Juice? Water?" I asked as we headed out to the kitchen, but Starr shook her head numbly.

Standing at the kitchen prep table, Starr pulled the journal out. While there *were* some windows back here, we could stand in a way that wouldn't expose anything should someone walk past. And foot traffic in the alleyway behind the café was minimal on a busy day, let alone after business hours were done.

Calista's journal had a few scratches, showing it was well loved. I stared at it for a moment, almost scared to touch it. I probably *shouldn't* touch it. Then I had an idea. I ducked down and reached for a box of food-safe, powder-free vinyl disposable gloves that I always kept on hand and slipped one on.

"What's that for?" Starr asked.

"I don't want my fingerprints all over it," I said. "I would have suggested you do the same but it's probably too late for that now."

She groaned. "That's exactly what the person who planted it would have wanted! I didn't even think."

I reached for the journal and flipped it open, thumbing to the first page that featured an entry. Calista's writing was messy, with curls and sharp lines that seemed at odds with one another, strange shapes and the weirdest Y I'd ever seen. It was almost like her brain worked too fast for her hand to keep up.

"Have you gone through it?" I asked, my eyes scanning the page. It was a list of ideas for future episodes: a restaurant inside a historic Boeing airplane, the oldest restaurant in the country, the original tiki bar, best spots for vintage cocktails.

"Yeah." Her eyes didn't quite meet mine.

"What did you find?"

Starr reached over and flipped a few pages ahead. At the top was scrawled *Azalea Bay, small town food mecca*. It was the original inception of her idea for episode 143. Baked by Chloe was the first dot point, followed by the words *more than just weed brownies*. She also seemed to tag the listed businesses with some important information. Next to my name were tags of *new business* and *woman owned* and *hot topic*. I wondered if these were notes for Destiny when she was uploading the episodes.

Further down the page was a dot point that read: *Stupid wellness café run by that bitch "Starr." This should be fun.*

Why was Starr's name in quotation marks? Whatever the reason, if the police saw this, it would definitely be another check against her for possible motivation.

"I knew the second she saw me it would be a totally bogus review," Starr said. "I could have ten Michelin stars and a James Beard award and Gordon Ramsay as my company mascot, and she would still hate whatever I was doing."

Following this list were a few pages of research notes, including information about the town in general—history, fun facts, famous former residents. Then there was a page with a roughly written recipe, another with a weekly template for social media posts, and another few pages of episode ideas along with research and interview notes.

Then we came across a page with an interesting header.

"*Performance review for Destiny*," I read aloud. It was dated two weeks ago.

"Oh yeah," Starr replied with a nod. "This chick was going to get the boot."

"The boot?"

"Fired."

My eyebrows shot up. That seemed in stark contrast with what Destiny had told me earlier that day.

"I was under the impression that Calista was going to bring her on as a coproducer," I said. "Destiny is Calista's assistant."

"Not for much longer if this has anything to say about it." She jabbed at the page. "According to this, Destiny was on her last chance."

I skimmed down the page. Starr was right. Calista's notes looked like talking points for a meeting, and they had a small yellow sticky note affixed to the top righthand corner that said: *video call, 1 pm Thursday.* The notes indeed showed that Calista wasn't happy with Destiny's performance, citing things such as editing errors in podcast episodes, her being late to meetings, and sharing *important trade information with affected parties*, whatever that meant.

"Do you think she killed Calista?" Starr asked.

Today I hadn't thought so, but now I wasn't feeling so confident. But what would killing her boss achieve, because the outcome would be the same. . . . Destiny would *still* be out of a job. Seemed like high risk for zero reward, unless it was a crime of passion.

"I don't know," I replied. "She made it sound like she was going to talk to some lawyers about taking over the podcast."

"That *totally* sounds like a motive to me," Starr said. "You go from working for a boss who's a major bummer to running one of the biggest food podcasts on the internet. Uh, jackpot! Calista must have been making a *fortune* from advertising."

I thought about this for a second. Starr made an interesting point.

"Wouldn't ownership of the podcast go to whoever was named in her will?" I asked.

"Do *you* have a will? Because I sure don't."

"No, I don't," I admitted.

Starr was about a decade older than me, which would mean

Calista was likely the same age if they had gone to college together. She wasn't married, didn't have any kids, and despite running an uber-successful business, she'd told me she was renting because the thought of buying a house and being stuck in one location was "stifling" to her. It was plausible that she didn't have a will.

"With Calista out of the way, Destiny could not only *not* get fired, but she could try to take the business for herself and have a huge leg up!" Starr's eyes widened. "It's kind of genius."

I chose to overlook Starr's opinion that murder was a "genius" solution.

"But *Starch Nemesis* would be nothing without Calista," I argued. "People listen because of her."

"Yeah, but if they had a few episodes prerecorded, Destiny could run it for a while and test the waters with a new host, whether that was herself or someone else. *Or* she could sell it off to a media production company or some, like, faceless corporation. Go all big corn, or whatever."

I wasn't exactly sure what it meant to "go all big corn" but I understood the implication.

"You think Destiny would use it to make a quick buck so she could then fund a project to branch out on her own?"

"Exactly." Starr nodded. "Not to mention it's a nice middle finger to the person who tried to fire you."

That seemed like an extreme move, but . . . well, people could do extreme things for money. And it certainly sounded like Destiny didn't have a wealthy upbringing based on her comments earlier today about Tristan and Annie.

"There was something here." Starr leaned over and motioned for me to flip a few pages. I don't know why she was worried about touching the journal now, given she'd had her hands all over it previously. But I did what she wanted. "Stop. There."

Most of the journal was written in black ink, but one section of writing was circled with red.

iListen exclusive miniseries.

iListen was a big deal in the podcast world and I'd heard the name pop up frequently as an "in conjunction with" partner on several of the shows I listened to. They even hosted some big awards every year, which were kind of like the James Beard awards of new media. I wondered if Calista had struck a deal with them.

"That could be lucrative," I said. "If Calista was planning a miniseries in partnership with iListen, then maybe that's why Destiny wants to take over. Especially if the episodes are already recorded."

"And *what* is the miniseries about? That's what I want to know," Starr said. "It would have to be something super interesting to warrant it being a miniseries rather than just episodes on the regular podcast, right?"

A memory sparked in my brain. Yesterday Tamika, the owner of the soul food restaurant Calista had helped put on the map, mentioned Calista was working on some exposé that was supposed to be even bigger than *Starch Nemesis*.

People get really protective when you go digging around their patch. She didn't listen. Calista never listened to anyone.

What if Calista had uncovered something scandalous in the food world and it had gotten her killed? I looked closer at the notebook and something grabbed my attention. Right at the edge of where the pages were bound to the spine, there was a tiny sliver of ripped paper. Using my gloved hand, I pushed down to open the spine up more.

"Starr, did you remove any pages from this journal?"

She shook her head. "You saw my name mentioned before. If I was going to destroy evidence, why wouldn't I take that out, too?"

Good point.

"Well, *someone* has." I pointed.

They'd done a good job too, ripping the pages out close to the join so it was concealed by the natural bend of the paper where it was bound. If it wasn't for that rogue scrap, I wouldn't have even noticed a page had been removed. I nudged the sliver of paper with my finger and it came free, but it was hard to tell how many pages had been torn out. One, two, ten? I had no idea.

Just when I thought we were done finding possible links to Calista's murder in the journal, I flipped over one more page. The word "stalker" was written in big block letters and out from it spiraled curling lines to cartoon clouds with questions and action points.

Does he know where I live?
Change email password.
Take different route to gym.
Can publisher supply security for book events?

"I'd heard that Calista had publicly shamed some guy for stalking her," I said.

"We never agreed on much but stalkers *do* deserve to be shamed." Starr nodded. "Nobody should have some creeper following them around."

"I wonder if she knew who he was," I mused. "Maybe we can find out."

I pulled out my phone and found my way to Calista's Instagram profile, the last post of which was a shot of Azalea Bay's gorgeous beach with Calista's hand holding out a giant cream-filled pastry in the foreground. The comment section was flooded with tributes and rest in peace messages. She posted frequently, sharing tidbits of her life in the Stories and Reels features and posting pictures of her foodie finds in the course of research for her podcast episodes. A recent post showed

Calista in headphones, with a microphone in front of her, her eyes sparkling with excitement. The caption read:

Hey listeners, I'm working on something VERY special! The food industry isn't as clean as you think and I'm not talking about food hygiene. Stay tuned for something different coming soon in partnership with @iListen. Bad people are about to be exposed. You won't want to miss it.

It certainly sounded like she was digging around in something messy. But there was no follow-up information on the miniseries. Further down, I found the post I was looking for. A photo showed half of Calista's face, mascara smudged, with an artsy black and white filter over the top.

This isn't my normal kind of post. Today . . . today has been a rough one.

I read the post out loud to Starr and it detailed how Calista had found a man lurking outside her hotel room at an event, trying to jimmy the lock. It wasn't the first time. She'd seen him before. Only this time she'd managed to find out his name because he was staying at the hotel and the idiot hadn't used a false identity.

"His name," I read, "is Niko Dragan Merković."

Starr's face paled. I didn't think it was possible for someone who loved fake tan as much as she did to look white as a sheet, but as the blood rushed out of her face, I shot a hand out to steady her.

"Starr, do you know that name?" I asked.

She nodded weakly. "That's . . . that's my brother."

CHAPTER 14

Starr's connection to Calista's murder was deepening at every turn.

"Your brother was her stalker?" I sputtered. "Are you sure? Maybe it's another Niko Merković."

"It's not exactly a common name here, Chloe." Her wide eyes were fixed elsewhere, and she shook her head back and forth as if her brain were rejecting everything that was going on. "I . . . oh, Niko. My big brother has always been trouble, but stalking? I can't believe it."

I had no idea what to say. With the way the connections were stacking up this was looking *bad* for Starr. Real bad.

"Niko had a gambling problem when he was younger. He's twelve years older than me, so I was a kid at the time." She shook her head. "He was a mechanic and very good with his hands, but he started boosting cars to fund his trips to the casino. It spiraled quickly. He stole a luxury car and the guy sent some thugs to our house to beat my brother up."

Her voice trembled.

"Then he got arrested. In a way I'm pretty sure that saved his life, though, because he was forced to stop gambling, and being in jail kept him safe from the guy whose fancy car he stole."

For a moment I barely recognized Starr. Gone was her breathy voice, gone was the gossipy twinkle in her eye, gone was the "give no f's" attitude. It was like I was talking to a person I'd never met before.

"My father never forgave him," she continued. "We moved here from Croatia when Niko was little, before I was born, and my parents were determined to build a good life for us. My father is a lawyer and my mother is a schoolteacher. They're upstanding people. Moral. Hardworking. They follow the rules and the law. But Niko . . . they were ashamed of him. He dragged our name through the mud."

"Oh, Starr, I'm so sorry."

"My real name is Zvezdana—it means star. So I changed it. I wanted . . ." She shook her head, tears glistening in her eyes. "I wanted to get away from the damage he'd done to our family's reputation. We were shunned by all my parents' friends. My father lost business. Other people in our community didn't want to be associated with us."

I'd known for a while that Starr Bright wasn't her real name—I mean, *who* would call their kid that? But I had no idea the story behind the name change.

"That's terrible they treated you like that."

"I know. But Niko served his time and he came out good. He was changed. That was five years ago." She wrung the fabric of her long dress between her hands, twisting it back and forth. "He reached out to me, wanting to rebuild our relationship. I've always loved my big brother, in spite of his faults and his bad behavior, and I missed him terribly when he was away. But when my father found out, he called me a traitor. He said Niko was no longer family and I was inviting trouble by seeing him."

"Is that why your father doesn't want to represent you?" I asked.

She nodded. "He'd already had one kid nearly ruin his reputation by getting into trouble with the law. Now he thinks my problem with all this is because Niko is back in my life. I told him he was a fool. Niko didn't even know Calista because he was in prison when I was in college. He never met her."

"But he must have."

"I guess he must have," she echoed, shaking her head. "But he never mentioned her name to me."

"Is he in town?" I asked, hoping that she would say no. That he was on the other side of the country and couldn't possibly have done it.

But she looked at me with a haunted expression in her eyes. "Yeah, he got in the day before the festival started."

The rest of the night went by in a blur. My head was swimming with all the possibilities of who was behind Calista's murder. Was it Destiny, who wanted to take over the podcast? Was it Dee, her former friend turned rival? Was it Tristan, ex-lover whom she treated badly? Was it Niko, her stalker?

Or was it Starr . . . who seemed to have more connection to the victim than anyone? I bit down on my lip, remembering the look of shock on her face when I'd named her brother as the stalker. Her reaction had seemed genuine. Nobody could make their face go pale like that on command, right? Unless she had some secret acting background that I didn't know about.

"Chloe?" Grandma Rose waved a hand in front of my face. "Would you like a side of apple crumble to go with that bowl of whipped cream?"

I blinked and looked down at the dessert in front of me that now had a giant, leaning pile of whipped cream sitting on top. "Oops. I got a little trigger happy there."

"Here, let's spoon some off." Grandma Rose took the bowl from me and used a spoon to scoop off the top of the pile and plop it onto another dessert. It looked decidedly less pretty than when it came directly out of the pressurized aerator can in a controlled little puff. "Stop worrying about how it looks. You know it won't last more than a few minutes anyway."

"How do you always read my mind like that?"

"I'm psychic." She winked at me and I snorted.

"You wish."

"I don't actually." She shook her head, the motion causing the silver strands of her wig to swish around her face. "I couldn't think of anything worse than knowing what was coming. It would be like standing on train tracks and looking at the headlights coming toward you."

That seemed like a morbid way of looking at it.

I frowned. "Are you okay?"

We were standing in Lawrence St. James's kitchen, preparing the dessert that Grandma Rose had baked. The scent of honey-poached apples mixed with a heavy pinch of cinnamon and nutmeg in the crumble topping, warm and fresh out of the oven. Her secret ingredient was a handful of candied walnuts sprinkled on top for extra sweetness and crunch, and a pinch of coarse sea salt to balance it all out. If love had a taste, it was this comforting, delicious and wholesome dish.

"The future seems bright at your age, Chloe, but it gets a little scarier the closer you get to the light." She placed a spoon in each dish, not making eye contact with me. "When I was young I used to want to race past every phase. Oh, I wish I was married, I would say. Then I wanted to have a baby, then I wanted that baby to be old enough to sleep through the night. Then I wanted to have a grandchild. It was like I was always wishing myself to the next step and now . . ."

My throat tightened.

"Getting old is a blessing, dear." She laid a hand on my arm. "I want it to last forever."

I slipped an arm around her shoulders and rested my head on top of hers. Her wig felt silky against my cheek and I noticed she had a new bruise blossoming on the back of her hand. She always seemed to be covered in bruises these days—a side effect of the chemo, we were told. It was hard to understand how something so powerfully good to rid her of cancer also caused such painful side effects like bruising, sores in her mouth, nausea and fatigue. She'd lost weight too, I'd noticed. Grandma Rose had always had that lovely plump grandma shape, but her clothes were hanging a little more loosely of late.

"I want it to last forever, too," I said, a slight feeling of panic gripping like a fist around my heart.

I couldn't imagine my life without her. Even trying to think about what it would be like caused my brain to shut down, like I couldn't handle even the hypothesis of it.

"Don't mind me, I'm just melancholy tonight." She gave herself a little shake. "Must be a full moon or something."

I laughed. "Don't turn into a werewolf."

She looked at me and made a scary face with her hands raised like claws and we both cracked up. That was one thing I truly admired about my grandmother—no matter how worried or stressed she might be, it was never long before she cracked a joke to pick herself and everyone around her back up. She was a realist, for sure, but she also had a deep-seated positivity and resilience to her that I wholeheartedly loved. Grandma Rose was strong, inside and out.

"What are you two giggling at in here?" Jake stuck his head into the kitchen, grinning. He looked so handsome tonight, his skin glowing with a tan from his first summer in the glorious West Coast sun. "Good lord, that smells incredible."

"She makes a *mean* apple crumble." I picked up two bowls and Grandma Rose did the same. Jake backed up to let us out of the kitchen so we could head into the lounge room.

Lawrence St. James's house was as quirky as one might expect from a retired writer. There were heaving bookshelves, along with a random assortment of statues, decorative pieces and a delightful mishmash of furniture he'd collected over the years. If Jake's place was "bachelor pad chic" then Lawrence's place was "eccentric artist maximalism." He had a brown velvet wingback chair by a fireplace, the mantel almost sagging with writing awards. There was a marble bloodhound—apparently a replica of Lawrence's beloved family pet from when he was a child—curled up at the foot of the hearth. A gold bar cart housed an interesting collection of decanters, cognac balloons, liquor glasses and vintage cocktail tools like a shaker, jigger and muddler. And the walls were covered in a textured wallpaper, with heavy velvet drapes hung at the windows.

Some might find it a little . . . much. But I thought it suited him to a tee.

"Ah, I found it!" Lawrence held up a book triumphantly. He was wearing green slacks and a tweed waistcoat over a rumpled white shirt, a pair of glasses perched on the tip of his nose. Antonio followed close behind, ears pricked skyward and question-mark tail bobbing happily with each step. "This was the book where I had to research scuba diving because my character finds a dead body trapped in some coral. He's missing a leg and has a diamond clutched in his fist."

"Oh, that sounds good!" Jake's eyes lit up.

"You can borrow it, son. Just don't dog-ear the pages." Lawrence handed him the book as we set the desserts down on the coffee table.

Jake looked almost offended. "I would never."

Antonio trotted around the coffee table, trying to get a look at what delicious-smelling food items had entered the vicinity.

That dog slotted right into our family with his serious sweet tooth. Since the table was above his head, he rose back on his hind legs, front paws tucked up, trying to see. We called this his "meerkat" pose.

Grandma Rose glanced affectionately at Lawrence and Jake, and leaned into me. "They get along well."

"Very well." I couldn't help but smile.

On the way over, Jake had told me he'd taken quite a shine to Lawrence, because he reminded Jake of his late grandfather. I knew he missed his gramps a lot. In fact, it was the reason Jake had left New York to move to the other side of the country when he didn't know a single soul out here. His grandfather had grown up in Azalea Bay, and when he passed he left Jake his vintage Chevy Camaro—which was in the process of being restored—and told him to get out of New York before his heart froze over for good.

Seeing the two men bonding and knowing how much it meant for Jake to have a grandfather-figure in his life, it made me feel all warm and fuzzy inside.

"So tell me, Chloe," Lawrence said as we settled down to eat dessert—he in his wingback, Jake on a footstool that served as an extra seat, and Grandma Rose and I on the couch. Antonio had found himself a cozy little nook in the corner of two bookshelves. "How's the ice cream festival going?"

"Good," I said, digging my spoon into my apple crumble and trying to get a nice balance of the apples, topping and cream in one bite. "We've had a lot of exposure from the podcast."

"That's the poor girl who died," Grandma Rose chipped in. "Such a tragedy."

"Oh yes, under the food truck, right?" Lawrence nodded. "Do the police have their eye on anyone in particular?"

"A local businessperson." I doubted Lawrence would know of either Starr or Sprout, given he was about as likely to eat an amethyst-charged smoothie bowl as I was to make brownies from a Betty Crocker packet mix. "But I'm not sure they're looking in the right direction. There seem to be quite a few people who could have had motive."

"As there usually are." Lawrence nodded sagely. "People who rise to the top of their field often collect a string of detractors along the way."

"Did you ever have to deal with that being a successful author?" Jake leaned forward, his eyes gleaming with interest.

"Oh, but of course! The publishing world can be cutthroat, especially when you're all writing about murder. I once had a very dear friend, but when my career started to take off he couldn't handle the feeling of being left behind, even though I would have helped him with anything." Lawrence sighed. "It was a sad loss. But he became so jealous that it ruined any chance we might have remained friends. He believed I took a publishing award that should have been his and it was that award which really launched my career . . . so he stole my fiancée as payback."

I gasped. "He did not!"

Grandma Rose didn't look surprised, so I figured she must know this piece of history.

"He surely did." Lawrence bobbed his head, his expression pained for a moment as if the memory caused him to physically hurt. "I could never forgive either one of them for that. It broke my heart."

I wondered if this was the reason why Lawrence had never married. He'd been single his whole life despite being a warm and lovely person, a dapper dresser, and sharp as a tack. He was a catch! But I also understood how a betrayal could make you withdraw from relationships. Perhaps Grandma Rose was just the right person to help him trust—and love—again.

"Why do you think the police are looking at the wrong person?" Lawrence asked. "I do love how you always get yourself embroiled in mysterious things."

"Don't encourage her," Grandma Rose grumbled, scooping up some of the apple dessert and making sure she got some whipped cream with it.

"This woman—Starr—she almost has *too* many connections to the crime," I said, ignoring Grandma Rose's comment. "Firstly, she has a history of a broken friendship with the victim. Secondly, she has a vase filled with the same yellow roses as the petals found next to the body at the murder scene. Thirdly, she claims someone broke into her store and planted an item—a journal—belonging to the victim. Then fourthly, her brother was apparently stalking the victim."

"That *is* a lot," Grandma Rose said. "But maybe there's a lot of evidence because she did it. Where there's smoke there's fire, after all."

I scrunched up my nose. "Why wouldn't she have tried to hide some of those connections then, if that was the case? Why show me the journal and leave the roses in plain sight?"

"That's a good point," Lawrence mused and I sensed a note of approval in his voice. "Do you think someone is trying to frame her?"

"It's possible." I nodded.

"Yellow roses could certainly indicate that." Lawrence's spoon had a loud clink as he chased a piece of apple around his bowl. "Come here, you silly little thing."

"I thought yellow roses indicated friendship," I said, thinking back to my visit to Heavy Petal.

"Possibly nowadays they do," he said. "But in Victorian times, yellow roses indicated jealousy or even infidelity. I briefly worked on a mystery series set in the 1870s where I had a lady sleuth who was a socialite and amateur botanist. Each of the books surrounded a particular type of flower. Sadly, they never sold well and the publisher dropped the series, as they're wont to do. But I learned a lot about the flower language of the era."

"That sounds like a fun series. I haven't read those ones," Grandma Rose replied.

"Nor did many people, I suspect." Lawrence sniffed. "It was such a departure from my long-running series, that perhaps the audience was not open to it. I spent hours researching proper etiquette among the upper class in England. There were so many restrictions on what was acceptable and what was not, which gave rise to creating a language of flowers. You could say things with a bouquet you could never say to someone's face."

"And yellow flowers symbolized jealousy and infidelity?" I asked. "I wonder why."

"From my research, the general suspicion is that the yellow roses of the time didn't have the same wonderful scent as red or pink roses. Therefore, the yellow roses were jealous of the red roses." He lifted one shoulder into a shrug and Jake shook his head in bewilderment. "It seems rather preposterous, doesn't it? But so do all meanings that humans assign to things. A color is a color—it doesn't inherently mean anything beyond the chemical compounds that make it so, and yet we associate red with passion and pink with love and blue with calm."

"So in Victorian times, if you suspected your husband was having an affair, then you would send his mistress some yellow roses to shame her?" I laughed. "I'm not sure I would want to waste my hard-earned money buying flowers for my scoundrel husband *or* his mistress."

"It was different times back then," Lawrence replied good-naturedly. "But I'm sure those meanings have changed over the years and, frankly, these days only people who have an interest in that period would even know of such information."

"True. But I totally want to read those books," I added.

"Oh yes, let me go find them." Lawrence placed his half-finished dessert on the coffee table and slowly got to his feet. "I'm pretty sure I have them here, somewhere."

As Lawrence pottered around his shelves, trying to locate the books, I thought back to what I'd learned at Heavy Petal. The card that accompanied the yellow roses had that rather cryptic message written on it: *Losing is not in my vocabulary.*

The message *could* be something to indicate jealousy—a warning from a rival perhaps? Or maybe the color of the roses meant nothing at all and the message was an indication of intent from a lover with whom she'd had an argument or tried to push away. Or maybe it could be a private joke or have some other meaning.

Or maybe there *was* something to Lawrence's research on the Victorian flower language and Starr had gotten herself an enemy.

CHAPTER 15

"Lawrence is so cool," Jake enthused as we walked up his driveway, carrying several books each.

After dropping Grandma Rose and Antonio back home, I'd offered to help Jake carry the books next door to his place. We'd left with a ton of loaners, on the promise that we would not dog-ear the pages. He was very serious about that. I couldn't wait to get started with the lady botanist mysteries—they sounded right up my alley.

"Grandma Rose is *totally* smitten," I said, chuckling. "I honestly never thought she would find another partner after my grandfather died. She hasn't showed any interest in romance for decades."

"I guess it takes the right person to come along." He tucked the books under one arm while he fished into his back pocket for his keys. "They seem to have a lot of fun together."

I thought back to the giddy way Grandma Rose had laughed at Lawrence's jokes and the sincere way he'd complimented how pretty she looked tonight. Ever since the chemo treatment caused her hair to fall out, and what little wisps of eyebrows and fine blond eyelashes she'd had before were now mostly gone, too, she'd been feeling self-conscious about her appearance. But he'd made her feel beautiful again with one heartfelt compliment.

It was a joy to see.

"I think being diagnosed with cancer has made her reevaluate things in life," I mused.

The lock clicked and Jake and I headed inside. He'd left a lamp on and it bathed the front of the house in a soft glow.

"How so?" he asked.

"Well, my grandmother has always been . . . deeply loyal. I think she felt that if she got into a relationship with another man then it might be disrespectful to my grandfather's memory. Like she was replacing him." I followed Jake to the lounge room, where we deposited the books on the coffee table. There were about fifteen in total and one of the piles teetered to one side. This would keep him busy for a while! "But I don't see it like that. She deserves to be happy and I think the cancer has made her see that we have to make the most of our time. Nobody knows how long they have, young or old."

"Ain't that the truth," Jake muttered.

I knew Jake understood that sentiment. Working on Wall Street had taken a toll on him. Long hours, constant stress, sky-high sales targets. A crystallizing moment had come when his best friend had a heart attack at thirty-five and then not long after Jake himself had ended up at the hospital with a panic attack, thinking he was going down the same path.

None of us liked to imagine our own mortality, but it was especially jarring to have it shoved in one's face. I tried not to think about Calista and how suddenly her life had been ended. Maybe there was something in Azalea Bay's air tonight—because this echoed the conversation I'd had with Grandma Rose.

"It could all be over in the blink of an eye," I said, shaking my head.

"Do you think you would have done anything different, if you knew you didn't have much time left?"

I laughed. "Uh, yeah."

"Like what?"

"Oh, I don't know. I might not chronically overthink every decision about my life and stress for so long before deciding to do something, or worry constantly about what people think of me. I might not agonize over having to make a phone call instead of texting someone. You know, the usual Millennial crap." I grinned and Jake laughed, nodding along like he knew exactly what I meant. "What about you?"

"I would have left New York sooner," he replied, nodding. "I knew *that* life was a dead end for me long before I got the balls to quit. But then, even if I would have moved out here earlier, I still would've had to wait for you to arrive."

A pleasant warmth pooled in my cheeks. "I don't know about that. Maybe you would have found some other small town girl next door to solve murders with."

"No way." Jake shook his head.

"No one else gets into trouble like me, huh?" I looked up at him and his hazel eyes were locked onto mine.

"No one else does *anything* like you." He reached forward and brushed a strand of hair back from my temple. "I think you undersell yourself, Chloe. A lot."

"I think I accurately sell myself," I replied. "I know I'm talented in some areas and very *untalented* in others. I'm just like anyone else."

It was a truth most people didn't want to admit—that on some level, the vast majority of us were ordinary, average folks. It was a disappointment I'd seen time and time again in the restaurant world—everyone wanted to believe that *their* business baby would become big and famous and change the world. But every year restaurants closed and new ones opened.

Some businesses failed while others thrived. Not everybody could be the star, the standout, the number one.

But that wasn't a reason not to swing for the fences. You had to try, in life. That was the whole point of living.

"You're not like anybody else I've ever met," he said. "And that's the truth as I see it."

It felt like the air was buzzing around us, electric energy shimmering like tiny sugar crystals on a perfect Christmas cookie. The way he looked at me—like I was someone special, someone desirable—it made me feel like I'd downed a glass of champagne too quickly. I was weightless. Fizzy. Giddy.

"I think you're a wonderful person," he said. "You stand up for people, you're brave. Talented. You care about your family so much."

I suppose some people would rather be seen as attractive or sexy, but knowing that Jake saw me for the person I was underneath all that superficial stuff had me floating on air. Because looks weren't the most important part of a person. Their heart was. Their soul.

And I felt like Jake could see mine.

"If I knew I didn't have much time left I wouldn't have been so afraid to give you a chance," I said. "*That's* the thing I would do differently."

Jake leaned forward, sliding his palm along my jaw and around to cup the back of my head. I didn't resist. Didn't want to resist. His nose brushed mine and my whole body filled with delicious, snapping anticipation. This was it. He was going to kiss me.

We hovered for a moment and I closed my eyes, relishing the warm puff of breath over my skin, followed by the soft yet firm pressure of his lips. My hands caught his shirt and a sigh rose up from inside me. I liked Jake a heck of a lot and it was time to let go of my fears of having my heart broken again. Life was for this. For living. For passion. For trust.

And I couldn't afford to waste a moment being afraid of those things ever again.

The following morning I woke up feeling like I'd slept on a bed of cotton candy clouds, with Jake's kisses still lingering on my lips. I was almost giddy as I got out of bed, and I couldn't help but dance around while I showered and then went back to my room to get ready—although I didn't turn on any music, because it was far too early to wake up Grandma Rose. But there was a spring in my step like I hadn't experienced in some time.

It felt good.

Outside my bedroom door, there was a scratching sound followed by a distinct "I know you're in there" whine. That's one thing they don't tell you about owning a Chihuahua—you will never have privacy ever again. Every breath you take? Every move you make? Every chip packet you rustle? Two beady little eyes will be watching you.

I found Antonio sitting in the hallway, staring up at me.

"What are you doing awake?" I asked as I bent down to pick him up and he scampered up my chest to snuggle against my neck. I was still wearing my toweling bathrobe and he *loved* the fluffy fabric. "It's far too early for a little guy like you to be up and about."

I carried him into my room and sat on the edge of the bed to let him snuggle for a few minutes. Since we were at the festival today, I actually didn't need to be in the kitchen quite as early as normal. But I was wound up—both from Jake's kisses and from all the happenings around Calista's murder.

Talk about clashing feelings.

"What do you think about Calista's murder?" I asked Antonio, who blinked sleepily from where he was now curled up in my lap. "Do you think Starr did it?"

How would I know, lady? I'm just a Chihuahua. My special-
ties are naps, snacks and demolishing stuffed toys.

In my head, Antonio had a funny little voice and I often found myself imagining what he would say back to me if he could speak. Was that weird? Maybe. But I still found it easier to talk through my problems with a willing ear available, even if there wasn't much back-and-forth.

"And who is sending me these nasty emails, huh? What the heck is all that about?" I let out a sigh. "Why would someone go to the lengths of sending me a photoshopped picture of my store with the windows busted? If they hate what I'm doing so much, why didn't they actually break the windows?"

It was such an odd situation, because it really seemed like the anonymous email sender was more interested in rattling my cage than actually following through with the threats. But to what end?

"If only my life was as simple as yours," I murmured, stroking Antonio's velvety ears. "If my biggest task of the day was finding the sunniest patch to take a nap, life would be pretty good, wouldn't it?"

I let him stay on my bed while I changed into my work clothes and put on a little light makeup. I didn't always wear makeup to work, because some mornings I really needed that extra ten minutes of sleep, but this morning I was feeling energized, so I slicked some shimmery stuff onto my eyes and brushed mascara through my lashes. I finished off with my favorite pink lipstick that I'd used so much it was barely a nub and the brand's name had totally worn off the packaging.

When I turned to say goodbye to Antonio, I saw that he'd made himself a cozy little nest from my discarded bathrobe. Chuckling, I left him to sleep. Before I headed out, I put a load of washing into the machine, tipped some dry dog food into Antonio's bowl, and turned the coffee pot on to brew so it would be ready for Grandma Rose when she got up. Then I went outside, hopped into the Jellybean and drove to the café.

Early mornings were always a peaceful and creative time for me. As hard as the early starts had been when we first opened Baked by Chloe, I had mostly acclimatized to the shift in schedule and now I really enjoyed starting my day alone.

I mentally ran through my to-do list as I walked from my car and let myself into Baked by Chloe through the back entrance. We still had plenty of ice cream left, but I also knew that Saturday and Sunday would be the busiest part of the festival. And Grandma Rose had always told me it was better to have too much than not enough. I figured making an extra batch of the chocolate ice cream would be a good backup, just in case we ran out. If not, I could add it to the specials board until it was used up.

First things first, I needed to decarboxylate the cannabis. I threw on my apron, set the oven to 240 degrees Fahrenheit and retrieved the most recent delivery of cannabis buds. I needed about forty minutes of heating time to make the cannabis psychoactive and be ready for infusion with the heavy cream required to make the ice cream. The process was actually rather simple—once the buds were decarbed, they were placed into a saucepan along with the heavy cream, simmered until the cream was fully infused, and then strained through a fine filter to ensure there was no debris messing up the silky, luxurious texture.

Our ice cream was made with full-fat cream. This wasn't only because of my love for rich desserts, but also because THC was fat soluble and when cannabis was consumed alongside a fat source, the bioavailability—the ability of the THC to be absorbed and used by the body—was increased. This meant better benefits and a more potent experience for the person consuming it.

And hey, any excuse for me to use butter and heavy cream was a win, as far as I was concerned. I'd even been toying with the idea of making a coconut-cream-based ice cream for our vegan customers, since coconut was naturally high in fat and would make a great alternative to cow's milk. Not to mention the fact that cannabis-infused heavy cream didn't *only* need to be made into a sweet dessert. I'd had an idea for a weed mac-and-cheese churning in my brain for some time now, too.

With ideas buzzing, I retrieved my pre-chilled bowl and set about making the ice cream in the heavy-duty machine that Aunt Dawn and I had purchased for the café some weeks back. It was a pricy investment, but a worthwhile one, since I was sure our customers would want to continue eating our cold treats during the long, hot Californian summer. I set the ice cream to churn in the machine and started cleaning up my preparation area by washing the pots and other cooking implements I'd used. Then I headed into the office to do some administrative work.

Usually, I played music through a portable speaker while I worked. I had a playlist with all my favorite nostalgic hits from when I was young—Britney Spears, Katy Perry, Beyoncé. But today I was enjoying the quiet. Maybe it was because my head was full of questions about Calista's murder and Starr's potential involvement. Or maybe it was because Jake and I seemed to be taking our relationship in a more serious direction and that felt exciting and scary and right.

Whatever the reason, the kitchen was near silent as I worked. Which was why I heard the faint sound of the back door handle moving as I stared at a spreadsheet of sales data on my computer. Frozen, I strained to listen.

Someone was trying to break into Baked by Chloe.

CHAPTER 16

My heart pounded like a fist was trying to punch its way out of my chest and it felt as though ice had been poured into my veins, freezing me to the spot. The handle jiggled noisily again, then it fell silent. I swallowed, my ears almost aching with the strain of trying to hear. Maybe the wannabe thief had given up. I listened for footsteps, muttering, anything.

But there was nothing.

Just as I was about to get out of my chair there was a soft scratching sound, like something pliable against metal, almost as if whoever was trying to get in was picking the lock.

Starr suspected it was the killer who'd broken into her café to plant evidence, so clearly they knew how to break and enter! I wondered if they thought Baked by Chloe was empty, since we had a sign out front saying we were closed for the duration of the festival and to come visit us at our stall. The scratching persisted. I reached down into the pocket on the front of my apron to grab my phone so I could call 911, only to find that my pocket was empty. Crap! I must have left the device sitting on the magnetic charging stand I kept near my portable speaker.

Glancing around the office, there wasn't anything to use as a defensive weapon. The closest thing I could find was the heavy stapler I used to attach my delivery invoices to purchase orders for our filing system, since many of the small businesses I bought from hadn't yet converted to digital.

I grabbed the stapler and stood, holding my breath and inching toward the small open doorway that led to the kitchen. As soon as I left the safety of the office, whoever was trying to break in would see me through the eye-level window on the back door. Prior to now, I'd appreciated the window because it allowed me to see who was knocking if there was a delivery due. In this exact moment, however, I wished it wasn't there.

I hovered in the doorway, holding the stapler firm while I mentally prepared myself to clobber someone over the head, should the situation call for it. It felt like every nerve in my body was pulled tight as cutting wire about to slice through a thick wheel of Gouda. But before I could convince myself to step into the kitchen, there was a loud burst of sound—glass shattering. The tension I'd been holding inside broke and I screamed at the top of my lungs.

I'd well and truly blown it now—whoever was trying to break in would know I was here. Holding my breath, I peered into the kitchen. The window on the back door was destroyed and a large rock lay among the sparkling, shattered remains. But there was nobody standing outside. I hurried forward, stapler still in my hand, stepping around any large chunks of glass lest they cut through my chef clogs.

With my heart in my mouth, I pushed the door open and cautiously peered outside. But the alley was deserted. Most of the businesses here didn't open for several more hours. It was light out, but quiet. An older woman in a loose tunic over capri pants was walking past the alley and paused to look at me with a concerned expression.

"Was that you?" The woman frowned. "I heard a scream."

"I'm okay. I, uh . . . saw a mouse." I cringed. It was probably *way* worse for my business to say there were mice around than to admit someone had been trying to break in and that I'd screamed in fear. I wasn't sure why I lied—it just popped out. I guess saving face came a little too naturally. "When I came outside, I mean. Not in the kitchen. We definitely don't have mice, I promise."

She eyed the stapler and then looked back at me, her eyes resting on my apron, which had the Baked by Chloe logo embroidered on it. Probably thought I'd eaten a little too much of my own product. "Right."

Without further word she hurried away, muttering to herself and shaking her head. Great. I'd convinced her that either my kitchen was rodent infested or that I was working while high. Neither was a good look. Dammit! I should have asked her if she'd seen anything. I hurried along the alleyway toward the street, hoping to catch her. Instead I almost ran into someone and skidded to a stop just in time. It was Dee, the podcaster.

"I heard someone screaming bloody murder," she said, pressing a hand to her ample chest in motherly concern. She was wearing another one of those maxi dresses with a dizzying print. Her hair gleamed with a generous coating of gel that she'd used to spike the short lengths in all directions, giving her an almost porcupine appearance. "Did you hear it, too?"

"I, uh . . . hey, did you happen to see anybody running this way?" I asked, ignoring her question. The other woman who'd stopped had already turned the corner, looking back over her shoulder at me like she hoped I wasn't following.

"There was a man. He almost ran me over." Dee harrumphed. "Not for nothing, folks could at least have a little decency on the sidewalk. Some of us don't have the agility we used to."

"What did he look like?" I swung my head around, but there was no sign of a man. "Which way did he go?"

"That way." She pointed toward the residential area. Her

nail was bitten down to the quick, but she'd attempted to cover it with nail polish, which only served to highlight the jagged edges. "He was a tall guy, built like a double door fridge. Kinda gray at the temples—salt and pepper, ya know."

She pronounced pepper like pepp-*ah,* giving a hint of accent—New York, perhaps. Maybe Boston or somewhere else in New England. But it was very faded, like she'd grown up there but had moved a long time ago.

"He was wearing a"—she moved her hands back and forth in front of her body, searching for the right word—"a jacket, thing. A blazer."

A tall, large older man in a blazer. That didn't ring any bells, especially not since blazers and suits weren't exactly common attire in Azalea Bay. Even in the businesses where folks might dress more formally in big cities—like lawyers' and accountants' offices—here, people dressed casually. Best you'd find was someone in slacks and an open-collared shirt, if they felt like dressing up. Blazers? Not so much.

"Might be an out-of-towner," I mused. But that didn't make sense, either. Why would an out-of-towner be worried I was bringing "sin" to Azalea Bay?

An idea popped into my head—could be a property developer who was working on a plan to build something here and they felt like a cannabis café was bad for property values or for whatever they were building. Maybe a worship center, or some other place with more conservative values.

"Uh, what's with the stapler? And why do you think someone was running?" Dee looked at me with narrowed eyes. "Was that you screaming?"

The quick-fire questions caught me off guard, and I stammered, totally giving away that it was, indeed, me who had screamed.

"What happened?" She grabbed my shoulders. "Are you okay?"

"Someone was trying to break into my shop."

"No!" she gasped. "Did you chase them out here? And what did you think you were going to do with a stapler, girl? Give them a puncture wound? Lecture them about taxes?"

"I wasn't really thinking," I admitted. "Just reacting."

"Let's get you back to your café so you can sit down and calm yourself." She steered me toward the back entrance to the café and I didn't have the energy to protest. I felt like I'd had the wind knocked out of me.

So much for naïvely thinking the anonymous email sender was simply trying to rattle my cage. Turned out they *were* planning to act. A thought niggled in the back of my mind.

You're assuming this is related to the emails and not *to Calista's death.*

What if I was wrong? It wouldn't be the first time someone had tried to harm me because I was sniffing too close to the truth. Perhaps the killer had seen me and Starr together?

Dee led me into the café, closed the door behind us and dragged my chair out of the office, plunking me down on it and divesting me of the stapler. Now she was fussing over the broken glass.

"Do you want to call the police?" she asked, crouching down and squinting at the rock without touching it. "I can ring 911."

"It doesn't really feel like an emergency now." I let out a breath. "And I'm pretty sure there are no CCTV cameras in the alley."

"I could give a description of the guy to the cops. Maybe they could do one of those . . . what do they call them? Composite sketch things." She frowned. "Someone was serious about breaking in with this thing. They could have reached in and unlocked the door from the inside, right?"

I nodded. I might have struggled to do it, being vertically

challenged, but someone who was taller with longer limbs could probably have slipped an arm through and reached for the lock.

"Do you think someone was looking for a drug heist?" Dee asked.

I hadn't even thought of that. I did keep a reasonable amount of cannabis on-site, so perhaps the break-in was nothing at all to do with either the emails *or* Calista's death. Aunt Dawn had said something about getting a security camera for both entrances, and she was probably right. One previous attack and now one attempted break-in were certainly enough to warrant upping our security a bit.

"It's possible," I said, nodding. "It could be anything."

Dee raised her eyebrow. "You think it might be something else?"

I could hardly tell her that I was snooping around looking for Calista's murderer because there was a chance Starr had been framed. What if Dee was the killer? Or what if she wasn't, but she seized the opportunity to blow the story up for her podcast? That would make everything worse and Starr would kill me.

Well, not really . . . I hoped.

"I've received a few unhappy emails since the café opened," I admitted, twisting the hem of my apron. "They're saying I'm bringing the town into disrepute, I should have been raised better. That I should shut the business down. Blah, blah, blah."

Dee's eyes widened like saucers. "That's terrible."

"I wish I could say I was surprised." I lifted one shoulder into a shrug. "I knew a cannabis café would be controversial."

"So did I, that's why I asked you that question during the interview." Dee winked, then a look of recognition flashed across her face and she slapped a hand to her forehead. "This is bad timing, but I was actually meaning to catch you today. The audio recording from our interview got corrupted and I lost the entire thing. My boyfriend is pretty good with computers, so he's taking a look. But he says I've likely lost it all. Any chance you would give me a do-over? Please, Chloe. It was going to be such a good episode. I really thought your festival menu was incredible."

It was the *last* thing I felt like doing, in truth. But Dee had been kind enough to walk me back to the café and sit me down and offer to call the police.

"Sure," I said, nodding. "Maybe after the festival is wrapped up tomorrow evening? It's going to be a busy two days."

"Of course. You good, kid?" She nodded and brushed her hands down the front of her dress. "Want me to wait with ya?"

"That would be great, thanks." I let out a sigh and went to grab my phone.

Why did it suddenly feel like I needed to have the police on speed dial?

A uniformed officer came to the café to take my statement, get the description from Dee and check out the damage. He also arranged for someone to dust for prints. Jake had arrived with wood, nails and a hammer to board up the back door window from the inside just in case the person came back, and Aunt Dawn and Grandma Rose had raced over to make sure I was okay. And I was. Shaken, yes. But okay.

Despite the scary morning, by lunchtime it felt like any other business day.

The festival was bumping and we had a steady line of customers keeping me busy enough not to dwell on any of the things cluttering up my brain. The Saturday of the annual ice cream festival was colloquially known as "kids' day," where all the main stage demonstrations were aimed at the little ones— including a lunchtime entertainment show featuring people in ice cream costumes dancing and singing—and other activities such as face painting and ice-cream-themed fair games like ring toss and tin can targets.

Given we were in the "adults only" marquee, none of this really applied to us, but it did make for some weary twenty-one-plus festivalgoers sneaking in for a moment of kid-free peace and quiet.

"I'm glad I made an additional batch of ice cream this morning," I said to Erica as I handed over another fulfilled order for her to call out. "At this rate, we would have been playing a game of chicken to make it to closing."

"Worst game of chicken *ever*." Erica chuckled. "Nobody wants to run out of ice cream, especially not with it being this hot."

I fanned myself. "No joke. It's roasting today."

The fans inside the marquee were working overtime and Aunt Dawn, Erica, Jake and I were taking turns standing near the refrigerator to keep cool. The weather had certainly drawn even more people into the festival—the promise of a smooth, ice-cold treat irresistible once the temperature shot past ninety degrees. For anyone who wondered how one small town could sustain a multiday ice cream festival, *this* was it:

Roaring temperatures + tourists + beach = ice cream sales.

"The weatherman said it could reach ninety-seven by this afternoon," Aunt Dawn said, pausing to fan herself. "Remind me why we've stayed on the West Coast so long."

"Because come winter you don't have to deal with the feeling of your eyelashes freezing," Jake quipped, looking totally at ease in the warmth. "I'll take this heat over an East Coast winter any day of the week."

"The man knows what's up." Erica nodded sagely. "Nobody wants frozen eyelashes."

The four of us fell into our easy working rhythm and I was grateful to be surrounded by the people who made me feel safe. Every so often I would catch Jake looking at me when he thought I wouldn't notice and when our eyes met, it sent a little frisson of happiness through me. Aunt Dawn checked in no less than every twenty minutes to see if I was feeling okay, mother-hen mode fully engaged. And Erica worked hard as ever, cheerfully calling out orders and eagerly jumping in to prepare the dishes when someone else needed a break.

When it came to relationships, I had an embarrassment of riches. And no jerk with a rock or keyboard would be able to take that from me.

Sometime around one thirty, my stomach was growling and Aunt Dawn convinced me to take my lunch break ahead of her. I'd forgotten all about my plan to have something substantial for breakfast after the break-in attempt and I hadn't eaten a thing all morning. Feeling a little lightheaded, I didn't argue and instead slipped off my apron and made my way to the green room tent. I could at least fuel up and hydrate for a moment while I got my head together.

But after only a few minutes there—just long enough to eat a granola bar and a piece of fruit, and have a hearty drink of water—I was already itching to leave. The last twenty-four hours had filled me with jittering energy and I was like a jack-in-the-box about to pop, so I decided to go for a walk. The center of the festival was thick with children who were all hopped up on sugary treats, wearing glitter face paint and generally exploding with joy. Cute as it was, I didn't feel like dodging the crowds. Instead, I left the festival through a "staff and vendors only" exit and walked along a trail that would eventually curve up to the lookout point high above the beach. This part of the park was more thickly wooded, but had a clearly marked path and signs to make it easy to follow.

It was quieter here. On days where a nice breeze rolled off the ocean this was a popular walking spot, but today most folks were either occupied with the festival or cluttering the sandy shoreline, ready to cool off with a swim. I could hardly blame them. I'd much prefer a dunk in the ocean over a sweaty uphill walk.

But clearly some people had decided to brave the weather. Up ahead, I saw two men walking, their backs to me. Both were tall—though one appeared muscular and athletic, wearing workout shorts and a baseball cap and sneakers, while the other was skinny with hunched shoulders, pale limbs and hair tied back into a coppery-red ponytail.

I blinked.

Something about the men seemed familiar. Hadn't I seen a tall, thin man with a ponytail hanging out with Dee in the adults-only tent yesterday?

The two men appeared to be deep in conversation, their strides slow as though they weren't in any hurry to get where they were going. Because of this, I began to catch up to them. Instinctively, I stepped off the trail and onto the grass, skirting around a tree as the men slowed to a stop. The man with the ponytail looked behind him, as if checking whether anyone was following, and I crouched down behind a bush, peering through the branches, hoping that they wouldn't catch sight of me. It was definitely the guy I saw yesterday.

What on god's green earth are you doing?

Thankfully, the voice shouting in my head could only be heard by me. But something in my gut told me this was important.

"You're paranoid," the man in the cap said to the other man with the ponytail.

"I'm cautious," he corrected. "Now, what did you want to talk about?"

The more athletic man took off his cap and raked a hand through his thick blond hair. Now that I could see his face better, it struck me who he was—Tristan Patrick. What an odd combination of people. I was surprised anyone in Dee's orbit would be connected to someone as famous as Tristan.

"I want to make sure we're on the same page," Tristan replied smoothly. He was practically glowing from the sun, skin tanned and smooth, especially when compared to the other man's pale, pock-marked face and scruffy red beard flecked with silver strands.

It was almost comical how different they looked.

"In regard to what?" the redheaded man asked, folding his arms across his chest. Everything about his posture radiated wariness. Distrust. These men were not friends, that much was certain.

"To what we agreed upon, earlier." Tristan was being cryptic, despite the fact that they were alone. Seemed the lack of trust went both ways. "That the job is done and we go our separate ways."

A cold, heavy stone settled in the pit of my stomach. What "job" were they talking about? It didn't sound like any traditional kind of employment, because what other job required a conversation on a nearly deserted hiking trail?

"What makes you think anything has changed?" Now the redheaded man was vaguely smiling, like he thought he had the upper hand. "Worried I'll go to the cops?"

"Now why would you have to say something like that?" Tristan pulled his shoulders back as if trying to match the other man's height. "It's almost like you're trying to make me worry on purpose."

"Never."

"Don't screw around with me, okay? I know you think I got where I am because of my looks, but I can assure you I had to scrape and scavenge for every drop of success I have." Tristan's expression was hard. "I didn't grow up with money. I was born in Red Hook. I know how to fight."

"No point knowing how to fight if you don't want to get your own hands dirty."

"Bottom-feeders get their hands dirty." Tristan looked the

man up and down, the edge of his lip curling with disdain. "I've moved beyond that."

What was it with men always needing to have a pissing competition? That was one thing I really liked about Jake. He didn't do any of that alpha-male BS.

"Be careful what you insinuate." The redheaded man took a step forward and tilted his chin, jaw set. There was something determined in his eyes. Something unshakable. "Good-looking guys like you don't do so well in prison."

"I haven't done anything that would put me there."

"Keep telling yourself that." He chuckled. "And at this point, you need my silence *far* more than I need your approval. In fact, I don't need you at all. I could find that pretty lady detective and tell her everything."

The air was thick with tension and it felt like my hair was almost standing on end. I didn't dare move. Barely even dared to breathe. For a second, I was sure they were going to come to blows, but then there was a shuffling sound, like hurried footsteps.

"Tris?" It was a female voice.

A second later, Tristan's fiancée, Annie, came into view. She was dressed similarly to the last time I'd seen her—her petite frame covered up with a striped shirt dress buttoned all the way to her throat. Over the top she wore a white blazer, despite the heat, which had a vintage-looking brooch on the lapel and a designer logo containing an anchor stitched onto the pocket in gold thread.

The outfit looked like a fashion spread for *Millionaire Yacht Life Quarterly*. Now that Destiny had told me about her family money, it made sense.

"You must be Annie," the redheaded guy said, sticking his hand out. "Pleasure's all mine."

Annie glanced at Tristan as if waiting to see whether he would make an introduction, but he didn't. Instead he stared stonily at the man, jaw twitching like he was grinding his teeth together. She tentatively reached for the guy's hand, likely out of ingrained politeness, and he turned her hand over and kissed it. Annie's nose wrinkled and she snatched her hand back.

"See you around, *Tris*," he said, mocking Annie's pet name. "I look forward to us working together again soon. I'll be in touch."

He walked away, heading back toward the festival with his hands in his pockets, whistling a tune that sounded creepy echoing through the quiet trees.

"What was that all about?" Annie asked, looking at Tristan with a frown. "You're *working* with him? He looks like . . ."

She shuddered. Apparently, the redheaded man looked so bad she didn't even have a word in her vocabulary to describe it.

"We're not working together. He meant it as a joke." Tristan waved off her concern and slipped an arm around her waist. "Now, what are you doing looking for me?"

They started to head back in the direction of the festival, but slowly, walking arm in arm. Annie leaned into Tristan, more at ease now that the other man had left, his long legs carrying him off into the distance rather quickly.

"I wanted to have lunch," she replied. "And we promised Daddy that we would meet him at the marina. They've got that restaurant, Foam. It's nothing fancy but we should spend time with him while he's here."

Foam was the fanciest restaurant that Azalea Bay had to offer, but I supposed to someone like her it probably didn't seem that exciting.

"You need to stop being so desperate for his approval." Tristan shook his head.

"I'm not!" she protested.

A faint buzzing caught my attention and I flicked a hand by my ear, thinking it was a fly. But a flash of yellow blurred in my vision as a wasp darted around my head. Crap! Those things could be vicious.

"He comes and goes as he pleases," Tristan said. "He should be the one desperate to hang out with *you*."

"Don't say that. He's being so generous with us! You wouldn't have this new restaurant if it wasn't for him."

The wasp darted around my head like it was a fighter pilot trying to confuse the enemy. I shrank back, waving my hand in front of my face, trying to quietly shoo it away. I hated the darn things. Little yellow demons they were! So angry and hate-filled, ready to stick a stinger in you for simply existing.

"You *really* think that's the only reason I'm getting a new restaurant?" Tristan sounded insulted.

"Oh, I didn't mean it like that."

The wasp, completely giving zero f's that I was trying to hide, decided to try to land right on my nose. Out of pure instinct—and fear for my life—I shrieked at the top of my lungs and stumbled backward, almost falling over, but instead tumbling into clear view on the side of the walking trail. Tristan and Annie whipped around to see me.

"Are you alright?" Annie came toward me.

"Wasp!" I gasped, waving my hands. Thankfully the tiny yellow spawn of Satan decided it'd had enough of my antics and promptly buzzed off.

I caught sight of Tristan eyeing me with suspicion, as Annie looked around, trying to locate the wasp.

"I think it's gone. Thank goodness," I said shakily. "I was coming back from a nice walk up to the lookout. Have you been? It's *very* romantic. Our most romantic spot in Azalea Bay, in fact! Worth the effort to get up there, although it's hot today."

I was rambling. Tristan's eyes narrowed, but his expression softened when Annie placed a hand on his arm, her huge engagement ring winking in the sunlight filtering through the trees. "Oh, we should go, Tris. What do you think? Maybe after lunch? We could get an ice cream and walk up."

"Sure," he replied curtly, his eyes still fixed on me as though he was trying to figure something out. Likely whether or not I had overhead his conversation with the redheaded man. "After lunch."

"Thank you for the suggestion." Annie smiled, looking rather pleased to have some afternoon plans.

"It's Chloe, right?" Tristan asked. "I came past your stall yesterday since Calista spoke so highly of your skills, but you were on break. Your ice cream was very good, indeed. Lovely texture."

"Oh." I blinked. "Thank you."

That was high praise coming from an acclaimed chef like him. Momentarily, I was dazzled enough to almost forget about his suspicious conversation with the redheaded man.

"We're having a party tonight," he continued. "Annie's father has a yacht that's docked in the marina and we're doing a little industry thing. Do you have plans? We'd love to have you join us."

Annie seemed slightly taken aback by Tristan's sudden invitation, but she covered it quickly with a practiced smile. "What a great idea. Yes, please join us."

Why on earth would Tristan invite me to their party if he had any suspicion at all that I was eavesdropping on his conversation? Something in my gut sounded a warning alarm. Looking at his now-smiling face, which was worlds away from the hardened expression I'd seen moments ago, I knew there was far more to this man than met the eye.

But the lure of an "industry thing" with successful people in the restaurant world seemed like too good an opportunity to pass up. What budding restaurateur *wouldn't* be foaming at the mouth to attend a party with a celebrity chef and the rich future father-in-law funding his next business venture? I could make contacts that could be vital to the success of Baked by Chloe.

"Sure," I said, sucking in a breath. "I would love to come. Thank you so much."

The people at this party would likely know Calista. Maybe I could kill two birds with one stone and dig up some information about her murder. Now *that* was my kind of two-for-one deal. And the more I kept an eye on Tristan, the better.

Because it sounded a heck of a lot like he wasn't the golden boy everyone thought him to be.

CHAPTER 17

For the rest of the day, all I could think about was the conversation I'd overheard between Tristan and the still yet-to-be-identified redheaded man, aka Dee's possible boyfriend. Not to mention every so often my mind flashed back to the terror of having my café almost broken into that morning. I would need to organize someone to come and fix the window properly. But right now, I had a party to dress up for and a yacht to get to.

After the festival finished, I raced home to have a shower and wash my hair. What *did* one wear to a yacht party? I looked through my wardrobe and everything felt a little . . . casual.

Unlike Annie, I did not look like I could be on the cover of *Millionaire Yacht Life Quarterly*.

"Grandma! I don't know what to wear," I called out.

Chuckling, Grandma Rose shuffled into my room. She was clearly settling in for a cozy, relaxing evening as she was wearing a faded pink Disneyland T-shirt that I was pretty sure she'd had since the '90s. She held Antonio in her arms like a baby. His eyes were squinted shut and he looked utterly blissed out at being carried all around the house.

"Not that," Grandma Rose said, nodding to the fluffy robe I was wearing. I laughed and shook my head. "You have so many lovely things. Where are you going?"

"To a party on a yacht." I frowned at my wardrobe. "I don't think any of this stuff is fancy enough."

"Oh, a yacht *is* fancy." She nodded, but then her eyes brightened and she thrust Antonio into my arms. "Wait here."

The dog blinked, annoyed that his nap had been interrupted. Down the hall, I could hear the bang of a cupboard door and rustling. A few minutes later, Grandma Rose appeared in the doorway with an armful of vintage dresses.

"Some of these were mine when I was young, and some belonged to my sister, your great-aunt Maggie." She laid the pile on my bed. "Maybe we can find something in here that will work."

"I don't know if I'd fit into any of your old dresses." I bit down on my lip.

Grandma Rose had been quite svelte back in her day and it was an impossible task to work as a pastry chef while retaining anything close to a model's physique. I'd made peace with that a long time ago, and I liked that I had curves. That did mean, however, Grandma Rose's lovely vintage dresses would likely have a hard time getting over my hips.

"Maybe not." She started to spread the dresses out. "But Maggie was bustier than me and she had broader shoulders and hips. Her dresses might work better. Here, what about this?"

The dress she held up was stunning. It was white, sleeveless and would hit me above the knee, but the stand-out detail was the line of large mother-of-pearl and rhinestone buttons that ran off-center down the length of the dress. I gasped at how pretty it was. I didn't even need to see the other options.

"There are also some snaps inside to help it stay properly closed." Grandma Rose looked pleased that I liked the dress.

"And, if I am not mistaken, I have some earrings that would match perfectly."

"I hope it fits."

"You try it on and I'll grab the earrings."

I placed Antonio onto the ground and he whined at me, already wanting to be picked back up. "Sorry, bud, I have to get dressed."

I slipped out of my robe, unbuttoned the dress and put it on. It was ever-so-slightly too big, but I didn't mind a little extra room in case they were serving some delicious treats on the yacht. The crisp white fabric made me look more tanned than usual and the hint of gold on the buttons matched my hair well.

"Oh, Chloe, it looks amazing on you." Grandma Rose shuffled back into the room and held out her hand. In her palm was a vintage gold bracelet with matching clip-on earrings. "How about these to go with it?"

"They're perfect!" I held my hand out so she could fasten the bracelet around my wrist.

It took a solid three attempts to get the clip-on earrings in the right position and I was already wondering how long I'd last wearing them, because the pinching sensation wasn't the most comfortable.

"How on earth did you get invited to a yacht party anyway?" Grandma Rose asked as I rummaged around in my cupboard for some flat sandals.

"The yacht belongs to the future father-in-law of a chef I met at the festival. It's a . . . networking thing."

My unfortunate and unintentional pause made Grandma Rose narrow her eyes. "What are you not telling me, Chloe?"

"Nothing," I squeaked. But I immediately felt guilty at the prospect of lying to my grandmother, so I spilled the beans. "I think the chef could be involved in Calista's murder."

Grandma Rose let out a disappointed sigh. "And here I was thinking you were just going to a nice party and all the while you're going sleuthing!"

"Can't a modern-day woman do both?" I asked with a hopeful smile. She folded her arms across her chest and it was clear that she wasn't buying what I was selling. "Don't worry, I asked Jake to come with me so I won't be alone. I promise I won't get into trouble."

"Don't make promises you can't keep," she muttered. "And why do you think the chef is involved?"

I had to stifle a smirk of amusement that even as she was lecturing me, she was still interested in the mystery I was trying to solve. Grandma Rose *loved* a good puzzle and that was the reason she enjoyed reading Lawrence's mystery books so much.

I filled her in on how I accidentally stumbled across Tristan talking to the redheaded man about a covert job he wanted to keep secret.

"What do you think the job was?" Grandma Rose asked.

"It sounded a heck of a lot like the redheaded guy was a hitman and Tristan had hired him to kill Calista," I said. That was my working theory, anyway.

"Doesn't that seem a bit"—she wrinkled her nose—"unbelievable? This isn't a Hollywood movie. This is Azalea Bay."

"People *do* hire hitmen in the real world," I said. "I listened to a true crime podcast recently about a woman who tried to hire a hitman to kill the wife of the man she was in love with. And that happened in a town smaller than ours!"

"Don't put yourself in harm's way," she said, looking at me with her lips pursed. "I worry about you."

"You'd worry about me no matter what I did." I leaned in to give her a peck on the cheek. "Even if I was just baking cookies."

"Yes, well, cookies won't kill to cover up a secret," she said sagely. "Remember that."

* * *

Jake and I walked through the marina, past a collection of bustling restaurants on the way to the area where all the boats were docked. The deep green-blue of the ocean bracketed the boardwalk and slatted wood pathways, the sound of tinkling laughter, chiming glasses and the gentle slap of waves beneath us a romantic soundtrack on a perfectly balmy summer evening. To our right, Azalea Bay's most well-known restaurant, Foam, sat in all its glass-fronted glory, the balcony overhead dotted with white-linen-covered tables and flickering candles. It looked like every seat was full and several small groups waited outside, enjoying the breeze rolling off the water while they waited for a table to become free.

It was still light out, but the sky was streaked with peachy-pink clouds, like tufts of cotton candy. At the horizon, there was a splash of red-toned gold where the sun was dipping down and silver-capped waves rushed the shoreline.

"I feel like I've said this half a dozen times already, but"— Jake looked at me—"you look incredible."

How could he even look at me with *this* view in front of us?

"That's the power of a good dress." I tried to make out like I was used to such compliments, although I wasn't. Jake was very free with his praise and his thoughts, and that was new to me. "Grandma Rose has quite the treasure-trove of lovely vintage things. This belonged to my great-aunt Maggie."

"People used to dress up so well back in those days," he said wistfully. I loved that Jake was enamored with old things. He appreciated the craftsmanship of a time before fast fashion and disposable everything, and my gut told me that appreciation was a good thing. He was a quality-over-quantity kind of guy— with food, with things, with people. "My grandmother was a seamstress and she would make all her own clothing. I remember watching her sitting at her sewing machine when I was a kid—the damn thing screamed like a freight train."

"I have similar memories of Grandma Rose." I laughed. We walked, lost in our respective memories for a moment. "So, are you excited to see the inside of a yacht?"

"Are you kidding? It's not every day you get to go on a yacht, let alone one belonging to one of the most prominent venture capitalists in Silicon Valley." Jake seemed impressed, but I crinkled my nose.

"Wait, *who* is he?"

"You don't know Henry De Vries?" Jake sounded shocked. "His firm has backed all kinds of tech businesses that are huge now—DoorDash, Groupon, Airbnb, Skype. You name it. He's got a knack for picking which ideas are going to blow up."

"Wow. The first time someone told me about the DoorDash or Uber Eats concept, I thought it was the weirdest thing ever. Shows what I know." I snorted.

"He's a capital B big deal." Jake was almost buzzing with excitement.

"You can take the boy out of Wall Street, but you can't take Wall Street out of the boy," I teased.

"Well, I'm guessing you didn't accept the invite for the chance to meet Henry De Vries, anyway," Jake replied. "You're trying to sniff out clues."

"Busted," I admitted. When I had shared the details with Jake after speaking with Annie and Tristan, I had said it was a networking event. But clearly he knew me better than that. "Although it will *also* be a good way to meet more people in the industry."

"Whatever helps you sleep at night," Jake said, slipping an arm around my shoulders and chuckling. I leaned into him as we made our way past the restaurant area of the marina, down toward where all the boats were moored.

It wasn't hard to spot Henry De Vries's yacht, because it made all the other boats look like toys you'd expect to find floating in a bubble-filled bathtub. The behemoth vessel gleamed white against the faded sky, the name of the ship—*Princess Anouk*—written in orange text along the side. He'd named the yacht after his daughter. That was sweet . . . in a one-percent kind of way.

Onboard, well-dressed people stood with champagne flutes in hand, music billowing softly into the night air. A ramp was set up to allow guests to board the yacht, at the base of which stood a slim woman with dark hair, holding a tablet. A small line of people waited while she checked names.

"My old colleagues at the investment firm would *not* believe this." Jake practically bounced on the heels of his shoes. "Who would have thought I'd leave New York to move to a small town and then meet someone like Henry De Vries!"

We joined the small line of people waiting to be granted access to the yacht and as I took my phone out of my bag, I noticed that a text had come through in the last five minutes.

ERICA: Did you hear the news??

I texted her back.

CHLOE: What news?

ERICA: Starr got arrested!!

Usually I would tease Erica about her predilection for double punctuation, but I was too stunned to do so. Starr had been arrested. When? Why? Well, I knew *why* in the grand scheme of things. But what piece of information had tipped the police over the edge?

CHLOE: How did you find that out?

ERICA: Mom was out walking the dogs past the station when they brought her in. She was in handcuffs and everything!!!!

The punctuation was multiplying.

"Starr's been arrested," I told Jake, showing him the text chain.

He let out a long, low whistle. "Still think she didn't do it?"

"I don't know *what* to think." I shook my head, feeling conflicted. "My head tells me there's too many connections to simply ignore them, but my heart says she didn't do it. If someone is trying to frame her, they're doing a bang-up job."

The people ahead of us were let through onto the ramp and the woman smiled at Jake and me as we approached. "Names?"

"Chloe Barnes, and this is my plus one, Jake Reed."

She looked down at her screen, scrolling with one manicured finger. "Ah, there you are. Welcome to the *Princess Anouk*. You'll be asked to remove your shoes before boarding and a crew member will supply you with a space to store them for the duration of the evening. There's no smoking of any kind on board. Restrooms are on the lower deck. If you're having trouble finding them, any of the crew members will be able to assist you."

"Thank you." I was a little too awestruck to say anything more than that. It felt like I was about to go off on a luxury cruise or something!

Jake held my arm as we headed onto the yacht, keeping me steady. There was something about being on the water, even if only barely, that made my legs feel a bit wibbly-wobbly. Although I doubted the yacht would feel like it was moving at all, since it was basically closer to a small island than a boat. At least, that was from the perspective of someone who had only ever been out on the ocean on a vessel closer to the size of the door that Rose wouldn't share with Jack at the end of *Titanic*.

I was still salty about that, all these years later.

As we got to the top of the ramp, we were greeted by a man who opened a sleek-looking cabinet hidden into the wall of the yacht, which housed rows and rows of shoes. Clearly Henry De Vries had built this yacht for hosting parties.

Now barefoot, Jake and I followed the crew members' directions further along the main deck. The yacht appeared to have three levels—the main deck, which had an indoor-outdoor entertainment area, the upper deck where some partygoers had already congregated, and the lower deck, which was where all the bedrooms and bathrooms were housed.

"This is wild," Jake said under his breath as a waiter approached us with a tray of champagne flutes. We each took one and gently clinked our glasses together. "A yacht like this is probably worth five million. Maybe more."

"He bought it for eight point three million, I believe."

A voice behind us made me jump and I whirled around, almost losing half the contents of my champagne flute. Thankfully, I steadied myself before I spilled anything. It was Destiny.

Jake let out a low whistle. "That's a pretty penny and then some."

"Small change to a man like Henry De Vries." Destiny lifted one shoulder into a shrug. I made a quick introduction between her and Jake. "So, how did you score an invite?"

I took a sip of my champagne. Something told me I'd need a little liquid courage tonight. "I ran into Annie and Tristan today. They kindly invited me."

Destiny raised an eyebrow as though this was unusual behavior, but she didn't elaborate. Today she was wearing her long black braids pulled back into a thick ponytail and she had on yet another fun, colorful dress. This one was black with cherries all over it.

"You have the most *fun* wardrobe," I said. "Every day I want to see you, just so I can check out your outfit."

Destiny smiled and it was one of the most genuine smiles I'd seen from her thus far. "Thanks. My mama always wore these big '50s skirts with petticoats underneath and I love that style. But not all clothing is made for my thick thighs and hips. So she taught me to sew and now I don't have to worry about fitting into some skinny person's size."

"You *made* that dress?" I was agape. "It looks so professional."

"With my own two hands." She nodded proudly.

Jake and Destiny started chatting all things 1950s—turned out Destiny had a huge interest in classic cars, so they hit it off right away. I handed my champagne flute to Jake and left the two of them talking to head in search of some food. If I was going to be drinking champagne, I needed something in my stomach. Stat.

The yacht's main floor featured a lounge-type area with several white leather sofas upon which people sprawled, talking and drinking. The decoration looked like something out of a design magazine, with harmonious soft white, blue and stone colors not daring to detract from the glorious view on all sides. There were so many windows that it still felt like you were floating on the water. A curved bar in pale ribbed wood was topped with a slab of white marble, and a man in a white shirt and black suspenders was making cocktails in a gold cocktail shaker, the sound of ice rattling almost lost in the din of conversation and music.

I walked through the space and came to a dining area, where more people sat. Turned out the food was being delivered by waiters, rather than simply being out on a table. So I hunted down one of the black-and-white-uniformed folks and took a few bite-sized pieces for myself. As I was making my way back to Jake and Destiny, someone called my name.

"Chloe!" A woman waved.

It took me a minute to recognize her. She was tall and willowy, with long red hair and a wide smile. It was Penelope, Calista's literary agent, whom Jake and I had met at the beach. She looked vastly different wearing a slim-fitting olive-green cocktail dress and smoky eye makeup than she had at the beach, bare-faced and playing with her daughter.

"Nice to see you again," she added as she walked over.

I nodded as I covered my mouth with my palm, still chewing on a canape. "Excuse me."

It came out more like *mphuse mhm.*

She laughed. "Don't rush on my account."

I swallowed and let out a laugh, feeling more than a bit out of my element on a multimillion-dollar yacht surrounded by people who'd probably spent more on their outfit than I did on college.

"Sorry, I was starving," I admitted. "And I'm a lightweight if I don't eat when I drink."

"For all the money these people have, they always seem to spend it on booze rather than food." She winked. "After some big publishing parties I make my husband stop at McDonald's on the way home."

I chuckled and used a napkin to make sure I hadn't left any crumbs on my mouth. "That *never* happens in my industry."

"I'll bet."

"Is your little girl with your husband tonight?" I asked.

"Yeah, having a daddy-daughter night while I'm out here schmoozing." There was something a little half-hearted in her voice. I could tell she wasn't exactly excited about being out at a party while her daughter and husband were having a night together. "I wish I was with them, to be honest."

"Not into parties?"

"When I was younger I loved getting glammed up and dancing the night away," she said with a wistful smile. "But I'm forty-three and honestly . . . I don't have the patience for small talk anymore. It's so draining."

I laughed. "That doesn't bode well for me. I'm twenty-eight and I already feel that way!"

"It only gets worse." She shook her head and laughed. "Thank goodness there's someone normal here. I don't think I could stand another one of Henry De Vries's cronies hitting on me like they're shopping for their third wife."

I wrinkled my nose. "Ew."

"Major ew." She sighed. "Calista and I would make fun of people like that when we went to events together. She kept it one-hundred-percent real, even when she got famous. I always appreciated that about her."

"It's an admirable quality, for sure."

"I heard they arrested someone this evening."

Word had clearly travelled fast about Starr. Penelope probably had no idea who she was, however, given Calista's review of Sprout had been brutal but brief. She hadn't even mentioned her name in the podcast, I don't think.

"It's a relief," Penelope continued with a sigh. "Just to know that it's over."

But was it, though?

"Can I ask you something?" I looked around to see if anyone was in earshot, but most people were sitting down and fully engaged in their own conversations. I still hadn't spotted Tristan or Annie, and it seemed that Destiny and Jake were still happily chatting outside. "Do you know what's going to happen to the podcast now?"

"Ownership will be transferred to the agency, actually."

I blinked. "The literary agency?"

"*My* agency, yes." Penelope nodded. "Calista didn't have any close family or anyone she trusted to run the podcast in the event of . . . well, her becoming unable to do it herself. We talked about it six months ago and she asked if I would ensure it was managed correctly in her absence. I agreed and she wrote it into her will."

So Calista *did* have a will after all.

"Did she think something was going to happen to her?" I asked. "Or was she just being prudent?"

Penelope looked down at her hands. "This isn't public knowledge but you seem like someone who genuinely had a connection with Calista so I guess it won't hurt to tell you. She was . . . sick."

"Sick?"

"Thyroid cancer."

"Oh my gosh, I had no idea." I pressed a hand to my chest. "That's so sad."

"She was having treatment and things were going really well. The tumors were shrinking and the oncologist was happy with her progress. But they did set expectations with her that there was a slight chance it could come back more aggressively in the future. Apparently, it can happen," Penelope said. "So she asked for my help in getting some of her affairs in order, just in case. We'd become close over the years of working together on her book, so I was happy to help."

"There was no chance that Destiny would take the podcast over?" I asked.

Penelope shook her head. "Calista was one of those people who thought that if you wanted something done right you had to do it yourself and she wasn't happy with Destiny's work. But I don't think *anyone* would live up to her standards."

"Did Destiny know she was sick?"

"I don't think so. Hardly anybody did."

"And what about her special miniseries thing? Did you know what it was about? I saw an announcement on her Instagram saying she was working on something exciting," I said.

Penelope shook her head. "Yet another area where Calista played her cards very close to her chest. She told me it was going to be big, but she said she didn't want to risk any bad luck by talking about it before it came out. All I know was that she dug up some dirt on *someone* and it was going to rock the industry. But I only represented her literary work, not her podcasts."

At that moment, Penelope's phone started ringing. She pulled it out of a small bag with a chain strap that was slung over one shoulder and saw her husband was calling.

"Sorry," she said. "I have to take this. I'll come find you later and we can talk. I represent quite a few cookbook authors, you know."

She answered the call and headed outside to talk with her husband, leaving me standing there in shock. What did she mean by that statement about representing cookbook authors? Did she think *I* could write a cookbook? It had always been on my list of life goals.

Buzzing, I suddenly became desperate to talk to Jake and see what he thought. A loud burst of laughter from outside made me jump and I whirled around. More people were boarding the yacht and divesting themselves of their shoes.

But Jake and Destiny were nowhere to be seen.

CHAPTER 18

I scoured the entire main deck looking for Jake or Destiny, but to no avail. They weren't anywhere to be seen. I spotted Tristan in deep conversation with someone I didn't recognize, his brow furrowed; he barely seemed to acknowledge his guests. Something was definitely going on with him.

But right now, I needed to find Jake.

I headed to the upper deck, where I found another small indoor sitting area and large open space with a sizeable hot tub. A few partygoers sat on the edge, feet dangling in the bubbling water, champagne flutes in hand. Two people were submersed entirely, possibly having brought swimsuits. I vaguely recognized one of the women as an Instagram food influencer who did these elaborate flat-lay images of rustic meals and baked goods. She'd run a workshop at the ice cream festival about food photography for beginners and tips for making easy but visually appealing desserts with ice cream.

I saw a cluster of older men standing at the pointy end of the yacht—was that the stern? Or the bow? Or maybe it was the port? I had no idea, because I knew nothing about boats—along with Annie. She smiled politely, nodding at something one of the men was saying. The man next to her was tall and barrel chested, with a loud voice. They had the same hooded eye shape and mousy brown hair, so I suspected he must be Henry De Vries.

But still, I could not see Jake.

Perhaps he'd gone looking for the restroom. I made my way back down the stairs to the main deck and then went further still to the lower level, where all the living and sleeping quarters were. It was quiet down here. I heard the flush of a toilet and a moment later a woman in a sparkly dress came out of a doorway, fluffing her hair and adjusting the strap of a tiny, glittering purse. She smiled at me as she walked past, heading straight toward the stairs up to the main deck.

For a moment I stood in the open space. A lounge room sprawled out around me, with couches and a television and a coffee table. There was a bar behind the couches with wine glasses hanging from an overhead rack and an espresso machine sitting to one side. If I didn't know I was on a boat, I would have thought I was simply in some rich person's basement movie room. It had every mod con one could need, although who would sit down here watching a movie when there was such a beautiful view on the main and upper decks? Certainly not me.

Nobody appeared to be coming or going from the bathrooms. There were two that I could see, facing one another, with sliding pocket doors that weren't properly closed, so I knew they were both unoccupied. Clearly Jake wasn't here either. I was about to turn around and head back upstairs when I heard a strange sound. Rustling, then a soft grunt. More rustling. The sound of a drawer being closed.

Someone was down here and they weren't using the bathroom.

Given I'd seen Tristan, Annie and her father already on the two levels above, it couldn't be any of them. What else was down here aside from the bedrooms? And who might have cause to be in any of those rooms? Perhaps it was a crew member. They probably stayed on the ship, right? After all, I'm assuming Henry De Vries didn't captain this thing himself.

The rustling continued.

Curiosity got the better of me and I crept forward. With my bare feet on a large, sprawling rug, my footsteps didn't make a sound and I inched along on my tiptoes, taking one careful step at a time, making my way through the lounge area. There was a small hallway that ran between the two bathrooms, leading toward what I assumed were the bedrooms. There were more than I expected—five doors in total, at least that I could see. Two on the left, two on the right, and one at the end. The first room on the left had the door ajar and I peeked in to find two twin beds, one of them rumpled in a way that told me the covers had been pulled up in a hurry. There was a book on a shared nightstand and a pair of glasses, along with a water bottle.

The other rooms all had their doors closed. I paused at the door on my right and gently pressed my ear to it, listening—silence. When I moved closer to the second one on the right, the sound became a little louder.

That's where they were, whoever was down here.

"Where is it?"

The voice caught me off guard—it was low, gravelly. Frustrated. Definitely male.

I hovered by the closed door, unsure whether I should leave or stay to find out what was going on. A tingling in my senses told me this wasn't simply someone looking for a misplaced pen or a set of keys. But before I could think of what to do, voices sounded from the staircase leading down to the lower deck.

"I don't know what you want me to say, Tristan. She was keeping the project under wraps."

It was Destiny. And I was far enough down the hallway that the second they got to the bottom of the stairs, they would see

I had gone well beyond the toilets. For a second I froze to the spot. But then I saw Destiny's feet appear on the steps and my brain finally kicked in like a tire gaining traction after spinning in mud. I couldn't go into the room next to me—as there was definitely someone inside—so I had to try my luck with the one on the other side of the hallway. I scurried over and slipped inside. Holding my breath, I quietly closed the door behind me, praying that it wouldn't make a sound. Now I was in a bedroom with a queen bed in the center and a small, high window showing the last vestiges of sunlight outside.

Maybe I could wait in here until they left.

The voices became louder and I glanced around the room, hoping I hadn't accidentally picked Tristan and Annie's room to hide in. But before I could even take a look around to see if there was anything to indicate *whose* room it might be, the door slid open and a figure crashed right into me, forcing me to stumble back.

"What the . . ." He slid the door behind him, blocking my exit.

It was the tall redheaded man with the straggly beard that I'd seen talking to Tristan earlier. The man who might very well be a contract killer! I opened my mouth to scream but the man came forward and grabbed me, clamping a hand over my mouth.

"Be quiet, or you'll regret it," he said in a low growl.

Outside, Destiny's and Tristan's voices grew louder still and I could tell they'd made it to the bottom of the stairs and into the lounge area.

"I don't know how many times I can tell you this," Destiny said, huffing impatiently. "She didn't share it with me. You know what Calista was like. Everything was locked up tight in her head until she was ready to make a move."

My heart fluttered like a bird trapped in a cage as I looked up at the redheaded man, who leaned menacingly over me, his large, bony hand wrapped tightly over my mouth and the other holding my upper arm in a viselike grip. His eyes darted back over his shoulder toward the door. It sounded like Tristan and Destiny were mere feet away.

"I can't risk anything coming out that might ruin the restaurant opening." Tristan's voice sounded high-pitched with worry. "God, Calista could be vindictive sometimes."

"Well, you *did* dump her for Annie."

"*After* she rejected my proposal," he snapped. "I asked her to marry me and she said no. So who dumped who, then?"

If I wasn't so terrified of potentially being in the clutches of a murderer, I would have gasped out loud at this new revelation. Tristan *proposed* to Calista? They weren't just dating for a hot minute, like I'd previously heard. It was serious. I wondered if Calista said no to Tristan because of her cancer diagnosis. Maybe she thought she was doing the right thing by not committing to him when she didn't know how much time she had—or what the outcome of her treatment might be. Perhaps he didn't even know she was sick.

The sound of a door sliding on the other side of the hallway muffled the voices. They'd gone into one of the bedrooms. The redheaded man narrowed his eyes at me.

"Don't you dare scream," he said, his voice barely a whisper. "I know a move that'll turn your lights out so fast you won't even be able to say your own name before you're unconscious."

That sounded *exactly* like something a contract killer would say!

He released me and reached for the door behind him, flicking a lock and trapping me inside. My hand shook as I touched the place on my arm where he'd grabbed me. Now that I wasn't in his grip, I could get a better look at him. His hair was scraped back from his face and he was wearing a black and white outfit. It took me a moment to realize it was a catering uniform.

"What are you doing in here?" he asked, keeping his voice down. "This area is private."

"I could ask you the same," I hissed.

Neither of us made a move or said a word for a few solid seconds. It was a standoff.

"I know you're not a caterer," I bluffed, still keeping my voice down. "Are you here to murder someone else, huh? Got another contract hit?"

Maybe it wasn't a good idea to antagonize a potential murderer, but I was so scared that my mind had turned into a bowl of Froot Loops. I scrambled back and went to the bedside table, looking for a weapon with which to defend myself. I grabbed the only thing on there—a magazine.

"What are you going to do with that? Roll it up and whack me on the nose?" He rolled his eyes. "I'm not a Labrador."

Admittedly it wasn't a great weapon. But options were slim.

"And I'm not going to kill you, little girl. I just need you to keep quiet so I can get out of here without anyone seeing me." His eyes flicked over me, hard and assessing. Lines bracketed his eyes, and underneath the patchy beard I saw hollow cheeks and pockmarks that might have come from acne or another skin condition. "And I haven't killed anyone, either."

"I'm not sure I believe you."

"You're clearly up to no good yourself, or else why would you be hiding in the captain's room?"

Okay, so that was one question answered.

"I heard you rustling through Tristan and Annie's bedroom," I whispered, bluffing again. I didn't know for sure it was their room, but figuring the room at the end belonged to Henry, it was an educated guess.

"And you were just being nosy?" His eyes remained on the door. Clearly people finding him here was more a threat to him than me and my magazine.

"What were you looking for?" I asked, ignoring his question.

"None of your business."

We were talking in stage whispers and more voices sounded outside the room. Two men laughed and made a crude joke about someone upstairs, their words slightly slurred. I heard a door slam, followed by more laughter.

"What was the job you were doing for Tristan that he doesn't want anyone to know about?" I asked.

His eyes narrowed and suddenly I had his attention. "Have you been following me?"

"No. But I hear things." I kept the magazine in front of me, not that it would do any good. "I knew Calista."

"I wish I'd never heard that goddamn name." He practically spat the words out. "I was supposed to be making better choices. Getting straight. Not letting money lure me into a cage again."

He was almost talking to himself, the words low and muttered. His eyes kept flicking back to the door. There were more voices now, people waiting for the bathrooms, perhaps. It looked like we might be stuck here for a bit.

"What if someone comes in here?" I asked, looking nervously toward the door.

"Captain's got shore leave today. First officer is in charge for the night," he replied, like that would mean anything at all to me. But if the captain was off the yacht, then perhaps he wouldn't be coming back to his room anytime soon. "No one else will come in here."

The words sent a chill down my spine. I didn't know what was worse—being sprung by the captain for hiding in his room, or being trapped in here with a strange man and not having anyone come to help.

"Look, I'm not going to hurt you, okay?" He glanced at me

and rather than looking menacing, all of a sudden he just looked tired. "Not unless you do something to jeopardize what *I'm* here to do."

"How will I know if I'm jeopardizing your mission if I don't know what it is?" I asked.

He let out an irritated sigh. "You're nosy. You know that, right?"

I lifted one shoulder into a shrug. "I prefer . . . curious."

"You said you knew Calista." He turned and leaned against the wall next to the door, relaxing a little but still standing guard in case I tried to make a break for it. "I'm trying to figure out who killed her."

I gasped and then clamped a hand over my mouth, hoping no one heard me outside. "Me too."

"You her friend, or something?" He ran his hand over his beard and I shuddered. It looked like it was made from steel wool.

"I was an acquaintance, really." I sat on the edge of the bed, figuring that if we were going to be stuck in here until the coast was clear then I should at least get comfortable. The voices of the slightly inebriated men outside—now singing a sea shanty—should cover the sound of our quiet talking. "But I don't think a murderer should go free."

"They have someone in custody," he said, looking at me closely as if to gauge my reaction.

"And yet we're both here still looking for clues." Then it dawned on me. If he knew that Starr had been brought in and yet he was on the ship sneaking around, looking for clues then . . . "Oh my god, are you Starr's brother, Niko?"

I expected him to be surprised, but instead a flash of recognition streaked across his face. "You must be Chloe. Short, blond, pushy do-gooder energy. Description fits."

"Hey." I frowned. "I'm not pushy."

"Zvez—I mean, Starr, she told me you were trying to help her."

"Seems you are, too," I replied. "But you were *stalking* Calista, weren't you?"

"I was being paid to . . . scare her. By Tristan."

So *that* was the job they were talking about earlier! Not murder, but contract stalking.

"Why?" I asked.

"She was working on some exposé for her podcast. When Calista and Tristan were together, he let slip about some less-than-aboveboard practices going on at a restaurant owned by a friend of his, and Calista decided it would make a great investigative project. He tried to convince her not to do it, but she wouldn't listen. Then they broke up. So he paid me to send her threatening letters and to follow her around and . . . try to scare her out of doing the podcast."

Paying someone to stalk and intimidate your ex-girlfriend? What a standup guy. Not.

"Why would you take a job like that?" I asked, shaking my head.

"Do you know what it's like trying to find work when you get out of prison?" His face was a hard mask of someone who understood that survival and determination were not always pretty. "I took responsibility for the crimes I'd committed. I pled guilty from the beginning because I knew what I'd done was wrong and I did my time. I paid those dues. But you're tarred forever. No one wants to hire an ex-con. No one wants an ex-con in their community."

I couldn't even begin to imagine what it would be like. My own brush with the law as a wrongdoer was limited to the single speeding ticket I'd received and the one time I got a slap on the wrist for parking too close to a fire hydrant.

"Starr took me to some food social influencer conference," he continued. "She was trying to get me involved in her business, but I didn't want no pity job. I got drunk at the bar one night and ended up talking to Tristan, who'd just broken up with Calista. He offered me a job that *wasn't* out of pity. I figured it was an easy payday. Easier than I'd get anywhere else and I wouldn't be in emotional debt to my sister."

"And you had no idea about Starr and Calista's past?"

"Oh, I knew. Calista was at that conference and Starr had made a passing comment about what a terrible friend she'd been for stealing her boyfriend. She was speaking more to herself than me, but I noticed it." He shrugged. "I figured I could kill two birds with one stone. Get some cash in hand and get some revenge for my little sister."

Starr probably had no idea how that one muttered comment under her breath had stuck in her brother's mind.

"How did you even sneak onto this yacht?" I asked.

Niko eyed me warily. "I can't tell you that. I had help, but I don't want to get anybody in trouble."

I wondered if he might have had a connection inside the catering company.

"Can you tell me what you're looking for?" I asked.

"The missing pages of Calista's journal. The ones that outline her plans to do the miniseries about the stuff that Tristan told her."

"You think he killed her to keep her quiet?" I asked.

"Damn straight I do."

It occurred to me then that it had gone very quiet outside the captain's bedroom. Niko seemed to notice it, too. He pressed his ear to the door, holding one hand up to keep me quiet while he listened.

"I think we're alone," he said. "But I didn't find anything in Tristan's room."

"Keep looking," I said. "I'll go back upstairs and see if I can get anything out of Destiny. I still haven't written her off as a suspect. She could know more about Calista's plans than what she's letting on." Then I remembered something. "I'd also wondered about Calista's podcast rival . . . Dee."

Niko's cheeks were tinted red. "I know for certain that Dee didn't do it."

I raised an eyebrow.

"We met at that same conference where Tristan hired me. Dee and I have an on-and-off thing. She was with me the night of the murder. We were, uh . . . otherwise engaged."

I wrinkled my nose. That was not a mental image I needed in my head.

But at least I could officially strike both Calista's "stalker" and her rival off the suspect list. I doubted very much that Niko was lying about not having any personal motivation to go after Calista, and he *especially* would not be setting up his own sister to take the fall. Not if she was the only one in their family who tried to make amends with him after he got out of prison.

"I'm sure Starr would be encouraged to know you're trying to help her," I said.

A grave look passed over Niko's face. "It's a drop in the ocean compared to what I owe her."

He slid the door back an inch and peered out. Looked like the coast was clear. We agreed that I would go first and then I would fake a coughing fit if anyone was coming downstairs so I could alert Niko that it wasn't safe to come out of the room. I slipped out into the hallway and hurried down to the area where I was supposed to be.

I got to the staircase just in time to see two bare feet dashing back up to the main floor.

Had someone been listening to us?

CHAPTER 19

Once upstairs, I almost immediately ran into Jake.

"Where have you been?" we asked in unison, then we both laughed.

I was still feeling rattled from the unexpected encounter with Niko and from the surprise of seeing someone disappear back up the staircase when we thought the lower level had been empty.

Was the murderer on board this boat?

"I was looking for you," I said. "I went to grab some food and then I turned around and you were gone."

"I actually bumped into an old colleague. Small world." He raked a hand through his hair. "Sorry about that. I came to find you so I could introduce you both, but I couldn't figure out where you'd gone."

"That's okay," I said, waving a hand. "There's so many levels on this thing."

"Speaking of which, I have something to show you." Jake grabbed my hand and led me toward the stairs going to the upper level. But just when I thought we were done, he walked me around the side of the yacht to one more small set of stairs that I hadn't even seen before.

Now we were on the very top of the yacht where a huge out-door sofa curved into a perfect circle. There were breaks between the modular pieces so you could walk through and sit down. In the middle was a circular table, a fruit and cheese platter sitting atop it. We managed to snag a seat facing right out to the ocean.

"This is spectacular," I breathed.

Jake slipped an arm around my shoulders and I allowed myself to lean into his side. Feeling his solid and steady presence beside me was a relief. A comfort. He lowered his head so he could talk to me without other people hearing.

"I know you're here for clues, but I figured you could take a quick break from sleuthing to watch something special."

"I think so."

The last sliver of sun was blotted out against the horizon as rich indigo blue finally overtook the sky. A few stars twinkled and it was like staring right into the universe. For a moment I felt impossibly small and insignificant—like a tiny speck of dust that was doing nothing more important than drifting through the air. I wasn't sure if it was a good feeling or a bad feeling.

In the scheme of vast existence, what impact did a single person make?

On the universe? Perhaps nothing. But on the other specks of dust? Everything.

Lost in a moment of deep contemplation, I jumped when the sky suddenly exploded. Flashes of colored light illuminated the inky darkness. The sound of fireworks combusting, followed by the spray of dazzling light, made the breath catch in the back of my throat. I'd forgotten that they always did a fireworks show on the Saturday night of the ice cream festival. It was Azalea Bay tradition, and year after year I had stood on the street with my grandparents, sitting on my grandpa's shoulders when he was still alive, shrieking with delight at the "sky glitter."

Fireworks rippled and popped for the next ten minutes, setting our town ablaze with shimmering and shattering red, purple, green, gold and white. Every boom echoed against the ocean waves and the yacht was hushed, its guests mesmerized.

"Wow," I breathed as the show came to an end. "I'm so glad I didn't miss that."

"As soon as I saw this spot, I knew I wanted to bring you up here," Jake said.

Was it the magic of the fireworks show or was I feeling the deep tug of something real inside me? Like the tingle of intuition that told me when a new recipe was going to work out exactly as I wanted it to. Like the flutter in my stomach when I had a new idea in the middle of the night that I had to write down so I wouldn't forget it. It felt like those things. Those real things.

"I'm really glad you moved in next door to Grandma Rose," I said.

"So am I, Chloe. It might be the best decision I ever made." He leaned forward and brushed his lips against mine, his arm tightening around my shoulders.

For a brief moment, I let myself be lost in his kiss. In his touch. There was no murder and mayhem. No sleuthing. No clues. No falsely accused. It was just us.

If only the world was filled with good things like this and nothing else. Like pastry and kisses and fireworks and balmy summer nights. *That* was a world I wanted to live in.

In the next few hours, talk of the arrest burned through the party and I overheard multiple people gossiping about it—although many did not seem to know Starr, personally. But it seemed Calista had been deeply ingrained in this crowd—a friend to some, acquaintance to others, admired by most, even if they didn't always agree with her methods.

I found myself standing on the outer part of the deck that wrapped around what I now knew to be the penultimate level of the yacht, leaning against the railing and staring out into the dark ocean view. Jake had caught up with his old colleague again, who'd offered to introduce him to Henry. Practically giddy with excitement, he allowed himself to be whisked away, and I'd told him to have fun and take as long as he wanted. I was perfectly happy having a moment alone with the top-class bubbles and my thoughts.

But I'd only been standing there for a few moments when I saw two familiar faces doing something similar—drinking and admiring the view. It was Penelope and Annie. I wandered over to say hello.

Penelope looked a little windswept, her long red hair less curled and a little more tangled from the persistent sea breeze bringing moments of sweet relief from the heat. Her cheeks had also gone pink, presumably from the champagne she was drinking, giving her a real English Rose look.

Annie on the other hand had not a hair out of place on her brown bob, the pin-straight strands falling flatly to her chin. Like usual, there was a vaguely nautical theme to her look, which was a white and blue striped shirt dress with a tan leather belt at her waist, the buckle fashioned to look like a gold sailing knot. A tiny anchor was embroidered on the collar. On her right breast pocket she wore a gold brooch which was ringed with pearls, and the middle was a picture of an eye.

It was a bit creepy, but I'd once worked with a woman from Greece who always wore those "evil eye" charms around her neck. Apparently, it was meant to ward off bad vibes and curses, or some such. Was Annie worried about something happening to her?

"Hi, ladies." I held my free hand up in a wave. "Did you catch the fireworks earlier? They were amazing."

"Yes, so pretty. We get such a great view from the upper deck," Annie said.

"Where's that handsome man of yours?" Penelope asked. "I saw you two canoodling during the show."

"He's getting an introduction to Mr. De Vries." I glanced over to Annie. "Jake's an ex–Wall Street guy. Big fan of your dad, apparently."

"Isn't everyone," she replied a little drily.

I wasn't quite sure what to make of the comment. I imagined that having the kind of wealth the De Vries family did, it would make it hard to tell who a real friend was and who was simply a hanger-on.

"I'm so glad we caught up again," Penelope said. "I was just telling Annie I wanted to catch you before the party was over so we could talk shop. Sorry, darling, more book talk."

"Perfectly fine. I'm used to it with Tris." She smiled good-naturedly. "But I might leave you two to chat. I should check in with the catering folks and make sure we're all good for the desserts to start circulating."

She gave a wave and continued on along the walkway that skirted the outer part of the level, disappearing around the corner.

"Is Tristan writing a cookbook as well?" I asked, turning back to Penelope. "That's exciting."

"He's actually writing a memoir. It's not common knowledge, but Tristan had a rough upbringing. His father had substance abuse issues and the kids were often only fed at school and through the generosity of their neighbors. He said it caused him to develop a bit of an obsession with food and cooking, and he promised himself once he was old enough to live on his own that he would do his best to make every single meal a special occasion because he knew that not all meals were guaranteed."

"That sounds like a heck of a story." I took a sip of my drink.

"Absolutely," she said. "I represent a wide array of nonfiction authors. Everything from biographies and memoirs, to self-help, business books, creative nonfiction, et cetera."

"And cookbooks," I said, trying to ignore the flutter in my stomach.

"That's right." Penelope smiled. "Do tell me about yourself, Chloe. I know you trained in Paris and have a cannabis bakery now. But I'd love to know more about your food philosophy."

My whole body was practically vibrating with excitement. This felt like a pitch! A possible pitch to a literary agent for my very own cookbook. It was something that had been on my dream list for as long as I could remember. When my life fell apart in Paris and I made the decision to sacrifice working in fine dining to move home and care for Grandma Rose, I thought that dream was dead.

"I never planned to make weed brownies professionally, but"—I sucked in a breath—"inspiration comes from the most unlikely places."

I spent the next hour telling Penelope about my professional experience, Grandma Rose's diagnosis and everything I knew about cannabis baking. We were still deep in conversation as the party had begun to slow around us and I got the sense that she would be a great person to brainstorm with, not to mention that she seemed super excited about my business and the possibility of representing me.

"I really think this could take off, Chloe. I mean, there are already cannabis cookbooks on shelves, of course, but I really think your twist would make it something unique. Weed *and* fine French patisseries? It's genius!" Her words were a little slurred, but I hoped it wasn't only the alcohol talking.

"I could have a whole section up front talking about the decarboxylation process and all the different types of infusion methods. I love the idea of having a repertoire of base ingredients upon which to build *any* cannabis recipe you like," I said excitedly. "I've even been experimenting with using a sous vide infusion method, which might appeal to more adventurous home cooks."

I could practically see it now, a picture of me in professional hair and makeup, holding a plate of pastel candy-colored macarons toward the camera, my name in pink text below the image.

Baked by Chloe: pastries with a higher purpose.

"I could have a macaron library of recipes, dozens of different cannabis buttercream, caramel and ganache fillings. I mean, that could fill a whole book by itself! Do you think publishers would want a specific cannabis macaron cookbook? Because I could do it. I could write a hundred recipes."

I could feel my excitement spiraling out of control, whipping up ideas like my stand mixer whipped butter and sugar into magic.

Way to play it cool, Chloe.

I had never played it cool in my life. Not once.

"I *love* your enthusiasm, Chloe." Penelope laughed as she dug something out of her purse. "This is my business card. After the festival I want you to send me an email so I have your details. Think about what you'd include in a first book and give me a one-paragraph pitch with a list of potential recipes. If you feel like sharing any of the recipes you use for Baked by Chloe, send a complete one along, too, so I can get a sense of your style."

I took the card from her, hands shaking. "Thank you."

Penelope looked past me and spotted someone. "Oh, there's Tristan. I need to speak with him. But please email me, okay? I'm very excited about your ideas."

She left me standing there in awe, staring down at the neatly printed white business card that said: *Penelope Hendriks, Senior Literary Agent and Co-Founder. Hendriks and Quinn Literary Agency.*

"What's that you've got there?" Jake came up beside me and slipped an arm around my waist, peering over my shoulder. "A business card?"

"Turns out Calista's literary agent is interested in receiving a cookbook pitch from me!" I whirled around, still holding the card with both hands like someone had handed me a precious white truffle. "I can't believe it."

"I can." Jake smiled down at me. "You're a force, Chloe."

For a moment it felt like my entire life had clicked into place—I was home with my family, I was running a business that people seemed to love and was growing at a rapid pace, I had found a man who respected and supported me. And now I might possibly tick off one of my lifelong bucket-list goals.

"What if it all goes away?" I whispered.

What if it was all a trick? A dream?

"Then you'll build something new." Jake squeezed my shoulders. "The only true end is giving up. So if you don't do that, then there's always a chance to try again. But something tells me this isn't the time for you to be trying again. I think you've hit something big here."

"Really?" I asked hopefully.

"Heck yeah, I do." He grinned. "Do you think literary agents go around offering their cards to everyone just to be nice?"

"No," I admitted.

"And do you think people like Calista would tell everyone to come visit your café if they thought it was mediocre?"

"Definitely not." I knew for a fact Calista had no qualms about telling people when she thought something was average. "She wouldn't have done that."

"So stop being afraid of success." He gave me a gentle shake. "Otherwise you're going to make me say something corny that I'll regret for the rest of my days."

"Oh yeah?" I laughed. "Like what?"

"Like, you miss one hundred percent of the shots you don't take." He gave me a cheesy wink, which made me laugh even harder. "Shoot for the moon. Even if you miss, you'll land among the stars."

I cringed. "Oh, that one's *real* bad."

"I'll do you one better," he said, trying not to laugh. "Yesterday is history, tomorrow a mystery and today is a gift. That's why we call it the present."

"No!" I let out a barking laugh that was so loud I startled someone walking by. "Okay, sir, you have won the battle of most cringiest motivational quotes ever. I dub thee, King Cringe."

"Thank you, thank you." Jake did a little bow and made a flourish with his hands. "Come on, we should probably get going. I promised your grandma I wouldn't let you turn into a pumpkin."

"Oh, pumpkin! You know a cannabis pumpkin pie would be pretty amazing. Maybe I should put that in my recipe list."

Jake slipped his arm around my shoulders and we made our way downstairs, falling into easy banter. Talk about a productive night! I was very happy I'd accepted the invitation to this party, even if my sleuthing hadn't turned up too much.

"I'm going to make a quick restroom stop before we go," I said to Jake. It wasn't a long trip home, but the few glasses of champagne I'd consumed had suddenly snuck up on me. "Meet you back here?"

"Sure."

I left him standing on the main deck to head below. Both bathrooms were occupied and I bounced on the spot, impatient. As I waited, I let my gaze roam down the hallway to the bedrooms, wondering what had happened to Niko. Hopefully he'd gotten off the yacht okay. Maybe he'd found what he was looking for.

It was then I noticed that one of the doors was slightly ajar and something was sticking out. It looked like Tristan and Annie's room. I took a step forward and then another, squinting. Was that . . .

Oh my god, it was a hand!

I rushed forward, bladder needs forgotten, crying out. The fingers of a hand were indeed sticking out in a small gap between the sliding door and the frame, and when I slid the door back I found a body crumpled on the ground.

It was Tristan.

He was slumped on his side. For a moment I wondered if he might be dead, but there was no blood. No immediate sign of injury. Then I heard a low groan come from him—it didn't sound good. I crouched down by his body and placed a hand on his arm.

"Tristan?" I asked. "Are you okay?"

"Help," he croaked. "Emergency."

I fumbled for my phone, fishing it out of my purse and dialing 911. "Just stay still. I'm calling for help."

As I waited for the call to be picked up, I noticed a small torn piece of paper about the size of a quarter on the floor next to his crumpled form. It appeared to be from a lined notebook. Black ink spelled out part of a word.

-mally.

Was it part of a name or just a word? I couldn't be sure. But then something struck me about the writing. It showed a very strangely shaped letter Y. The weirdest Y I'd ever seen . . . well, actually I'd seen it once before.

It was from Calista's journal.

CHAPTER 20

It was close to midnight by the time Jake and I finally made it home. Paramedics had arrived on the yacht to check Tristan over and see if he needed to be transported to the hospital. Meanwhile, Henry De Vries had seemed more upset that the EMTs were traipsing onto his yacht with their shoes on than that his future son-in-law had been knocked out cold. Annie had been fussing over Tristan, shooting frustrated glares at her father every time he tutted at one of the EMTs.

Talk about awkward.

In the end, the party had been declared over and we'd all been unceremoniously kicked off the yacht.

"So, how was it meeting the great Henry De Vries?" I asked, lazing back in the passenger seat and watching Jake as he drove us home. The streetlights flickered past us, showing flashes of his profile—the straight nose, sharp jaw, and the warm tones in his thick hair. "Did you fanboy all over him?"

"I conducted myself like a mature adult," he said, smirking. "No fanboying at all . . . at least, not in front of him."

I laughed. "What did you talk about?"

"He was interested in what I used to do on Wall Street and how I'd set up my financial consulting business here. He said it was refreshing to see young people with ambitions and a mind for financial responsibility."

"Did you ask him how many yachts he owns?" I teased.

"I did not. But he owns two. I didn't have to ask." Jake chuckled. "It's wild being around someone like that. He's so wealthy and famous—at least in tech and finance circles—but he's also just a normal guy. He has immigrant parents and he was raised to work hard."

"De Vries . . . where is that name from?"

"The Netherlands," Jake replied. "Sounds like he has a home in Amsterdam, which he goes back to frequently."

"I never got to visit there while I lived in Europe. It's still on the bucket list." I'd travelled as much as my busy study and work schedules would allow. I'd even done some work trips to experience incredible restaurants in Italy, Spain and Portugal. But the Netherlands remained unexplored. "Looks like a cool place. What else did you talk about?"

"Boats, watches, and sports. They're really into soccer—although they call it voetbal there." Jake looked at me, as if waiting for me to pull a face or fake a yawn. He knew I was *not* a sports person. "Actually, here's an interesting story. He told me about the only time he ever made a truly bad investment. His daughter convinced him to back this startup, which was apparently a social network for people to connect with fictional characters."

"What on earth? That's so silly."

"You never wanted to friend Thor or Batman on Facebook?" He chuckled. "Yeah, the idea was pretty wild but apparently his daughter was dating the guy who created it and she twisted his arm. Said it was the stupidest investment he ever made."

"So you spent all that time talking about money, huh?" I teased. "How very Wall Street of you."

"Actually, we had a really interesting discussion about vintage restoration. I told him all about my grandfather's car and how I'm fixing it up. He and his wife collect antiques, mostly jewelry and furniture. He told me about a cameo brooch they bought for their daughter's twenty-first birthday that dates back to the nineteenth century and is made from lava from Mount Vesuvius!"

We continued chatting about the night, eventually turning back to my cookbook proposal, and we were still brainstorming recipe ideas when Jake pulled into our street. The lights were on at home and I detected movement behind the gauzy curtains.

"Grandma Rose must be waiting up for me," I said, shaking my head.

"That ruins my plans to ask you in for a drink," Jake said, looking at me with a cheeky smile that obscured whether or not he was telling the truth. "I couldn't make your grandma worry about you being gone all night."

All night? I felt my face grow hot.

It wasn't that I was uncomfortable with sex. . . . Truly, I wasn't. But his comment had stirred something in me that now felt a whole lot like disappointment that I had to do the right thing and head home so Grandma Rose didn't worry. I *wanted* to go in for a drink with Jake and see where it led.

I might possibly want to stay all night.

"Come on," he said, clicking the button to release his seat belt. "I'll walk you over."

"Maybe you can come in for a drink at mine," I suggested. "It's not 'all night,' but I'm happy for the night not to be over just yet."

His hazel eyes seemed to glow with warmth and he nodded. "I'm happy for it not to be over yet, too."

We got out of the car and headed over to my side of the

fence, and the front door swung open before we even made it halfway up the driveway. Grandma Rose was in her pajamas and a robe, her head wrapped up in a silk scarf.

"Did you hear the news?" she asked, eyes wide. "Starr was arrested tonight!"

It wasn't like Grandma Rose to let someone outside the family see her in her pajamas, without at least a robe over the top. I wasn't sure if that was because A, she was distracted by gossip; B, Jake had practically saved her life at one point so her jim-jams seemed inconsequential; or C, because she figured him being my boyfriend made him family. Whatever the reason, I was happy that she was comfortable in his presence.

"We heard," I said as the three of us headed inside. Antonio was fast asleep in his doggy bed in the lounge room and although I desperately wanted some doggy cuddles, I didn't dare wake him. That dog was chill AF ninety-nine percent of the time.

But woe to anyone who woke him from a deep sleep.

"It's all anyone is talking about." Grandma Rose continued on toward the kitchen and Jake and I followed. There would be no gossip without tea. She put the kettle on to boil and pulled three cups down from the cupboard. "I ran into Luisa on the boardwalk while I took Antonio out for a stroll."

Luisa is one of my grandmother's oldest friends.

"She said that the police had some major piece of evidence linking Starr to the murder," Grandma Rose finished. "Can you believe it?"

"What evidence?" I asked.

"A notebook or a journal or something."

My eyebrows shot up. "How does Luisa know that?"

"I think her granddaughter's fiancé works for the police. Or maybe it was her son-in-law? Or a nephew, perhaps? They have such a big family I can't keep them all straight." Grandma Rose shook her head. "But she said the police received a tip-off about Starr being in possession of it. That's what they call it, right? A tip-off? I'm pretty sure I heard that word on *Law and Order*."

A tip-off. That could only be the person who planted the journal, because nobody else knew Starr had it aside from me. Someone was trying really hard to make sure she got put away for this.

"Maybe she really did it?" Grandma Rose said.

I shook my head. "Starr isn't stupid—she wouldn't keep the journal in her possession if she killed Calista. What purpose would that serve? It's nothing but evidence against her, and if she *did* kill Calista, she would have burned the journal or disposed of it some other way. Someone planted the journal and then called the police to tell them she had it."

"But why would someone try to frame Starr?" Jake asked, scrubbing a hand over his head. "Why take on extra risk by planting the journal and calling the police? Surely the murderer would rather just get out of town and minimize their contact with law enforcement."

"You're right, which means it *has* to be personal," I said, biting down on my lip. We all fell into contemplative silence, which was then shattered by the whistling of the kettle, which made us all jump. "Someone wanted Calista dead *and* they wanted to make Starr's life miserable."

Grandma Rose got up to make the tea and soon three mugs of steaming peppermint were brought to the table.

"In any case, we can cross both Calista's stalker *and* her podcast rival slash former friend off the suspect list," I said. Then I filled Jake and Grandma Rose in on my chance meeting with Niko during the party. "He was looking for the missing pages of the journal to help clear Starr."

"What is on the pages?" Grandma Rose asked.

"We believe they outlined the inside information Tristan gave Calista that launched her investigative podcast miniseries."

"*Someone* has those pages. Presumably they took them from Tristan and then knocked him out so they could escape," Jake said. He had both elbows on the table and his chin in his hands, eyes far off in the distance. "Maybe it was Niko who knocked him out and not the killer?"

"That's possible," I said. "I didn't see him as we all left the boat, but maybe he'd gotten away before I found Tristan."

"Who else might have wanted those pages?" Jake asked.

I blew on the steam curling up from my mug. "Honestly, I'm not sure. I would have thought Tristan would want them more than anyone. They provide a motive for him to be the killer, because it proves he leaked confidential information to Calista. That would probably get him blacklisted from a whole lot of things in the industry, if people think he can't be trusted. But if he is the killer, why would he still have those pages in his possession? Like the journal, why would a killer hang on to evidence that would incriminate them? It doesn't make sense. And if he's *not* the killer, then why would the killer care that he might be incriminated?"

"But what if the miniseries and the journal pages don't actually reveal that Tristan gave up the information?" Jake suggested. "Calista could have positioned it like *she* found it all out on her own. It's plausible—she had *a lot* of industry contacts."

"It seems like everything is tied to this secret podcast project thingamajig," Grandma Rose mused. "It must have contained some juicy secrets."

"It seems so. But we don't know what, since the pages were already torn out of the journal before it came to be in Starr's possession."

"I wonder what happens to the podcast now that Calista is dead," Jake said, rubbing a hand along his jaw.

"It goes to her literary agent," I said, remembering back to my conversation with Penelope earlier. "Calista listed her agent in her will, since she doesn't have any family that she's super connected to and she and Penelope became close while Calista was writing her book."

"She had a will? That's very responsible." Grandma Rose nodded in approval. "Not many young people have wills, when they should. You never know what might happen."

"She was sick." A strange feeling was beginning to settle into the pit of my stomach. "Thyroid cancer. When she was diagnosed she wrote a will, but the cancer treatments were helping her get better."

Jake frowned, like he was starting to make the same connection that I was making. "So if Calista got better, then Penelope the agent wouldn't gain control of the podcast."

"No, she wouldn't." I shook my head. "She also represents Tristan. He's writing a memoir, so perhaps she wouldn't want any bad press involving him that might affect book sales."

Whatever high feeling I'd been experiencing that night about the potential cookbook pitch, it all came crashing down around me. I stared down into my peppermint tea, my reflection wavering like the confidence and excitement that had fueled me earlier.

What if Penelope was a killer? What if the person whom I'd thought could help me make my cookbook dreams come true was actually a cold-blooded thief and murderer? What if she knew I'd been snooping around and that was why she wanted to get closer to me?

She'd been on the boat. Had access to Tristan. Was in town the night Calista was murdered. The only connection I couldn't see was how Penelope was linked to Starr.

I felt a resolve harden inside me, like all the broken shards of a possible dream came back together with grit and determination. After all I'd been through this year, there was no way I was going to wallow and feel sorry for myself. I started my life over and look how well it was going! I could face this challenge.

My cookbook dreams *would* come true, one day, and I *would* catch Calista's killer. Whoever they were.

Sunday was the final day of the ice cream festival. It was also the day where the festival opened late, at one p.m., due to there being a parade through the center of town. It wasn't anything grand—especially not by the standards of anyone who lived in a big city. Let's be real, Macy's Thanksgiving Day Parade it was not. But Azalea Bay put on quite the show for our young residents and visitors, which included several floats, a performance from our local high school's marching band, and people dressed in all manner of costumes.

I remembered going as a kid and standing on the sidelines, jaw practically on the ground, as a wild rainbow of color, sequins and merriment rolled past. There were people handing out balloons and I knew we'd see children clutching the brightly colored helium-inflated gifts for the entire rest of the day.

I'd planned to sleep in a little after the eventfulness of last night, but instead I was woken by a phone call just after nine a.m. Groggily and still within the clutches of sleep, I slapped my hand onto my nightstand looking for where my phone was sitting, plugged into the charger. I didn't recognize the number.

"Hello?"

"Chloe?" An unfamiliar voice greeted me, male. "It's Niko, Zvez—uh, Starr's brother. Sorry, I'm still not used to her having another name."

I sat up, rubbing my eye with my free hand, trying to force the fog of sleep away from me. "Oh hi. Did she give you my number?"

"Yeah. She called just now. I, uh . . . thought you might want to know."

"What did she say?" I asked.

"The police really think she did it." He sighed. "She said they questioned her for hours yesterday, showing her the journal and other evidence like some ribbon or string or something that was the murder weapon. They pulled up her Facebook post."

There was a scraping at my door and I went to let Antonio in. He scampered through the opening and rushed straight up to the edge of my bed, rearing up on his hind legs and slapping his paws against the side in silent request. I scooped his little body up with one hand—a benefit of Chihuahuas—and placed him on top so he could snuggle while I sat and talked to Niko.

"It doesn't look good," he concluded.

"But you found the missing pages of the journal, right?" I thought back to the scrap on the floor next to Tristan's crumpled body, which I had left on the ground since it didn't say anything of use. I'd thought about phoning the detective to tell her what I found, but what would I say?

Hi, Detective Alvarez, I found a tiny scrap of paper with four letters on it next to Tristan. No, it didn't say anything useful. Yes, anyone could have dropped it. No, I have no idea what it means.

All that would do would get me a telling off for meddling like last time. I couldn't let the police know I'd been investigating until I had something useful for them.

"No," he said. "I didn't find the pages."

I blinked. "Really?"

"Why would I lie?" Niko sounded confused. "I searched that room high and low before you and I met in the captain's room. Afterward, I went back in but I still couldn't find anything. All I can think was that he must have kept it in the safe. It's the only area I couldn't access."

I frowned. Something wasn't adding up. "Did you have a fight with Tristan last night? In his room? Around eleven, maybe eleven thirty?"

"What are you talking about? I couldn't let him see me, because he would *know* I wasn't part of the catering staff and kick me off the boat. I did my best to avoid him. Thankfully someone self-important like him doesn't pay attention to anyone in a worker's uniform, and I managed to dodge him all night. I snuck off the boat before ten."

Huh. If Niko hadn't knocked Tristan out, then who had? Penelope had left me with her business card right before saying she needed to go and speak to Tristan. That's when I caught back up with Jake and we decided to head home. Only a few minutes later I'd found Tristan barely conscious on the ground.

I didn't like where this was going.

"*Someone* has those missing journal pages," I said. "Tristan got knocked over the head and there was a scrap of paper by him. It had Calista's handwriting on it."

"You sure he wasn't faking?" Niko asked. "The guy's a natural-born actor. He's used to manipulating a situation to get what he wants. I don't know what Starr saw in him."

"Wait, *what*?" My surprise startled Antonio, who snuggled closer against my leg, seeking comfort. I took one of his velvety ears and rubbed it gently between my thumb and forefinger. That always seemed to soothe him. "Don't tell me they dated, too?"

"Not sure I'd call it dating. They . . . hooked up." I could practically hear the disgust in Niko's tone, though whether it was because he hated Tristan or because the thought of his sister hooking up with anyone would gross him out, I wasn't sure. "It happened at that conference I told you about, where I first met him at the bar. Turns out I wasn't the only one he propositioned that night."

Starr and Tristan? Wow. Given what Starr had told me about her and Calista stealing each other's boyfriends and generally trying to get back at one another, it certainly didn't seem off-brand that Starr would sleep with her rival's ex.

This whole thing was a soap opera episode waiting to happen!

"They didn't keep seeing each other after the conference?" I asked.

"No idea. I didn't *want* to know. That guy is bad news and I told her that." He grunted. "Not that she would listen. She'd just tell me I was also bad news but she still loved me."

I could practically hear the words in Starr's sassy voice.

"But you still did the job for Tristan."

"Like I said, I was desperate for cash."

Could Tristan have been the one who sent Starr the yellow roses? Maybe he wanted them to stay friends?

Or maybe he thought she was the perfect patsy.

But I also couldn't shake Penelope the agent from my brain. Or Destiny. They were all connected to one another *and* to Calista. But Tristan was the only one connected to Starr. At least, that I knew of.

"Does the name Penelope Hendriks mean anything to you?" I asked.

"Nope, never heard it."

"Destiny?" I tried.

"That's Calista's assistant, right? I saw her a few times where I followed Calista to her events. But I don't know anything else about her."

Hmm. I was missing something key.

Tristan could have killed Calista to quash the exposé and make sure his reputation wasn't ruined. Even if the bad stuff happening in the industry wasn't about him specifically, if people knew he'd snitched . . . well, that could have him cut out of a *lot* of important circles.

On the other hand, Penelope could have killed Calista to inherit the lucrative *Starch Nemesis* podcast via her will. She *also* could have done it to quash the exposé, since she was *also* representing Tristan and his memoir project. In this case, Tristan's success was Penelope's success. Perhaps that motivated her to ensure nothing brought him down.

And Destiny could have done it out of rage, if she found out that Calista was planning to fire her. Maybe she didn't know about the will and she thought she could stake a claim on the podcast, without knowing it would go to Penelope in the event of Calista's death. This option seemed the least plausible, but I wasn't willing to cast it aside just yet.

I chewed on my bottom lip and something else struck me—what about Henry De Vries? He was investing in Tristan's next restaurant and therefore was also motivated to ensure nothing brought the burgeoning celebrity chef down, otherwise he would lose his investment and that would be *two* bad investments Annie had roped him into. Would he kill to avoid another bad investment that might tarnish his near-pristine track record? What would the world think of him if they knew he allowed himself to be swayed into bad investments? I didn't know what Henry thought of his future son-in-law, but the man knew money.

And plenty of people killed for money.

Last night, Henry had definitely seemed more perturbed by the EMTs wearing shoes on his yacht than the fact that his future son-in-law had been attacked. Perhaps he *didn't* think much of him.

"Did Starr say anything else that might be helpful?" I asked. "*Someone* has those journal pages and I bet they're the key to all this. Whatever Calista found out, it got her killed. But nobody seems to know the particulars. Well, nobody except Tristan and I doubt he'll talk. He's probably hoping those pages are lost for good."

"All she said was that Calista would happily use her clout to bring anyone down who dared cross her. The chick seemed vindictive like that."

Vindictive or not, it wasn't an excuse for anyone to be murdered.

I finished the call with Niko no closer to feeling like I had answers. I needed to think.

Antonio was curled up on my bed, half dozing, his eyes blinking slowly and his rib cage rising and falling with even breaths. He was as peaceful as peaceful could be. But I knew one thing that would perk him up.

"Want to go for a—"

He leaped to his feet, ears pricked upright and almost vibrating with excitement, the earlier moment's sleepiness evaporating like a puff of steam into the air. His question-mark tail was straight up and he stamped his front paws one, two, one, two, like he was marching on the spot.

"Walk?" I finished.

The little dog sailed off the bed, clearing an impressive amount of air as he jetted toward the door, landing soundlessly on the carpet and taking off into the hallway, collar jingling, undoubtedly heading to where his leash and harness hung by the front door.

I smiled in the direction where Antonio had vanished out of my room. "I'll take that as a yes."

CHAPTER 21

After throwing on leggings, a baggy Disney T-shirt, sneakers and a pink baseball cap, I helped Antonio into his harness and we set off. Our town was in overdrive preparing for the parade. The main street had been cordoned off with signs rerouting both road and foot traffic, and people in bright blue and yellow vests bustled about, helping with directions and answering questions. Two uniformed police officers stood near the entrance to the main street, keeping an eye on things.

The weather was Goldilocks perfection—not too hot and not too cold, with an azure sky and marshmallow fluff clouds. It would get hotter as the day went on, but for now I was enjoying the cool sea breeze and mellow buttery morning sunshine.

No less than five people stopped to coo at Antonio as I walked him, and several polite youngsters asked if they could have a pat. Antonio lapped it up and I thanked the universe, yet again, that he was such a relaxed and sociable dog. Since I couldn't walk through the main area of town, I took a detour down a quieter street and realized that I was actually heading in the direction of the police station. I wasn't sure if Starr was being held there or somewhere else while she awaited arraignment.

Instead of peeling off toward the beach I headed on toward the station, my gut instinct tugging me forward. I had no idea what I was hoping to see. But I was totally at a loss about who murdered Calista and it felt like the deeper I dug, the more confused I got.

The police station appeared quiet, probably because most of the officers would have been dispatched to help with the parade, ensuring that people stayed safe and that there were no traffic incidents.

"Maybe we can ask if Starr is here and if she can have visitors," I said to Antonio. "She might like to see a friendly face."

I didn't even make it to the door, however, when someone pushed through, marching with purpose and almost bowling me over. It was Destiny. Instead of her trademark colorful full-skirted dresses, she was wearing cropped yoga pants, a flowing tank top and flip-flops, and she looked madder than a wet hen.

"Oh, Chloe." She stopped short, causing Antonio to skitter out of the way. He let out a yip of annoyance. I stooped down to pick him up and cradle him against my chest. "Sorry about that."

"Everything okay?" I asked. Her eyes were bloodshot and her full lips were pressed into a grim line. Today her braids hung loose down her back.

"If by 'okay' you mean I've been accused of assaulting Tristan Patrick, then yeah." She snorted. "As if I would. The guy isn't worth my time."

I gaped. "You're talking about what happened on the yacht last night?"

"That's right. Someone said they saw me go into his bedroom on the yacht not long before he was found, but it's not true!" Her angry demeanor dissolved and I saw a flash of fear.

It stripped years from her face and suddenly, without her colorful armor, she appeared vulnerable. "I didn't do it."

"Who told the police they saw you?" I asked.

"I have my suspicions, but I don't know for sure. And they wouldn't tell me a thing." She pulled her shoulders back as if trying to regain her composure. "I might have dropped out of law school before finishing, but I learned enough that the police won't hold me without the right paperwork. If they're gonna arrest me, then they better be damn sure they got the right person. And they don't."

"Why would someone set you up?"

I immediately thought of Starr—she couldn't be blamed for last night, since she was already in custody. And if someone had set her up to take the fall for Calista's murder, then perhaps they weren't above blaming Destiny for Tristan's attack? But to what end? Maybe the attack on Tristan wasn't planned and they knew they couldn't blame Starr, so they'd pointed the finger somewhere else.

Or maybe Destiny was lying. I couldn't rule that out, either.

"I've been trying to get access to Calista's accounts to keep the podcast going, but so far no luck. Clearly someone is trying to keep *something* under wraps." She huffed. "And they're not above trying to paint me as violent to do it."

If Destiny had wanted to take over the podcast, then surely she would have obtained Calista's passwords and account information *before* she murdered her. And now knowing that Penelope's literary agency was going to inherit the rights to the podcast, which would leave Destiny totally out of the running, it made me less convinced that she was involved in her boss's murder. Perhaps the attempt to gain control of *Starch Nemesis* was nothing more than an opportunistic grab.

"Did the police ever question you about Calista's murder?" I asked.

Destiny looked at me warily. "Yeah."

"They're not trying to link these two things, are they?" I asked, making out like I didn't have much of an idea of what was going on. I felt Antonio judging me with his dark brown eyes, or maybe that was simply my own conscience projecting. "They don't think you did that too, surely."

"Maybe they did for a hot minute, but no. Turns out the creeper who owns the Airbnb I'm staying in had a damn nanny cam in the house for spying on his guests. Can you believe it!" She shuddered. "I saw some video on YouTube about using your phone camera to do a sweep of any places you rent, and I've been doing that for years now. This time I actually found something. Looked like a regular old USB charger but it had a camera in it! Turns out it was the alibi I needed, and I told the Airbnb host I wouldn't press charges if he let me use the footage to prove where I was the night Calista died."

That officially crossed Destiny off the suspect list.

"What are you going to do now?" I asked.

"Lawyer up. I know how to protect myself and if the cops want to come after me then they better be prepared for a fight."

Destiny began to walk away and I had a feeling that this would be the last I saw of her.

"Did you know Calista was sick?" I called out.

Destiny halted and whirled around, brows furrowed. "Sick?"

"She had cancer."

Her eyes glanced up as if she was remembering something, then she let out a sharp humorless bark of a laugh. "Makes sense."

"How so?"

"Calista left her phone in my car one day after we'd been on the road for an interview. Tristan was texting her—something about a ticking clock and a last chance to make things right. I wasn't sure what it meant at the time, but it makes sense if she was sick. Time was running out."

"What do you think he was talking about?"

"I'm pretty sure he was trying to convince her not to go ahead with that investigative piece. Maybe he thought that if she was sick and her time was running out, she might be influenced. Like a deathbed change of heart."

I cringed. "That's a hell of a time to try to manipulate someone."

"He loved her and she broke his heart and then betrayed him with this investigative podcast. He probably felt there was nothing to lose." She shrugged. "Now he has to make sure he doesn't lose access to his future father-in-law's funding. That relationship is his cash cow."

There were two ways to look at the relationship between Tristan Patrick and the De Vries family: On one hand, Tristan could have killed Calista to preserve his reputation, protect his book deal and make sure his new restaurant—and his future father-in-law's investment—didn't fail. But if he truly had loved Calista at one point . . . would he be able to end her life?

On the other hand, wasn't it possible that Henry might have killed Calista to protect his investment and his *own* reputation? A man who was famous for making the right investments might do anything to keep his track record clean by ensuring Tristan's restaurant was a success. Even kill. But would he risk all he had built by murdering someone?

Out of the two, only one option felt right.

"We have to speak to the detective," I said to Antonio. "Otherwise that yacht will leave town and any chance the police have of seizing those missing journal pages will be gone with it."

It took almost half an hour sitting in the bland waiting area of the Azalea Bay police station before Detective Alvarez motioned me into an equally bland interview room. She looked tired. Dark circles cupped her eyes, and her glasses—which today were a pale pink plastic with a pearlescent sheen to them—had slipped down her nose.

"Take a seat." A table was surrounded by four chairs. The rest of the room was sparse, with a glass wall on one side that allowed people to see in. I guess that was supposed to signal transparency between the police and the community. "You said you had information about Calista Bryant's murder?"

She lowered herself into one of the chairs across from me, sliding a stylus out of the leather cover on her tablet and preparing to take notes. The piece of technology seemed out of place. The rest of the station appeared behind the times, by comparison, with clunky fax machines and cork notice boards and ancient desk phones dotted around.

"I know who did it!" I said as I sat down, placing Antonio on my lap. His large ears were pricked skyward and his little buggy eyes darted around, as though he was wary of the unfamiliar surroundings. I stroked his head to let him know he was safe. "And it's not who you think."

Detective Alvarez put her stylus down. "We've already made an arrest, Chloe."

"You have the wrong person," I argued. "Starr didn't do it."

"I understand she's your friend—"

"Technically, she's not," I said, shaking my head. "Starr and I . . . we're more like acquaintances. But she's being set up! The killer is trying to make it look like she did it, but she didn't."

The detective let out an exasperated sigh and pulled her glasses off, letting them dangle from her pinkie finger while she pinched the bridge of her nose. "We have overwhelming evidence against her. People don't get arrested in real life like they do on television. If we bring someone in it's because we've done the work and found enough to support our actions."

"You've only found that evidence because the real killer wanted you to find it!"

"So you're saying Starr didn't write that Facebook post?"

I cringed. "Okay, well, she *did* do that. But the journal was planted in her possession."

"How do you know about the journal? That hasn't been released to the public."

"Starr showed it to me." I knew I was in the doghouse the second the words left my mouth.

"She showed you the belongings of a murdered woman and you *didn't* think to bring that to my or the chief's attention? Chloe, Dios mío. You do know that could be considered obstruction of justice, right?" She shook her head and her disappointment hung heavily in the air. "The chief said not to go investigating or meddling, but he did *not* ask you to keep evidence quiet."

"But did you notice there are pages missing from the journal?" I continued, barreling on ahead and not at all heeding her warning. "Somebody tore them out."

"People tear pages from notebooks all the time. Maybe she wanted to write a grocery list?"

I wasn't sure whether the detective was aware of the missing pages or not prior to this moment and her tone was hard to read. "Those pages contain information about a secret project Calista was working on for her podcast, I'm sure of it. A secret project that was going to expose things in the food industry." I knew it sounded vague when I said it out loud, but I was confident the missing pages were linked to Calista's murder. "Did you know she dated Tristan Patrick?"

"Yes, Chloe," the detective said in an exasperated tone. "I know that because I interviewed him myself and he told me. He was at Foam the night of the murder and the security footage has his alibi completely confirmed."

Oh. Well, that was that.

"Well, he told Calista a bunch of secret things that she was going to turn into a podcast after they broke up," I said. "It would be super bad for him, because people in the industry might know he snitched. But he didn't murder her."

"I know that already. I just mentioned his rock-solid alibi."

"Aren't you even a *little* bit curious about what I think?" I asked. Antonio whined in my lap and the detective's eyes dropped down to him, softening for a minute.

"Fine. Who do you think did it, Chloe?" she asked, and though I could tell she was simply humoring me, I had to forge on.

"Henry De Vries."

The detective laughed. "Henry De Vries who owns the superyacht currently parked in our marina? The same Henry De Vries who is known world-wide for his incredible investment strategies and his success in funding start-ups? *That* Henry De Vries?"

"You think that successful people don't commit murder?" I asked.

"No, they don't. They hire other people to do it for them, for one. For another thing, Henry was giving a talk that night."

"A talk?" I squeaked.

"In Silicon Valley. There was a big conference up there and he was the keynote speaker. He had a driver take him there and back—I know, because he had a police escort. Two vehicles, in fact. We had to assign two of our officers to make the trip after he received a threat on his life. The chief said it would be good for all of us if we complied. Money talks. That's how I know that A, he didn't do it; and B, even if he wanted to, he wouldn't have done it himself."

I didn't say anything. That was two people I was sure were involved and both had alibis. But to the detective's point—just because he didn't do it himself, doesn't mean he wasn't involved.

"How can you entertain the possibility that he would hire someone to commit murder but not that he would frame someone for it?" I said, tossing my free hand in the air. The other kept a secure hold on Antonio.

"Because there's literally no evidence to support it. And what would his motivation be?"

"To stop Tristan's new restaurant from flopping when it opens, because he invested in it," I supplied. But my confidence was waning by the second.

"Chloe, the man is rich as a king. Do you think he cares about one bad investment enough to kill a person and put *everything* he owns on the line? That's ridiculous."

"Rich people get away with stuff all the time because they can afford good lawyers," I argued.

"True, but the man is a billionaire. An actual billionaire. Do you have any idea how much money that is? He could buy three dozen restaurants and have them all fail and it wouldn't make a lick of a difference to him."

I sagged back against the chair. No matter what I said, the detective wasn't going to see where I was coming from. Okay, a billion dollars *was* a lot of money. Maybe it wasn't about the money. Maybe he was doing it for his daughter's sake, so her fiancé's reputation wasn't ruined.

But even as I thought it over in my head, that sounded pretty weak.

Would a man as well-known and wealthy as Henry De Vries really murder a podcaster to keep something hidden that wasn't even directly related to him? To protect money when he had squillions more where that came from?

"What about Calista's literary agent?" I asked, thinking about the only person left on my suspect list. "Did you know she's due to inherit the podcast?"

The detective's brow furrowed and she made a note on her tablet. "Penelope something, right? I don't have her name on me."

"Hendriks," I said, thinking of the business card burning a hole in my pocket.

"How do you know this?"

"She told me. Does she have an alibi? Did you question her?" I asked.

"Chloe, I'm not sure what I can say to get this through your head. Investigating crimes is the job of the police, not of civilians. You should *not* be going around questioning people. This work is dangerous, as you well know from not only one incident but *multiple* incidents." She shot me a pointed look. "I don't want to receive a call one day that a nosy twentysomething blonde has been found face down in the water because she asked the wrong person the wrong question."

"I wouldn't have to do this if you just listened!" The second the words were out of my mouth and I saw the detective's expression turn hard, I knew I had stepped over a line.

"If you continue to involve yourself in this investigation—or any other investigation—I'll have no choice but to book you for obstruction of justice," the detective said, her mouth set into a grim line. "It's for your own good. Stay out of it."

This was pointless. I appreciated that police work was a difficult job—something I had even *more* respect for since solving a murder or two of my own. But I also found the detective's stubborn refusal to listen to be infuriating. They'd gotten it wrong before. Couldn't they see that it was possible Starr wasn't a killer?

"Starr has been framed," I said, pushing back on my chair and standing, Antonio clutched to my chest. He trembled in my arms, obviously picking up on the tension in the room. "You have the wrong person."

As I walked out of the interview room and into the main foyer area of the station, I saw a very tall man with big shoulders and intense, heavy-browed eyes walk up to the reception desk. "My name is Dragan Merković and I am here to see my client, Zvezdana Merković."

Starr's father. He came for her.

Despite feeling at my wit's end with the investigation, knowing Starr's father had come around and was going to help her left a tiny seed of hope in my heart.

I'll do everything I can to get you out of here, Starr. I promise.

Feeling somewhat deflated, I began to trudge home with Antonio. The day was warming up and the noise in the town had started to swell, marching band music drifting on the ocean breeze and calling folks to the center of town. In the next two hours the parade would be over and the ice cream festival would open up for the final few hours of trade. Then Azalea Bay would empty out once more for a brief lull before the next big summer event rolled into town.

Ahead of me, a little girl skipped along the pavement, twin blond braids fluttering like ribbons behind her. Her father followed behind, clutching the chubby hand of a young boy in blue overalls and sneakers with flashing lights in the soles. How simple life was when you were young, where the biggest drama was which cereal to eat for breakfast and what toy to play with.

Something churned in the back of my mind while I walked—puzzle pieces that didn't want to click together. The list of suspects was growing shorter.

Tristan, Henry, Niko, Destiny and Dee were all clear.

That left one person. Penelope.

But the more I tried to think about her as the murderer, the harder it was to get everything to make sense. Sure, she stood to inherit something valuable with Calista's death. But how long would *Starch Nemesis* continue to *be* valuable without Calista's voice? She was the life and soul of that podcast and there was no guarantee it would continue to make money without her.

Not to mention that Penelope had genuinely seemed upset by Calista's death. She might have been the only person who genuinely mourned her.

The only other motivation I could think of was that perhaps she murdered Calista to keep the investigative miniseries under wraps in order to protect Tristan and, by extension, his memoir. But given Calista was also one of Penelope's clients— and her book was certain to make a pile of cash—wouldn't an explosive exposé make Penelope *more* money if it brought more people to Calista's work and, therefore, her book? It might potentially even boost sales of Tristan's memoir, even if it didn't help his reputation.

I couldn't be sure if this reasoning was logical, or if I just desperately wanted Penelope not to be a murderer for my own selfish reasons.

As I neared the area where the parade was about to kick off, my phone rang. Well, it vibrated anyway. How many Millennials actually have their ringtone volume turned on these days? Not me, anyway.

I fished the phone out of my bag and swiped my thumb across the screen, not recognizing the number. "Hello?"

"Hi, Chloe, this is Caterina from Heavy Petal."

"Oh hey. What's up?"

"Marty just called to check in about his shifts for next week, and I haven't been able to stop thinking about your visit the other day. So I asked him if he remembered who ordered the yellow roses."

I sucked in a breath. "And? Did he?"

"Yeah, he said it was a strange transaction. That's why he remembered it. The client was a woman wanting to send flowers to a friend, but she paid cash and was adamant about not leaving a name on the card. She also said the roses *had* to be yellow because it was her friend's favorite color."

"Huh." So it wasn't Tristan who sent the roses, then. I re-

membered back to when I'd seen the roses at Sprout and Starr
had commented how she wasn't a fan of yellow because it
clashed with her hair. Okay, so clearly the yellow color meant
something . . . and it wasn't because Starr liked it. "Did he say
what she looked like at all?"

I crossed my fingers, hoping he might have noticed some
distinguishing factor . . . like whether she had red hair.

"He didn't mention that. He said he didn't think she was
local, but there was nothing distinctive about her . . . only that
he got a weird vibe. Sorry that's not much to go on, but I figured you'd want to know."

"Thanks, Caterina, I really appreciate it."

"No problem. Chat soon!"

We ended the call and I continued walking, something stew-
ing in the back of my brain. The yellow aspect of the roses
seemed important. Why else claim to want that color because
it was your friend's favorite when that person actually avoided
it? Lawrence had made a comment about yellow roses being
used in Victorian times to signal jealousy or to shame someone
for having an affair.

But who on earth would follow the language of flowers in
this day and age? I mean, you had *multiple* ways to call someone out. You could email, tweet, DM, TikTok, vaguebook. You
could send a passive-aggressive meme or even insult someone
with only the use of an emoji. Remember that whole Taylor-
Swift-and-the-snake-emoji thing? Heck, you could simply
leave their texts on read—reading the texts without responding so the person knows you've read them—and *that* alone
would send a message.

Who would use their own time and money to send flowers
to someone when they probably wouldn't even get the meaning behind it?

Something in my brain clicked.

Starr didn't act like there were any negative implications behind the flowers—she actually blushed when I mentioned them. But what if the meaning of the yellow flowers wasn't really *about* her. Rather, it was simply a way to connect her to the murder, thus framing her.

After all, the first place I had seen the yellow roses was in the petals scattered around Calista's body. What if the message of the yellow roses was nothing to do with Starr, and everything to do with Calista? What if *she* was the one being shamed for having an affair?

And who would know enough about the Victorian time period to understand the societal language of flowers?

Someone with an interest in historical times and vintage things. Perhaps someone with a collection of cameo brooches. I brought up the browser on my phone. With intuition humming inside me, I typed into the search engine: *in what era were cameo brooches popular?*

The first article that popped up confirmed my suspicions.

Cameos, most often worn as a brooch or necklace, have been popular throughout history. However, when we think of cameos we usually think of its most popular period during the 19th century, also known as the Victorian era.

The same era as the language of flowers.

And it wasn't the only thing linking the De Vries family to the yellow roses. A vision of the yacht flashed up in my mind, with its name written in bold orange letters. Orange was the official color of the Netherlands—a sign of national pride. The note Starr had received with her flower delivery had contained a quote from a world-famous Dutch soccer player, and Henry's family was from the Netherlands. In fact, Jake had mentioned last night that they'd even talked about soccer! That quote would probably be known to them.

But if it wasn't Henry De Vries . . .

It must be Annie.

My mind started to comb through all the evidence again at full speed.

What if Tristan's text message referencing the ticking clock and "a last chance to make things right" wasn't about the investigative series at all? What if Tristan was still in love with Calista and finding out that she was sick had made him question whether he wanted to marry Annie? What if the "last chance" was about them as a couple . . . and Annie found out? Niko had also said that Starr and Tristan hooked up at some conference. Was he dating Annie yet? Maybe she thought she could kill two birds with one stone—off the competition and frame the one-night stand?

Then all she had to do was stand back while the police danced like puppets.

"We have to get to the marina," I said, bending down to scoop Antonio up. "If those journal pages are anywhere, they'll be on the yacht. I'm sure of it! And we don't have much time left."

The sounds of the parade starting up filled the air as I got closer to the main strip, which meant time was ticking down. I only had an hour and a half before the festival opened for the last time. Unless Tristan was scheduled to do anything else as part of his engagement, then the yacht might not be docked for much longer. I headed quickly in the direction of home so I could drop Antonio off and pick up the Jellybean. No way was I getting my little man *anywhere* near danger.

As I hustled along the street, I typed a text to Niko with one hand.

CHLOE: We need to meet at the marina ASAP. I think the missing journal pages are still on the yacht.

I wanted to call the police and tell them what I'd figured out, but the detective had already threatened me with obstruction of justice. It was clear they weren't going to listen until the evidence told them otherwise. So I would just have to find the evidence and hand it over. Then, I wouldn't need to convince them of anything. The truth would be apparent.

I had no idea how we would get onto the yacht to find the missing pages. But if we didn't try something, a killer might just sail off into the sunset.

CHAPTER 22

It took me a good twenty minutes to drop Antonio at home and race the Jellybean over to the marina. Time was running out. Grandma Rose had left me a note saying she'd gone to her friend's house for lunch, so I texted her to let her know where I was going . . . just in case.

I tried calling both Jake and Aunt Dawn on the way, but neither of them picked up. Aunt Dawn's phone went straight to voicemail and Jake's rang out. I knew he had a few meetings this morning for his business, so he was likely chatting with a client. I would have felt better with some backup, but since the police were determined to keep looking at the wrong person I had no other choice.

We needed to get our hands on those missing journal pages or *something* that might tie the murder to Annie.

Niko was waiting for me in the parking lot. He looked rough—with bags under his eyes and his beard even more straggly than usual—and he stood with his shoulders hunched and his arms crossed over his chest. When I got out of my car, he walked right over.

"That thing is a tuna can on wheels," he said, nodding to the Jellybean. "It's a death trap."

"We don't have time to talk about my transport of choice," I said, marching past him toward the entrance to the marina. "I'm pretty sure I've figured out who killed Calista and set up your sister."

Niko's long-legged strides caught up to me without issue. "I already know who did it."

"It's not Tristan," I said. "But he's connected, for sure. I think his fiancée did it."

"Annie? She's like the human embodiment of . . . beige."

"All the better to fly under the radar."

We walked past the restaurants on the way to the area where the boats were docked. In the day, the marina had a different vibe. It was still beautiful, no doubt, but rather than feeling soft and romantic, it felt more cheerful and upbeat. It was quieter, since the lunch rush hadn't yet started and most folks were currently distracted by the parade going down the main street. The restaurants were not yet open.

Today the green-blue of the ocean looked bright and jewellike, stretching endlessly from the boardwalk out to the horizon; and overhead, wispy white clouds were draped across the aquamarine sky. My sneakers slapped against the wood slats as I hurried toward the area where the *Princess Anouk* was docked.

"Don't rush, you'll draw attention." Niko grabbed my arm and slowed me down. "And what do you think you're going to do? Walk right onto that yacht without an invitation in broad daylight?"

"It's *got* to be her," I said. "Nothing else makes sense with the clues. And, for the record, Tristan has a rock-solid alibi. The police have him on camera."

Niko blinked in surprise. "I was sure he did it."

We slowed our pace so it looked like we were any other two people strolling around the marina, checking out the luxury yacht that made all the other boats look like dinghies. The little ramp that we'd used to walk onto the yacht the night of the party had been removed. Onboard, someone in uniform pottered about.

"There's no way we're getting on that yacht," Niko said. "And even if we do, we don't have the cover of a party distracting people."

He was right. Not only was there a crew member in eyesight, the ability to board the yacht had been removed *and* I noticed a marina security guard wandering around. They must have put extra people on because it was going to be busy today with the parade and it being the last day of the ice cream festival.

"What are we going to do?" I asked, desperation creeping into my voice. "The police won't listen to a word I say and if we don't find something to help your sister, these guys will sail off and that will be that!"

Right at that moment, I caught sight of movement on the yacht. There were two crew members now, and they were setting up the boarding ramp. Behind them, two figures appeared. Both women. It was Annie and Penelope. It looked like they were having a tense conversation.

"Quick, get out of sight." I grabbed Niko's arm and pulled him back, and we scurried back along the walkway, partially hiding ourselves behind a large sign that had the layout of the marina printed on it to help people find their way around. "What are they doing together?"

"Who's the redhead?" Niko asked.

"That's Tristan and Calista's literary agent, Penelope. I don't know what she and Annie would have to talk about."

We watched as the two women alighted the yacht. Penelope was wearing a long black dress and a floppy sun hat, her red hair hanging in a single braid over one shoulder. She had a large straw bag over one arm and flip-flops on her feet, as though she was ready for a day at the beach. By contrast, Annie looked starchy as usual in a stiff white collared shirt, clunky leather loafers and a skirt that came to her knees. She had an expensive-looking bag with a shimmering gold chain hanging over one shoulder and her diamond engagement ring glittered in the sunlight. Sure enough, she wore a cameo brooch at her breast pocket.

They walked past us, completely oblivious to being watched, heads bowed and whatever conversation they were having continued. Once they were a few paces in front of us, I turned to Niko. I caught a glimpse of something very unsettling—a bunch of yellow roses nestled inside Penelope's beach bag.

Had Annie given her the roses or was I totally wrong and Penelope was behind the murder all along?

"Something is about to go down," I whispered. "I can feel it."

We stepped out from behind the sign and walked at a distance behind them, so as not to attract attention. Annie and Penelope headed past the restaurants and continued toward the exit of the marina, out to the parking lot. They stopped in front of a lipstick-red hatchback and Penelope pulled a set of keys out of her bag.

"We have to follow them," I said. "I'll drive."

"Forget it," he said. "Your car sticks out like a sore thumb. *I'm* driving."

I had to give it to Niko—the man could tail someone.

And it wasn't an easy task, because Penelope drove like a drunk squirrel chasing a nut down a hill. She barely indicated when she turned and would swerve last minute around corners, not going superfast, but so erratic I had to wonder *where* her head was at. While we drove, I filled Niko in on everything I'd learned and he, in turn, did the same for me.

But it didn't give us any answers about what was going on right now. What the heck were Annie and Penelope discussing that looked so tense? And why were we heading out of town?

I glanced nervously at the clock on the dashboard of Niko's car. Although calling it a car seemed a little generous, because if the Jellybean was a tuna can with wheels, then this was an oversized suitcase on wheels. The back seat was littered with clothing from T-shirts to hoodies to sweatpants. I saw a pair of work boots thrown haphazardly back there and it occurred to me that I'd just jumped into a car with a man I barely knew and whose identity had only been confirmed by him. What if he was someone else entirely?

Outside the ocean view was a blur of blue and white, the rugged landscape of scattered trees and rocks slowly building up as we curved gently inland. Niko could take me anywhere and my only means of escape would be diving out of a moving vehicle.

"You got nervous all of a sudden. Why?" His wary eyes flicked over to me, though he stayed facing the road, hands at ten and two.

"I, uh . . . I didn't," I lied.

"Yes, you did. I can feel it." He grunted. "One of my cell-mates said I was, like, an empath or something. I feel other people's feelings."

One of my eyebrows shot up. "That seems very new age for a guy like you."

"Starr isn't the only one who likes crystals and stuff," he mumbled. Then he gestured to a small piece of amethyst that was stuck to his dashboard. "She gave me that when I got out. Said something about it being a protective stone and keeping it close would mean she was always watching over me."

I felt some of the anxiety melt out of my muscles. If he wasn't really her brother then he was a damn good actor.

"She's a good person," I said. "We didn't always get along, but I can tell she really cares about you."

"I don't deserve as much, being how I put her and our parents through hell."

I sensed his shame. "Everyone makes mistakes."

"Not according to my dad. I should have been perfect at everything." He let out a breath. "And I was *far* from perfect."

Up ahead, the red car suddenly turned off down a road and we were going too fast to catch it. Niko overshot the turnoff and swore, thumping his fist on the steering wheel. "Hold tight."

He indicated and swung the car around into an aggressive U-turn, earning us a honk from the people behind us. I squinted my eyes shut and forced myself to breathe through a wave of nausea as my stomach lurched, but soon we were on the right track and following the red car down a quieter road.

"It's going to get hard for us to stay out of sight," he said. "If they stop, I'm going to keep driving past. Just take note of where they are and we'll circle back. Hopefully they won't realize it's the same car."

"Good plan."

We were just on the outskirts of town, on a tree-lined street with newer houses. It looked like a recently developed area, and I hadn't actually been here before. It might not even technically be classed as Azalea Bay, depending on where the town boundaries were drawn. But the houses were big and fancy and modern, not like the quaint modest homes on the street where I lived.

The red car slowed and pulled into a driveway of one of the homes. The women got out of the car. Niko slowed down some but didn't stop, and we cruised past as Penelope and Annie headed up the driveway.

"Penelope said she was staying at an Airbnb, so maybe this is it?" I said.

Niko turned off at the next street and we did another U-turn, pausing at the end of the road before crawling back onto the same street. He parked on the side of the road, a few houses down from where the red car was parked. The two women had disappeared, presumably inside the house.

The street was totally empty, not a car coming or going. Nobody was mowing their lawn, or walking their dog. It was a little creepy.

"My grandma said there are a lot of these vacation rental homes popping up now. She thinks it's bad for the community because it means people aren't really living in the houses and contributing to the town, *and* it's driving up the housing prices," I mused.

"Capitalism is a bitch," Niko agreed.

We got out of the car and Niko dug around for a cap in his messy wardrobe of a back seat, tucking his hair away and slipping some wraparound sunglasses over his eyes, which didn't really do *that* much since his beard was very much still on display. I was even less prepared with a disguise, but had a large pair of sunglasses in my bag, which would have to do.

The house that the two women had parked at was big and white and boxy. The second level probably had a partial view of the ocean from here, and a large white wooden mailbox sat out front, decorated with a starfish and a gold number in a script-like font. *Definitely* a tourist house. No actual self-respecting resident from this area would decorate their mailbox with a starfish.

"Let's go this way." I indicated to the side of the house, where a small path ran, mostly covered by overhanging trees, some of which had small orange fruit nestled among the leaves.

We crept along the side of the house, which was no easy task since it was mostly made of floor-to-ceiling glass. At any moment, someone could have seen us. But the rooms appeared empty. I spied fairly basic furniture—IKEA, most likely, but decorated to look more expensive than it was with beach-themed items like large shells and rattan and wrought-iron anchors. A large sofa seat covered in beige fabric had a navy and white striped throw draped over the back of it, some cushions containing motifs of whales and boats scattered across the surface.

We crept further down the side of the house, not daring to speak. As we got closer to the backyard, faint voices could be heard, possibly through an open window.

"I didn't sleep with him. You're paranoid." It was Penelope and she sounded at her wit's end. "One, I am *happily* married with a child. Two, I don't mix my business with pleasure and Tristan is a client."

"I saw the way he looked at you." Annie sounded close to tears.

"If you're worried about how he looks at other women, you should take that up with him."

The voices became muted, as if the women had walked away from the window. I motioned for Niko to follow me around the corner. I stayed low, sticking close to the wall of the house. The backyard was nothing special, simply a space with an outdoor table setting and a small fire pit surrounded by a few chairs painted in white and blue.

The back of the house was also mostly glass and it provided a view into the kitchen area. The kitchen was *gorgeous* with a big center island and large open shelving. There was a bottle of wine on the island with two glasses next to it. But what really caught my attention were the two bags sitting on the large dining table on the right side of the room—one straw bag with roses poking out of it and one expensive-looking designer purse. I snuck over to the door and tried the handle—it moved.

"What are you doing?" Niko asked in a stage whisper.

"I'm going to see if they have the missing journal pages on

them," I whispered back. "If you hear people coming, make a distraction and I'll hide."

"I don't want to get caught breaking and entering—it'll be a violation of my parole." Niko swore under his breath. "Zvezdana is going to kill me."

"Stay outside. If they call the cops, I'll say I came here on my own." I shooed him back. "I'll only be a second."

I held my breath as I eased down the handle of the door, praying the hinges wouldn't squeak as I opened it. Mercifully the owners of this house had either invested in quality hinges or some WD-40, because the door opened as silently as my prayer. I slipped into the kitchen and left the door slightly ajar in case I needed a quick getaway. Then I tiptoed toward the table where the bags sat.

From somewhere deeper in the house, I could make out both women's voices.

"I don't know what to say that will reassure you, Annie. There's nothing going on between Tristan and I. Come on now, we're all supposed to have a nice lunch together to discuss Tristan's book. Let's keep it to business."

I tiptoed over to the table and hooked my finger over the edge of Penelope's straw bag to pull it open. The inside could have rivalled the back of Niko's car in messiness—crumpled receipts and gum wrappers and several small tissue packets and the shiny outer foil of a candy bar. There was a small spiral-bound notebook with a shopping list, a pen without a lid and at least five different lip glosses and lip balms, plus a bottle of sunscreen. I didn't see anything resembling the missing pages from Calista's journal, although it would be easy to miss it with the disorganized chaos.

"What about the podcast?" I heard Annie ask, her voice trembling. "The one Calista was working on based on the information Tris gave her."

"The one about how his mentor almost killed a dining guest by purposely putting something he was allergic to into his meal? The same guy who was known to sexually harass his female workers and who injured a staff member for making a mistake, all while being praised on national television for being an inspiration to young chefs everywhere?" Penelope snorted. "*That* podcast? Yeah, that guy is going down."

Ah, so Penelope *did* know what the miniseries was about!

I carefully and quietly twisted the locking mechanism on the front of Annie's purse—it was the kind where the lock was also the brand's logo—and then I eased the top flap of leather up to peer inside. Unlike Penelope and Niko, Annie was meticulously organized. Her wallet sat straight, nestled between her phone and a slim sunglasses case. There was a single lipstick with a shiny gold lid, a vintage mirror and a powder compact. I didn't see any papers.

"You can't publish it," Annie pleaded. "It'll *ruin* Tristan's relationship with him. Not to mention everybody knows how close they are and that he and Calista had a thing. They'll know he told her everything. He'll be an outcast and his new restaurant will fail."

"This is incredible publicity for his memoir," Penelope said, her tone dismissive. "You can't pay for the kind of buzz that's going to come out of all this."

There was a zip in the back part of the bag, hiding a small pocket away, and I gently tugged it open. Inside were the telltale jagged shreds of paper torn from binding. Holding my breath, I clasped them between my forefinger and thumb, easing them out of the pocket. Crap! I should have thought to bring gloves or tweezers or a plastic bag or something to preserve the evidence. A CSI expert I was not.

"You don't understand." Annie was close to tears, her voice wavering. "His mentor invested in this new restaurant. Half a million dollars. He'll pull out and my father . . . he only agreed to back Tristan if there was another investor on the hook."

I unfolded the pieces of paper and sure enough familiar handwriting looped across the pages, the strange Ys grabbing my attention immediately. But the contents of the pages were not at all what I thought they would be. There was no mention of the podcast miniseries.

Dr. Yamato Akiyama June 21st 2 p.m. Remission checkup.

So Calista's cancer had gone into remission. She was better—or getting better, at least. The notes continued down the page.

Call Tristan.
What on earth am I going to say to him? I love you. I need you. I'll lose everything, even this deal with iListen if it means we can be together again.
Who am I right now??

It was more like a journal entry, her thoughts and emotions splashed across the page in ink.

My therapist told me to write things down when I feel muddled . . . but this feels stupid. I feel stupid.
Can I let a bad person get away with terrible things to keep the confidence of the man I love? How much will I give up for him? All I know is that I can't keep pushing him away. If I do, he'll be gone for good. The last time . . . it was more than sex.
But I'll only be with him if he comes clean with her. I won't do it behind her back again. I feel terrible about that. But breaking up with him was the worst thing I have ever done in my life. I thought I was saving him from watching me die. I never thought I would get better.

It was proof of motive alright, just not the kind of proof I thought I was going to find. I folded the papers back and slipped them into my crossbody bag. It would be better for the police to find them on Annie, of course, but I couldn't risk her destroying them. Now the police would find my prints there, but hers would be, too. It was better than nothing.

I was about to back out of the kitchen when I heard a strange noise. An unfamiliar click.

"Annie . . . ?" Penelope's voice raised an octave. "What are you doing? Why have you got a gun?"

CHAPTER 23

"I didn't want to do *any* of this." Annie's voice floated into the kitchen, where I was half standing, half crouching next to the dining table. "But you're all giving me no choice."

I glanced toward the back of the house, through the big glass windows that showed the yard. Niko was gone. I stifled a curse.

"Annie, please. Don't be rash."

I looked longingly at the door, desperate to get the heck out of there and keep myself safe. But Penelope was stuck in here with a killer and the police had turned a blind eye to what was going on. Annie had killed before, and she could do it again. I couldn't let Penelope's little girl grow up without a mother.

I knew that feeling intimately and it wasn't something I would wish on anyone.

Creeping across the kitchen, I looked for something with which to defend myself, but to say the kitchen was sparse was putting it lightly. There wasn't even a knife block on display! What kind of a kitchen was this? I slipped around the side of the island, keeping low in case the women returned. Sliding one drawer out as slowly as possible so it didn't make a sound,

I peered inside. Loose cooking utensils floated in the drawer and one look at the knives told me they were blunter than the thick end of a baseball bat. How the heck was anyone supposed to cook with knives like that?

But I didn't have time to mentally berate the owners on the fact that dull knives were actually more dangerous than sharp ones.

There didn't seem to be much else of use, however. So I grabbed a knife and made my way to the wall of the kitchen, inching along the white wood paneling until I reached the open doorway that led into the next room. I didn't dare peek around the corner in case I exposed myself. Inside, I glanced, at an angle, to where a large mirror hung on the wall reflecting a sliver of what was going on. I couldn't see Penelope, but I *could* see Annie.

She indeed had something small and silver in her hands and was holding it out, aiming in front of her. At the last second, I had an idea. Grabbing my phone out of my bag as quietly as possible, I set it to record and laid it down on the floor near the doorway so it wouldn't be disturbed. Annie might say something incriminating that I could use to free Starr!

"Please," Penelope pleaded again. "I have a family. A little girl."

"You should have thought about your little girl before you decided to support a woman who was determined to bring down everyone around her," Annie said. Her voice was shaky, almost like her emotions had totally overtaken her. "Calista was a bad person."

"She *wasn't* a bad person."

"She hurt people," Annie argued. "She hurt me! You have no idea what she did. The lies she told."

"Did you . . ." Penelope gasped. "No, tell me you didn't kill her."

"It had to be done. I had to protect Tristan. She was going to release that podcast and ruin his entire career."

Only Calista had been thinking about canning the whole thing if it meant she could have Tristan back. Annie probably didn't want anyone to know about *that*—hence why she removed the pages from the journal. It wasn't about protecting Tristan. It was about protecting her and making sure nobody found out that she had motive to kill Calista.

"You would really kill another person to save your fiancé's career?" Penelope's voice was dull with shock and disbelief. "It wouldn't even do him that much harm. He'd profit from the notoriety, if anything. And so what if the other investor pulled out? He'd find more."

"But I promised my dad . . . I promised him this was a good investment, that it would be a worthy thing for him to add to his portfolio. I *begged* him." It sounded like there were tears in Annie's eyes now and I saw the gun shake in her hands. "I asked him to trust me one more time. This wasn't going to be like last time when I screwed up and picked the wrong man and he lost all that money on that stupid social media site. I can't make that mistake again. Tristan is different. He loves me. Someone finally loves me."

Oh.

Now it all made sense—this actually wasn't about Tristan. Not really. It was about Annie and her father. Her need to be loved. Because if she had convinced Henry to invest in Tristan's restaurant and then her relationship with him fell apart and the restaurant failed, her father would lose money and she would have, once again, steered him onto a bad investment. She would have failed him, again. Sure, it might not bankrupt him by any stretch, but money was a secondary motivator here.

Her father's love and approval was the main gig. I'd heard Tristan say as much the day I'd followed them on the walking trail.

You need to stop being so desperate for his approval.

"Of course he loves you," Penelope said, though it was very much in the voice of someone who didn't want to be shot.

"We are going to get married and then I will be a real grown-up who makes good decisions. I'm going to prove my dad wrong. I'm going to show him I'm smart and have a good nose for business, because the restaurant will be a success and my marriage will be a success and *I* will be a success. And then my dad will see me. He will see I'm the daughter he always wanted."

It sounded like she was talking to herself—convincing herself that everything in her plan would work out as she had intended.

"I didn't want to do any of this. But I had to. I had to kill Calista. I had to knock Tristan out last night before he . . ." Her voice trailed off, like she had gone to another place in her head. "Thank god he didn't see me. I'll tell him it was you. Yes, I'll say it was you who hit him."

So *she* had attacked him! I wondered if he was going into the safe and that's where she'd stashed the journal pages. I had no idea why she would have kept them. A reminder, perhaps, of why she was doing these terrible things? Or maybe it was insurance, in case Tristan tried to leave her? Then she could expose him as the one who'd leaked the information to Calista.

"Annie, please put down the gun," Penelope begged.

"No," she snapped. "Because you know too much now and you'll tell people. I can't have Tristan knowing that I killed her. I can't have anyone knowing! I'm sorry, Penelope. But you're a problem now and problems need to be fixed. I have to fix this."

"Please." Penelope was crying now. "Don't hurt me."

"I'm going to fix this. Yes, I'm going to fix this."

The almost out-of-body babbling sent a chill down my spine. Whatever was going on in Annie's head, she was in damage control mode and that was bad news. I had to do something. The knife in my hand was no more effective for cutting than a paperweight, but maybe I could use it as a distraction. If I could distract Annie, then I might be able to tackle her and knock the gun out of her hand. Then it would be two against one.

"You have the roses, so the police will make the connection. I can say you came at me with the gun, there was a fight. The gun went off. You tried to kill me," Annie said. "You killed Calista because you wanted to protect Tristan, your client."

"Annie, no!"

"You framed the blond woman, but then I figured out what you were doing so you tried to kill me. Yes, that will work. I'm so glad I bought the flowers. I thought you were trying to steal my fiancé and now it doesn't matter if you were or if you weren't. All that matters is that the police think you pulled the trigger."

I stopped the recording on my phone and dialed 911 with the volume on low—they would be able to trace the call and send someone. Putting the phone into the pocket in my leggings while it dialed, I hurled my knife through the doorway straight at the mirror. I was hoping for it to shatter and distract Annie, but instead it bounced off the glass with a useless *thunk*. Still, she jumped and turned around. I didn't have much time. I raced into the room and plowed into her, sending her stumbling back.

But instead of being knocked over, she caught herself against the back of a couch and slipped out of my grasp, keeping ahold of the gun and remaining upright.

"Chloe!" Penelope ducked behind a chair. "What the heck are you doing?"

Annie moved the gun to me and I froze on the spot, raising my hands in the air.

"Yes, Chloe. What *are* you doing?" Annie asked, her eyes wild and smudged. "Uggh! Can nobody mind their own business in this backward town? First that nosy blond woman starts hanging around Tristan, only for me to find out he *slept* with her! Then you start sniffing around. He didn't date you, too, did he?"

I shook my head vigorously.

"Get down on the floor." Annie held the gun steady, determination hardening her dull brown eyes. She was in solution mode now. Her panic had abated now that she had a plan. "We can make this work. When the gun went off, you were in the line of fire. It was a tragic wrong place, wrong time scenario."

Fear trickled down my spine as I slowly lowered myself to the ground, my hands planting on the cool bleached floorboards and my shoulders tensed. Then I heard a soft voice, so faint I almost missed it.

"9-1-1, what is your emergency?" It was coming from my phone.

"Help please, she has a gun! It's Annie De Vries and we're at—"

"Shut up! Shut up!" Annie shrieked but she didn't pull the trigger. Instead she rushed forward and used the butt of the gun to crack me across the skull. Lights burst like fireworks in front of my eyes and I crumpled, pain spearing through my brain like a hot-tipped fire poker. "Give me your phone now!"

"Penelope, run!" I shouted as I tried to scramble away from Annie's grabbing hands, twisting and turning so she couldn't reach my pocket. "Call for help!"

I saw Penelope dart toward the kitchen and Annie's eyes were drawn momentarily to the movement. I took the opportunity of her distraction to roll away, out of her grasp, but she lunged quickly, her nails raking across my arm. I kicked out and the gun fell to the floor, discharging and causing us both to scream. I stilled for a moment, waiting for the pain to kick in. But there was nothing.

Then why was there a large pool of blood spreading across the floor?

"Oh crap."

Annie lay on the floor, clutching her leg as blood oozed through her fingertips. The gun lay on the ground and I smacked it out of the way, sending it sliding across the polished boards so that it landed under a piece of furniture butted up against the wall. Snatching my phone out of my pocket, I brought it up to my ear just in time to see two figures rushing through the front door as sirens began to wail. It was Niko and another man, and they both held baseball bats.

"Police are on their way," Niko panted. "I ran to get help when I saw she had a gun."

"I thought you'd left," I said, slumping down to the ground.

Annie was sobbing on the floor, still clutching her leg. "He really loves me. He said it, he promised. He really loves me."

I grabbed my phone and brought it up to my ear as I moved to sit in front of where the gun was secured under a sideboard, to make sure no one could touch it until the police arrived.

"Hello? Miss?" The voice came from my phone. "Are you okay?"

"I think so," I said, my hands shaking. "But someone has been shot. We need an ambulance."

The other man rushed into the kitchen calling Penelope's name in a panic. It must be her husband. Niko stood over Annie with his bat poised, but I held out a hand to tell him to cool it. Her face was white as a sheet and her eyes were glassy from shock. She wasn't going to hurt anyone now.

It was all over.

The murderer had been caught.

* * *

I never made it to the final day of the ice cream festival. A quick call to Aunt Dawn solved the problem and everyone I knew had pitched in to help—Erica, Jake, Maisey, Sabrina and Cal had all gone to our stall to take turns serving customers and helping Aunt Dawn to run the show without me while I stayed at the Airbnb and waited to give my statement to the police.

Paramedics were called to tend to Annie's wound and she was shipped off to the hospital to get stitched up, but not without an officer there to guard her. As of now, she was about to be under arrest for murder and possibly attempted murder for pulling a gun on Penelope and me.

"What brought you to Ms. Hendriks's Airbnb?" Detective Alvarez asked.

Niko and I sat on the couch while another officer took a statement from Penelope in another room. She was with her husband and in a state of shock over what had happened. The paramedics had checked on both of us—but I was feeling surprisingly numb to it all. This wasn't the first time I'd faced a murderer, though something inside me hoped it was the last.

Having a gun pointed at you was certainly one way to bring life into sharp focus.

But instead of my life flashing before my eyes, I'd seen something else. The future. Holding hands with Jake and hugging Grandma Rose and tossing rose petals at Aunt Dawn's wedding. Things that hadn't yet happened. Things I would have missed out on if Annie had pulled the trigger.

A life that might not have been lived.

"I had a suspicion that Annie was involved with the murder. Niko and I went to the marina to see if we could find her and we followed her and Penelope here." I could feel Niko squirming uncomfortably next to me on the couch. "It was my idea. He only drove the car."

"And you broke into the house?" the detective asked, one eyebrow raised.

"The door was open." I met her gaze, confident and without any shame for what I had done. If it wasn't for Niko and I coming here, Penelope might be dead. "Niko waited outside and I entered alone."

The detective glanced at him as though she wasn't sure whether to believe me or not. "And what happened next?"

I relayed the whole scene, including playing the recording from my phone. It was fuzzy, but Penelope had used Annie's name enough to identify her. That coupled with what would have been recorded on the 911 call should be enough to put her away.

"And I also found these." I handed the missing journal pages over to the detective. "You'll find they match Calista's journal and it's clear that Tristan cheated on Annie with her. That's motive enough, even without him being entangled with her father's money."

The detective motioned for another officer to take the pages from me with a gloved hand, slipping them into an evidence envelope. She glanced at my bare hands but didn't say anything. Yep, my fingerprints would be all over those bad boys, but I wasn't worried about suddenly becoming a suspect. The case was closed now.

Another twenty minutes of questions passed while the detective took down all the notes she needed. I answered every question and didn't make a single comment about how she hadn't listened to me earlier that day when I'd come to her to plead Starr's case.

"I'm glad things didn't end differently," she said eventually, looking up from her tablet after she closed the case and tucked her stylus away. "Because I could very easily have been making a terrible call to your grandmother's house tonight."

"I know."

I didn't want to think about what might have been, but my brain seemed stuck on a loop thinking about my future and everything I could have missed out on. Rushing toward an armed person was a stupid, reckless act and I knew it. I could have died. I could have caused my grandmother the most terrible kind of grief there was, losing someone whose time wasn't supposed to be up.

"At least my sister won't be rotting in jail for something she didn't do," Niko said, his jaw clenched. The baseball bat he'd pulled from the back of his car—apparently used for some volunteer baseball games he played with at-risk youth— lay on the floor at our feet. "She might have had her life ruined for nothing."

"We'll be reviewing all the new evidence immediately," the detective said, not giving a thing away. Starr would have to be released in due course, but I also understood that the law moved in mysterious ways. There were rules and processes and procedures to be followed, which certainly gummed up the timeline.

The detective left us sitting there, going to round up the other officers who'd shown up, and they all vacated the Airbnb. Penelope and her husband came out of the room where they'd been making a statement.

"Thank you, Chloe." She rushed over to me, arms outstretched, her makeup completely smeared around her eyes. She enveloped me in a tight, trembling hug. "God, I might have died if it wasn't for you."

"I can't thank you enough." Her husband stood close, protective.

"Where's your daughter?" I asked, worried.

"None the wiser, at the festival," the husband replied. "Her aunt drove up from San Luis Obispo to take her to the parade and then spend the day with her. I'd gone out for a run and was on my way back when I saw this man running down the side of our house, waving me down and saying someone had a woman hostage inside the house."

"What a day." Penelope finally released me, her eyes watery. "I don't know how I can ever repay you."

"Maybe remember this when I send you an email with my book proposal," I joked, trying to lighten the mood.

"Oh, Chloe. I really *am* excited about your ideas and it has nothing to do with all this." She shook her head. "Although it's not every day I get to pitch a client and tell the publisher she's a real-life Millennial Miss Marple."

"I should leave you two to have some time alone," I said. Then I glanced at Niko. "Any chance you can drive me back to the marina to get my car?"

"You saved my sister," he said with a stoic nod. "I'll drive you anywhere you want."

On the way to pick up the Jellybean I learned more about him and Starr's family—all the difficulties of their childhood with parents who demanded perfection and the challenges of growing up in a country different from your own. Starr had made her own way and flourished, blending in and making friends, while Niko had struggled to figure out who he was.

"What are you going to do tonight?" I asked. "I'm hoping they let Starr out soon, but it might take a day."

"I, uh . . . I'm actually catching up with Dee." He flushed. "She was supposed to have an interview for her podcast but she said the person never showed up."

"Oh no!" I gasped, clamping a hand over my mouth. "That was me! I was supposed to be meeting her to re-record our episode. Oops. Please let her know what happened and that I totally got caught up."

A strange look crossed Niko's face. "*You* were the person she was interviewing?"

"Yeah, I run Baked by Chloe. It's a cannabis café. Starr never mentioned that?"

Niko shook his head and rubbed a hand along his straggly, red, gray-flecked beard. "She just said she knew you from around town and that you ran a business. I didn't know it was a cannabis café."

"Right."

"I, uh . . ." He swore under his breath. "You helped my family a lot today, Chloe. I didn't know if anyone would care about my sister's plight as much as I did. But you cared a lot. Enough to put yourself in harm's way."

I shrugged. "People don't deserve to be locked up for something they didn't do."

"Maybe don't have that interview with Dee." He cringed. "You didn't hear this from me, but she, uh . . . she was sending you emails."

"What emails?"

"Nasty emails pretending to be people trying to run you and your business out of town."

I blinked. The rude, anonymous emails I'd been receiving . . . they came from her? What the heck? "I don't understand."

"She was looking for a big story like what Calista found with Tristan's mentor. She copied Calista a lot, even though she would never admit it. She thought if she could find something juicy it might help her podcast go big, but when she couldn't find a story, she thought she would try to manufacture one. I told her it was wrong, but she said people in media did this stuff all the time." He shook his head. "She even photoshopped a picture of your store to make it look like the windows were broken. I saw her working on it when she thought I was asleep after we'd . . ."

He didn't need to finish that sentence.

"I can't believe it." I shook my head. "All this time I was thinking people were really trying to run me out of town."

"I think she owes you for an actual broken window as well." He cringed. "Sorry about that."

"Dee was the one who tried to break into my café?" I gasped. "That is just . . . that is going too far!"

I thought about how I ran into Dee on the street and she pretended to be concerned and waited for the police with me. I didn't suspect her even for a second.

"Look, she's a good person, just . . . a bit misguided." He sighed. "I can't judge. I've done some dumb stuff when I was desperate to get ahead. I made mistakes. But, uh . . . I don't want you to be thinking any of it's real when it's not. No one is trying to run you out of town. Please don't tell her I told you."

"I won't," I promised. "But I won't be taking her calls now. That is not okay!"

We sat in awkward silence for a moment. Why were people so darn complicated? We could be selfish creatures, we made bad decisions like we didn't know any better, and we were all fueled by the same things—a desperate need for love and acceptance, a fear of failure, and a survival instinct that sometimes led us to behave in a way we weren't proud of.

I wasn't going to hold it against Dee. But I sure as heck wasn't going on her podcast again.

"I hope you patch everything up with your parents," I said as Niko pulled his car up behind the Jellybean. "It's never too late to start over, you know. I mean, I didn't go to prison or anything but I made a mess of my life a while ago. Now it's great and I can't imagine what it would be like to lose it."

"Maybe don't go chasing any more killers around, if that's the case," he said. "You'll live longer."

"Wise words."

I got out of the car and waved him on, exhaustion suddenly flooding my body. My muscles ached, the scratch on my arm burned and my heart felt heavy. The detective might not have been right about who killed Calista Bryant but she *was* right about one thing. . . .

Today could have gone in a completely different direction.

CHAPTER 24

Two weeks later . . .

If there was one thing I felt compelled to do after having a gun pointed in my face by someone who'd killed before, it was to celebrate life. And what could be a better celebration of life than throwing a birthday party for Grandma Rose?

Seventy-five was a big deal. Three-quarters of a century lived, hundreds of meals shared and endless pearls of wisdom granted to those she loved. I wanted to shower her with love and throw her the best surprise party possible. Aunt Dawn, Maisey, Sabrina and I had been working hard all day, while Lawrence took her on a lovely drive up the coast under the guise of going to a special spot for lunch.

They were on track to return in half an hour and people were due to arrive any minute so we could assemble the surprise.

The backyard had been transformed into the perfect garden-party venue. We'd created a long table for our guests to eat at, by pushing two smaller tables together and covering them both with a gorgeous embroidered red linen tablecloth. Grandma Rose's seat at the head of the table was decorated with a large pink bow hanging off one side, and we had a pink party hat waiting for her.

Maisey was quite the wiz with flowers and had created an incredible garland centerpiece that ran down the middle of the table. She'd woven lavender from Aunt Dawn's front garden with wild grasses and several types of pink flowers including plush roses, carnations and azaleas. We'd strung fairy lights, dotted the table with pink tea light candles, and put together a beautifully eclectic set of vintage plates, bowls and glasses sourced from Grandma Rose's own collection, that of her friend Betty, and a few additional pieces borrowed from Baked By Chloe.

We'd even managed to find some gorgeous pink faux cut-crystal water jugs at a charity shop recently, which I had been saving for a special occasion. We'd filled them with water and different types of berries to make a yummy, fruit-infused summer drink. Of course, Aunt Dawn had insisted on some of our canna-gria, so we'd made up a large batch of that as well, complete with nonalcoholic sparkling pink wine.

"It looks amazing." Sabrina threw an arm around my shoulders as we surveyed our hard work. She had generously driven over some extra chairs from the bed-and-breakfast. "Your grandma is going to *love* it!"

"I just hope she takes the surprise well," I said. "She likes to be in control most of the time. But seventy-five is a huge deal. It's worth celebrating!"

"Absolutely."

The food was ready to go. We'd made up big salads full of yummy things like toasted nuts, blue cheese crumbles, dried fruit and more. I had baked two large quiches from scratch—one leek and bacon and one goat cheese and spinach—and we planned to cook some chicken and sausages on the barbecue as well. Dessert was really the main course, and I had baked a multi-layer cake with a Turkish delight–inspired flavor of rose and raspberry. The whole thing had been frosted with a gradient buttercream going from pale baby pink to a rich fuchsia. Admittedly, it was perhaps not the most even ombre as I would have liked, but cake decorating was one of my lesser baking skills and I knew the taste would more than make up for it.

"People are arriving!" Aunt Dawn called out from the house, and Sabrina and I rushed inside to greet people and lead them out to the backyard.

The doorbell buzzed and Sabrina beat me to it, opening the door as if the house was her own. She'd spent enough time here when we were kids that it practically was.

"Come in, come in!" She stepped back, beaming, her black curls hanging around her shoulders and her face alight as she let people in. "Oh, Chloe, sorry I am totally taking over. I'm just so used to doing this at work."

I chuckled. "No need to apologize."

Matt and Ben from the Dungeons and Dragons group came inside, one carrying a bouquet of flowers and the other carrying a gift wrapped in sparkly silver wrapping paper. They both stopped to give me a hug, and I directed them through to the back. We hadn't even closed the door before more people arrived. The ladies from Grandma Rose's weekly cards night— Ida, Betty, and Luisa—were all dressed to the nines. Luisa was wearing a full leopard-print jumpsuit with a sparkly gold belt that looked like she'd stolen it straight out of that '90s sitcom, *The Nanny*.

"Everyone through to the back," I said. "We're T minus twenty-five minutes."

It didn't take long for the backyard to fill up. The rest of the Dungeons and Dragons crew arrived—Cal carrying a gift, Archie looking frazzled and lacking sleep, and Erica with a beaming smile on her face, like always. There were two friends Grandma Rose had made at the place where she was getting her chemo treatments done, our next-door neighbors and Grandma Rose's hairdresser.

Antonio was racing around the backyard with Aunt Dawn's border collie, Moxie, and Maisey's Papillion, Annabel. The dogs were keeping everyone amused. Sabrina waited by the front door, keeping a lookout for Lawrence's car while Aunt Dawn and I made sure everyone was settled. Jake scurried over at the last minute, fresh off a work meeting, and paused to plant a kiss on my cheek that left me tingling inside.

A second later, Sabrina sounded the warning by waving her hands as she rushed out of the back door and into the yard. "They're pulling up now."

"Everyone in place," I said. "And keep quiet."

People in the yard moved to the sides so they couldn't be seen through the back windows of the house. Since there was a gate to the backyard, it was easy to hear what was going on at the front of the house, which was why we needed everyone to be extra quiet. The sound of doors slamming mingled with my grandmother's laughter. She sounded relaxed and happy.

It felt like everyone was holding their breath, waiting for Lawrence to lead Grandma Rose out the back. We'd planned for him to offer to make her a cup of tea while she got some sunshine. Shadows moved in the house and I heard the squeak of the handle on the old door being turned.

Grandma Rose stepped outside, smiling and looking blissfully unaware.

"Surprise!" everyone yelled in unison.

"Oh my—" Grandma Rose clapped a hand to her chest, a surprised laugh shooting out of her mouth. "What on earth is going on here?"

I rushed toward her, arms out, so I could embrace her in a tight hug. "Happy seventy-five, Grandma. With many more to come."

After we cut the cake, I was finally able to relax. Our guests had enjoyed a good meal and, most importantly, Grandma

Rose was having a blast. She sat like a queen at the head of the table and everyone was lounging around, talking and sharing, and slowly enjoying dessert. Erica, ever the saint, had helped me make coffee, tea and CBD chai lattes for everyone who wanted one.

Between the CBD chai lattes and the canna-gria, along with some weed brownies I'd made the previous day, which we'd also decided to serve, on request, everyone was feeling quite mellow. There were plenty of options, whether people wanted to indulge in cannabis goodies or not.

"I shouldn't have seconds." Betty eyed the remainder of the birthday cake with interest. "But it really is *very* good."

"Want me to cut you another slice?" I offered. "I made it for people to enjoy, so no need to feel guilty. There's plenty to go around."

She grinned. "Alright."

"Don't worry about your figure so much, darling." Luisa dabbed a napkin to her mouth, being careful not to smudge her red lipstick. "That's why God invented elastic waistbands."

Grandma Rose chuckled. "I'm going to need elastic everything after all the wonderful food I've had today."

"Good day?" I asked, reaching for her hand. She squeezed me.

"The best. Thank you, Chloe. This is a heck of a party."

"I'm glad you're happy."

I looked around the yard, my heart full to bursting. Lawrence was regaling Sabrina and Cal about something wild that happened at a writers' convention he went to in the '70s; Matt, Ben and Archie were sitting on the grass, throwing tennis balls for Annabel and Moxie. Antonio had found his way into Matt's lap and was happy soaking up all the love and attention he could get. The little dog's body was practically melted into a puddle. Grandma Rose's friends from the chemo center were sharing stories about their recovery with Erica and our next-door neighbors, and everyone was getting along great.

Next to me, Jake leaned over. "Hey, any chance we can steal away for a moment?"

"Sure. I probably need to get the coffee machine and kettle going for another round of drinks anyway," I said, pushing back on my chair.

We headed inside and a strange flutter of intuition came over me. Something big was about to happen. The way Jake was looking at me . . . it wasn't like anything I had experienced before. With my ex, he'd looked at me with passion, yes. With wanting. But there was always a shift in the power dynamic that meant he was the one in the driver's seat. The leader. The instigator.

But with Jake every step we took felt like partnership. We were on the same level as equals.

"Chloe," he began, digging his hands into his pockets. Nervousness made a shallow line form between his eyebrows. "I've been thinking about my life a lot lately and how much I enjoy having you in it."

"I enjoy having you in my life, too," I said. It had taken me a while to get comfortable with the idea of entering another relationship when my last one had exploded in such spectacular fashion, but Jake had earned my trust with his kindness and respect and patience. "A lot."

"I'm glad to hear that because"—he swallowed—"I want you around all the time."

He pulled a box out of his pocket—it was small and round and made of the kind of flocked material used at fancy jewelry stores. For a second I couldn't breathe. Was he going to propose? We'd only been together a short time! I liked him a heck of a lot and yeah, I could see us forming something really beautiful. But getting engaged felt like . . . a lot.

I wanted to take things slow with Jake and make sure that we enjoyed every step rather than skipping ahead. But when he opened the box, there was no ring inside. Only a simple gold key.

I blinked in surprise.

"Ah, crap. It's too corny, isn't it?" He flushed. "I, uh . . . I haven't done this before. I never dated anyone that I felt serious about and you're . . . well, I feel serious about you, Chloe. I wanted you to be able to come to me whenever you need. If you need an ear to listen or a shoulder to cry on or someone to listen to you talk about your day, I'm here for you. My door is always open."

My heart felt so full that it might burst. "That is so sweet."

"I know you want to take things slow," he said, as if he'd been able to read my thoughts. "And I respect that. I'm not asking you to move your whole life in with me, but if you want a second place that feels like home . . . that could be with me. Antonio is totally welcome to come visit, too."

"I would love that." I sucked in a breath. The last two weeks had made me think a lot.

About how I'd avoided things in my life because I was scared they wouldn't work out.

About how I'd held people at a distance.

I wound my arms around his neck and pressed up onto my tiptoes so I could brush my lips against his. "Taking it slow doesn't mean not progressing things. I want to keep taking steps with you, Jake. In fact, maybe we could take another step . . . tonight."

His lips came back to mine, soft, tentative. Teasing. "Tell me you're not talking about another murder investigation."

"I'm not." I chuckled as I stepped back, releasing him. "I think I'm done with murder investigations, at least for a while. I'd rather get my excitement exploring life with you and planning new recipes."

I had to send Penelope my proposal for the cookbook. Now that I knew she wasn't a murderer, I could get back to pursuing this particular dream with gusto.

"Frankly, between trying to write a book and growing Baked by Chloe and spending time with the people I love . . . I'm not sure I have time for solving mysteries anymore. I want to focus on the good things in life for a while."

"I like the sound of that." Jake closed the box containing the key and pressed it into my hands. "This definitely feels like a 'good thing' to me."

"That makes two of us."

Out of the corner of my eye, I saw Grandma Rose and Aunt Dawn peering into the kitchen window and not even attempting to be subtle about it. Aunt Dawn elbowed my grandma in the ribs and they were both grinning from ear to ear, probably already picking out baby names to suggest. I didn't know where the future would take me—whether it involved babies and marriage or if I'd spend the next decade of my life trying to figure it all out and still being unsure of what lay ahead— but I knew one thing for certain: family was everything.

And my family included all the amazing people here today. Grandma Rose, the Dungeons and Dragons group, my grand-mother's best friends and her cancer support group, Aunt Dawn and Maisey and their dogs, Lawrence, Antonio and, of course, Jake. I was surrounded by good people—and ani-mals—with big hearts, and opportunity seemed to be blossom-ing like the roses in our garden.

Life was whatever I could make of it, and I intended to give it my very best shot.

EPILOGUE

One month later...

I sat in the waiting room of the oncology clinic, my butt starting to go numb from their stylish but uncomfortable plastic chairs. I had read just about every trashy magazine that was sitting on a square table in the middle of the room, and had learned far more about the Kardashians and Jenners than I ever wanted to know. Now I'd resorted to scrolling on Instagram to keep my mind occupied while I waited for Grandma Rose to come out of her appointment.

She hadn't let me go in with her. Today we were due to get an update from the doctor on how the last course of chemo infusions had gone. She was nervous. So was I.

I had a feeling her wanting to keep me out of the doctor's office was just in case it was bad news. I knew what my grandmother was like; she never wanted to burden me with her emotions, even though it was a burden I would gladly carry. But she was old-school like that. In her mind, the elders took care of the younger ones, even when those younger ones were adults themselves.

JAKE: Text me when you get out. Keeping my fingers crossed for good news.

I smiled as the message flashed up on my screen.

CHLOE: Will do. Hope you have a great day xx

The last month had seen me spending even more time with Jake and I was sleeping over a few nights a week. Just thinking about how we'd woken up this morning together, neither one of us rushing to get out of bed since I wasn't working today, had made me happy in a way I hadn't known in a long time.

But even the great memory of that didn't work to quell my worry in this moment. I glanced at the door again, but it didn't budge. I tried scrolling on my phone, bouncing my leg in irritation when my Instagram feed declared there were no more new posts to read. Around me, there were half a dozen nervous faces. A woman in her seventies with silver hair like Grandma Rose and a woman I assumed was her daughter holding her hand. There was a woman in her thirties with a toddler in her lap, an older gentleman in a Hawaiian shirt and two women, twins, who looked around my age.

I sucked in a breath. Cancer touched so many people. Aunt Dawn and I had already talked about doing a big event in October for Breast Cancer Awareness Month. I would bake pink macarons and cupcakes with cannabis-infused buttercream, and we'd sell a pink version of our CBD chai lattes and cannagria. We would give away information about the benefits of cannabis for those undergoing chemo treatment or experiencing pain from their cancer. I wanted to raise as much money as I could to help people like Grandma Rose and those sitting in this oncology office.

As I anxiously looked around the office, hoping for something—anything—to distract me, I saw movement at the end of the hallway that led to the office. A door opened. Grandma Rose and her doctor were saying goodbye. Then she turned and started walking toward me. I spotted the tears in her eyes immediately.

My stomach dropped.

For a second, I couldn't move. I was rooted to the spot, heart in my throat. Was it bad news? Had the cancer spread? Was she . . .

No, I couldn't think like that.

I stood as Grandma Rose got closer and a smile blossomed on her lips, warm and bright like a ray of sunshine. She threw her arms around me and squeezed. Neither of us said a word for a moment. We stood there silently, embracing.

Then she whispered, "It's going away."

I closed my eyes and sagged against her. After a few more beats, she pulled back and grabbed my hand, her blue eyes misty.

"Is that what the doctor said?" I asked.

She nodded. "He said the tests show a significant reduction, even better than he had expected. I'm going to beat this, Chloe. I'm going to well and truly beat it."

As we stepped out of the oncology office and into the bright California sun, I swear the world looked even more beautiful than ever before. The trees were greener, the sky bluer, and hope sparkled like champagne in my veins. Grandma Rose was going to survive. My family was all together, where we belonged, and my business was thriving. Even more, we had Jake and Lawrence waiting at home for us, our house filled with more love than I'd ever known possible.

As we walked to the car, Grandma Rose filled me in on everything the doctor had said. She would need one more round of treatment, but they were hopeful that would be it. Just one more round. Then Grandma Rose could hopefully be cancer-free.

As we got to the car my phone vibrated with an alert. An email. It was from Penelope. Gasping, I opened it up, my hands shaking.

"What is it?" Grandma Rose asked.

"It's about my book proposal. She wants to talk about representation," I said, my eyes flying over the words. Penelope loved my ideas, she thought I had talent. She wanted to set up a call to talk about her becoming my agent. "She thinks publishers will want my book. What a day! Good news all around."

"I never had any doubt." Grandma Rose's smile was as wide as could be.

"About the cancer?"

"About any of it, Chloe." She leaned in and rested her scarf-covered head against my arm. "Good things happen to good people. And I might be a little bit biased, but my family is goodness through and through."

"You might be biased, but so am I." I grinned. "So I totally agree."

"We can do anything as a family," she said. "Anything at all."

For the first time in my life, I truly believed it. Jake might think me corny for using this phrase, but the sky was, well and truly, the limit.

RECIPES

Cannabis-Infused Cream

Yield: 2 cups

Infused cream can be used in a variety of recipes, sweet or savory! Try mixing with salmon and fresh herbs for a delicious creamy pasta or follow the recipe below to make your own cannabis ice cream. Beginners can reduce the amount of cannabis-infused cream by supplementing regular cream to make up the correct quantity.

A note on substitutions: the higher fat content of cream allows greater absorption of cannabinoids, so this method will not work in the same way with a fat-free or low-fat cream. For nondairy substitutions, you should look for a cream alternative with a higher fat content, such as full-fat coconut cream.

Ingredients
  1–5 grams decarbed cannabis flowers depending on
  personal preference (decarbing method below)
  2 cups heavy cream

Directions
Note: these ratios are only a guide. How much cannabis you use will depend on the particular strain you're using, how experienced you are with using cannabis and your personal tolerance levels. If unsure, use less.

Begin by decarboxylating your cannabis to make it psychoactive (the process which allows you to experience a high from consuming it). You may decarb more than you need for your recipe. If you do, simply store remainder in an airtight container out of direct light for 3 months.

1. Preheat your oven to 245 degrees F / 120 degrees C with a rack in the middle of the oven.
2. Line a baking sheet with parchment paper.
3. Break up the cannabis flower into smaller pieces to allow it to bake evenly.
4. Now, you have two options. You can either:
   A. Arrange them evenly across the baking sheet and create a pouch with the parchment paper, or
   B. Place them into an oven/turkey bag. This option might require buying some bags, but it will help, better than option A, to avoid making your kitchen smell during the baking.
5. Bake for 30 minutes. The cannabis should now be a brownish color.
6. Remove from the oven and allow to cool in the bag or parchment pouch.
7. Store in a cool dark place if not using immediately. It's recommended to use within three months.

Now it's time to infuse the cream.

1. Combine decarbed cannabis flowers and heavy cream in a saucepan and place over low heat.
2. Bring the mixture to the boil and then reduce to a simmer.
3. Simmer for a minimum of forty minutes, up to one hour, stirring regularly and checking the heat to ensure the mixture doesn't burn.
4. Strain infused cream through a cheesecloth or fine paper strainer.
5. Allow to cool, then store in an airtight container in the fridge.

Vanilla Cannabis Ice Cream

Yield: 4-6 servings, depending on desired dose.

This simple recipe is a great start for making cannabis ice cream! Once you're comfortable with your dosing, you can experiment with mix-ins and other flavors to customize your cannabis ice cream exactly to your liking.

Note: This recipe is designed to be made in an ice-cream machine. Not all machines are the same size, so feel free to increase or decrease the quantities below (maintaining ratios) according to your machine size. Allow room in the canister for your ice cream to expand while freezing.

Ingredients
    1 cup cannabis-infused heavy cream
    1 cup whole milk
    ¾ cup granulated sugar
    ¼ teaspoon salt
    4 pasteurized eggs (these eggs are safe to be eaten without
        tempering)
    The seeds of 2 vanilla pods

Note: the addition of eggs to this recipe makes for a rich, creamy ice cream that won't develop crystals in your freezer. However, it is possible to make the recipe without the eggs if desired, though this will result in a less rich flavor and texture.

Using unpasteurized eggs in this recipe is not recommended.

Directions

1. For best results, completely dry your ice cream canister and place in the freezer to chill overnight. Follow any other preparation instructions according to your specific machine.
2. In a large bowl, whisk eggs. Then add sugar and vanilla; mix to combine.
3. Pour heavy cream and milk into egg mixture and mix.
4. Pour mixture into your ice cream machine canister.
5. Churn according to the instructions for your specific machine until a soft serve consistency is achieved. You won't achieve full chilled regular ice cream consistency in the machine; this takes place in the freezer.
6. Once churned, turn off your machine. Now you can add any mix-ins you like. For a more pleasant ice cream experience, ensure mix-ins are small enough to be eaten without much chewing.
7. Transfer ice cream mixture to an airtight container and place in the freezer until firm, usually a minimum of 2–3 hours.

IDEAS FOR FUN WAYS TO SERVE YOUR CANNABIS ICE CREAM

- Pair with your favorite cookie recipe to make an ice cream sandwich.
- Serve with an espresso coffee poured over the top for a fun twist on an affogato.
- Add to a large glass with your favorite soda to make an ice cream float.
- Top with a banana, hot fudge sauce, crushed peanuts, whipped cream and a maraschino cherry to make a delicious cannabis banana split.

Note: remember that the cannabis in edibles can take some time to kick in! To avoid overconsumption, use a dosage calculator to determine the correct dose for your preferences and don't go back for seconds. Always have non-cannabis snacks on hand to satisfy cravings without overconsuming.

Acknowledgments

This series was written and came out during a challenging personal time. Having a world to escape to like Azalea Bay was a huge comfort. Knowing that I could go to a safe place filled with wonderful people where problems always have a solution and everyone (except the murderer!) gets their happy ending was so precious. This is the power of books. I know now, more than ever, that during hard times we need stories of hope, security and love, and I hope this series has been able to bring readers that comfort, as it did for me.

Thank you to my family, who are an endless well of love and support. No matter the distance, I know that you're all here for me through the ups and downs of life and publishing. Mum, Dad, Sami, and Albie, I'm blessed to have you all in my life. And thank you to the Littles, my family by marriage, for being such a warm and wonderful group of people.

Thank you to my Canadian found family: Shiloh, Jannette, Myrna, Madura and Tammy. I can't believe I moved all the way across the world and made the best group of friends I could possibly imagine. I love that we're always the loud table in a restaurant, that we're never without something silly to laugh about, and that you all love food, travel and the good life as much as I do. And thank you to my friends wide and far, who prove true friendship doesn't require proximity: Becca, Violet, Jen and Taryn.

Thank you to my agent, Jill Marsal, Elizabeth Trout, Larissa Ackerman, Carly Sommerstein and the rest of the hardworking team at Kensington for giving Chloe, Grandma Rose and Aunt

Dawn a home. Being able to write this series and see it on shelves has been such a delight!

Most of all, thank you to my amazing husband, Justin. Twenty-two years together this year! It's gone by in a blur and while life has thrown us many challenges, I couldn't have asked for a stronger, kinder or more passionate partner for this grand adventure. Thank you for always making me laugh and for drying my tears.

And finally, to the readers who all took a chance on Chloe and Azalea Bay, thank you. Without readers, books don't have meaning. To every reader who's contacted me, tagged me in a review or photo, who plucked my book off a shelf . . . you're all amazing. I'm blessed to have a space on your bookshelf.